LASCAR

SHAHIDA RAHMAN

Indigo Dreams Publishing

First Edition: LASCAR

First published in Great Britain in 2012 by:
Indigo Dreams Publishing Ltd
132 Hinckley Road
Stoney Stanton
Leics
LE9 4LN
www.indigodreams.co.uk

ISBN 978-1-907401-71-8

British Library Cataloguing in Publication Data. A CIP record for this book can be obtained from the British Library.

Designed and typeset in Minion Pro by Indigo Dreams Publishing Ltd.
Cover design by Ronnie Goodyer at Indigo Dreams

Printed and bound in Great Britain by: The Russell Press Ltd.
www.russellpress.com on FSC paper and board sourced from sustainable forests

‘The absence of truth-telling, ignorance flourishes. When the truth is told, society and humanity grow wiser, stronger, and more compassionate. It is with these thoughts in mind that I spin this epic tale.’

DEDICATION

For my four dear children: Ibrahim, Imran, Aniq
and Aminah.
The fragrance of flowers spreads only in the direction of the wind. But the goodness of a person spreads in all directions.

For the Lascars; the forgotten seamen.

ACKNOWLEDGEMENTS

Thank you to everyone who have made this book possible. Sincere thanks and gratitude to Eric Shapiro, the first editor of the book, for his invaluable help. Rabina for her special friendship, Duncan and Jan and for their kind help and faithful support. Jon Breakfield for his mentoring and pushing me as far as he did. David Thurlow for his help with the final edit of this book. My dear family for their support and patience. Thank you to all those for reading. Finally, a very special thank you to Ronnie and Dawn at Indigo Dreams Publishing for making this happen.

LASCAR

Introduction

Borne out of a rich and unique aspect of world history, the word "Lascar" originally referred to a sailor from South Asia, East Africa, Arabia, South Asia, Malaysia or China. Over time, the term has evolved to mean any servile non-European who toiled aboard British sea vessels.

The story that follows is about an Eastern Indian, named Ayan, who becomes a Lascar in the hope of a better life. Only to suffer prejudice, dislocation and inhumane conditions.

CHAPTER 1

Ayan gasped for breath and panicked, disoriented by the darkness. He stared, eyes opened wide, hoping to see something, yet fearing what might be there.

It moved. The darkness undulated. At least it seemed that way.

A spasm of heavy coughs racked his body. He fell to his hands and knees and coughed hard to clear the mucus from his lungs. He gulped, searching greedily for fresh air and then retched as he clawed his way forward.

The black prison inexplicably narrowed and Ayan felt a wall to his right and a wall to his left.

The darkness pitched and rolled under his feet, causing him to lose his balance and hit the floor hard. A vile stench forced him back up. He must still be alive. He knew pain and stench from the orphanage. Being alive meant pain and stench. A wave of relief swept over him. He only needed to move beyond the darkness, and then he would find his brother.

Then he became aware of something different. A cool tangy scent tingled in his nose - salt.

The floor shuddered once more beneath his feet.

Could this be? No, it couldn't! He was aboard a ship. It didn't make sense. He couldn't be on a ship. Men worked on ships. People paid to ride on ships. Boys did not belong on a ship.

A scream tore from his throat. Saltwater washed over his feet. He knelt, tears burning trails down his cheeks. There was no caretaker to tell him what to do.

"Help me," Ayan screamed. "Please. Hear my cries."

He stood and inched his way forward, measuring distance by the water level on his calves, then his knees and finally, his thighs.

"Kazi?" Ayan listened for his brother's breathing. "Kazi?" The word echoed endlessly, swallowed in the dark.

"Brother. I need you."

The water rose higher making it impossible to stand. Ayan treaded water until a flailing hand struck the ceiling.

And then the water closed over his head. He lost all sense of direction, touching the floor and walls, struggling to find the surface.

A small square of light pierced the blackness. Ayan swam desperately upward. Somehow he just knew that salvation lay beyond the light. Flailing wildly he struggled forward, never closing his eyes for fear the light might disappear.

Ayan thrust hard with his legs, broke the surface and sucked in the sweet air. He could just make out the outline of a large man. Ayan couldn't focus on any details except for a brilliant red wrapping.

"I am trapped in here. Help. I am trapped in here. Someone please. Kazi!"

The man continued to stare down into the darkness. He never beckoned or spoke, just stared. The stranger never took his eyes off Ayan. He never blinked, never moved. He did not recoil from the stench. He didn't wrinkle his nose up at Ayan's filthy clothes like the people in the streets often did.

Ayan held his breath with trepidation. The man did not close the door. He would not disappear leaving Ayan alone in the darkness.

The stranger's head tilted sideways. Something sweet emitted from the man's gaze, maybe compassion, or even stronger, love?

"Wait." Ayan gasped for breath. "Wait. I hurry. I hurry."

Determination enabled him to drag himself through the water. Another step closer to his beloved father. His father stood in the door, waiting for him. His father died when Ayan was very young. Now they were together.

"Praise be to Allah! My father," Ayan cried. "Father. It is I, Ayan. It is your boy. Ayan. Wait father. I am coming."

This is why Ayan was on a ship. It all made sense now. Kazi's stories about their father working aboard a ship explained it all.

For years, he worked so hard that his back grew hard with muscle. Men praised their father whose powerful hands could lift bundles of concrete without a shiver. Ayan saw those arms now, bands of steel, the size of a man's thigh.

The water vanished. Ayan stumbled once and ran. Beneath his feet, the ship faded into ground, not quite solid but not water. He walked on air.

"Father," he yelped. "It's me, your little boy. Do you recognise me?"

The man in the doorway did not return Ayan's smile.

Something was wrong.

He cried again. "How long I've wanted to meet you, father."

The man drew closer; at the same time, the distance between them widened. Ayan sped up, desperate to lunge into his father's arms. Ayan ached for a hug, dreamed of being embraced by the loving touch of his father. The image of Kazi looking at him and shaking his head made it hard to focus. He pushed thoughts of Kazi away. But they would not leave. Ayan tried harder. Kazi took good care of him, but brothers are, after all, only brothers. Ayan wanted his father.

His father's hand reached out and only inches separated them. Ayan's mind screamed, to run harder. Somewhere deep inside, he knew that something bad would happen if he didn't run faster.

His father's face twisted into a frightened frown. White froth oozed from between his lips. The trickle of spittle dripped and started to run. Ayan's hand withdrew. The darkness swirled faster then pulled him back. There was something important he had to remember. His blood turned ice cold as Ayan remembered; When Kazi spoke of their father, he said that he had drowned.

Panic widened his father's eyes as the distance between them increased. His father opened his mouth to cry out. Instead, he unleashed enough water to flood the darkness. The current dragged at Ayan's deadened legs, pulling him under, swirling him around. Ayan surfaced. His father opened his mouth again. Another wave filled the darkness. Ayan pushed against the ceiling He fought the water, desperately searching for an air pocket. He forced his mouth close to the ceiling and gasped for air. He struggled as cold water filled his mouth, his stomach - his lungs.

"Father, don't leave me!"

Ayan lurched hard, throwing himself onto the hard floor. He struggled and coughed, fighting for another moment before realising that the darkness was dry. His clothes and hair were dry.

A bed creaked and then another. Large curved windows at the end of the long dorm let in a thin grey stream of light. Beyond the window, the Bengal city lay silent. Dark colonial buildings blocked the view from the ancient mission orphanage. Ayan listened for the soft pad of caretaker footprints on the wooden floor. Silence filled the room. He sighed in relief. The mission teachers were not pleased when a child disturbed the routine.

Ayan touched his throat. He greedily gulped the hot summer air, desperate for coolness to ease his parched tongue. The Eastern Indian summer air refused to offer any comfort. It filled the dorm room, hot and humid. He padded down the long row of beds, careful to avoid bumping into the steel frames. He reached the court window and squatted by the bucket, empty. He licked the dry cup and then dropped it. The wooden clang echoed down the room.

Ayan spun, frightened. Several long minutes passed before he realised no one heard. His nose pressed against the dirty glass. The large moon turned the courtyard into a collage of blue shadows. The stone edge of the water-well stood grey against the flat grass of the yard. The moonlight rippled on the water that filled the outside bucket almost to overflowing. Ayan dismissed the thought of fetching water without being accompanied by a caretaker. Going out at night was not part of the routine.

The white mission teachers only came to the orphanage last

year. Until then, no one cared about a routine. He might go out for water at night. In fact, he could even go into the street and watch the strange white people from the east. They dressed strange and the way they talked sounded funny to his young ears. They brought the mission teachers with them. They talked about making the boys respectable.

Ayan knew about being low-caste. His father was low-caste. His grandfather was low-caste. He didn't understand what it meant, except that his father's death meant he went to an orphanage. It meant that he sat on a bench all day listening to the white teacher talk about things that would make him respectable. Ayan wondered why going for water at night made him less…respectable.

His tongue moved around the inside of his mouth to alleviate his thirst. He sighed. Why didn't he remember not to recoil in terror when his father started to drool? He knew, in his heart, that he must touch his father before the water came. That would make the dream real. If he could do it, just once, then they would all be together again. Ayan would make everything right again.

His memory was good, better than Kazi's. He would keep this dream in his mind. It was a good dream. He smiled. He almost touched his father this time. Next time, he would forget the pain in his feet. Forget the stink and the blackness. He would move faster and reach the door before the foam came, before the blackness drew him back.

He once told the caretakers about the dream where his father came to him. At that time, Ayan thought his father gave him directions on how they could be together again. The caregivers rolled their eyes and flapped their lips. Then they gave Ayan a beating. They dragged him before the mission teacher who talked a long time about a white place where good people went when they died. It didn't make sense. Good people enjoyed a better life. He wasn't sure he wanted to go to a place in the sky. His father wasn't in the sky. He was on a ship.

Ayan only ever told Kazi about his dreams now. The teasing of his brother was less painful than the stick from the caretakers.

At times, the dream felt more real than the hot sticky days spent listening to mission teacher's talk about strange things like mathematics and figuring numbers. He relived the dream again, drawing on the strange comfort, and the haunting knowledge that his father still lived. They would talk and share fruit and drink pitcher after pitcher of ice-cold water. How safe and cosy Ayan felt in the world inside his mind. It was much better than the real world where everyone said, "your father drowned in the sea," when his heart knew that they lied.

Ayan continued to build a picture in his mind adding richly coloured rugs he saw in the markets, and gold jewels or silks, just like the merchants wore. The table changed from long wooden planks in the orphanage, to a heavily carved teak table. He saw one through a garden's lattice wall. A thin young woman in a yellow silk sari danced for several men. The men ate a giant mound of fruit and talked about their rice harvests.

The excitement grew so strong he turned and slapped Kazi's round belly.

Kazi was a lucky one. They ate so little, but Kazi enjoyed a belly almost as large as the fat rice merchant. Kazi never agreed, claiming his belly hurt. But he did hold his head up when the mission teacher spoke in low tones about something being different about him. A doctor arrived to look at him one day and pronounced in an important voice that Kazi was special. He warned the mission teacher to be careful around Kazi.

Ayan looked like the other boys. He could push two fingers between his bones and make them move. Not Kazi. He was special. He held his hands apart showing everyone what a big baby he had been. He told stories of how grown-ups laughed and pinched his chubby cheeks. Everyone listened intently to Kazi's stories about being a baby in a real family. He told fantastic stories about his father's pride in his fat son. He told great stories of being in the high section of the city, away from the oppressing heat that filled the dock areas.

"One day, I walked the road with my father. Criers walked ahead of a litter. They announced that a great lady, wife of a very wealthy man wanted the road cleared. My father protectively pushed me back and shielded me from the crowed as they pressed away from the street."

Kazi let the introduction sink in while he prepared the rest of the story. "Tall men with curved swords and shields walked solemnly before the litter. Thick jewelled broaches clasped their clothing and adorned their turbans.

"Their thick black beards shone with rich oils. Smooth as a raven's wing, they shone. But, they were not worth looking at. The woman's servants came next. Fine women with beautiful eyes and soft skin, walked sedately, averting their eyes from the rough world they must walk through.

"Their silks were so fine they fluttered like a flower petal blowing on the breeze. Rich perfumes scented their hair and they rubbed saffron and sage into their skin. But, they were not worth looking at.

"Behind them came a beautiful litter. Gold gilded with rich carvings. The silks curtains fluttered as thin as a spring rain. A man might look hard and see the beauty that belonged to the wealthy. The pungent oils and fabrics wafted through the streets masking all other scents. The woman had been bathed in rose petals and oils. The handmaidens spent hours brushing her hair and rubbing fine oils into her skin. But she was not worth looking at."

Kazi paused until his audience coaxed and begged for more. He leaned forward and whispered. Every boy leaned forward in anticipation. "Elephants. Great beasts larger than any on earth. Gifts from Allah. They walked slowly, masters of the world. Gold balls adorned the ends of their long tusks. More wicked than swords and longer than spears.

"Their bodies were painted in blue and gold. Designs that took artisans many hours to create. A man rode each beast, his position of honour signified by the wealth he wore. A golden pike directed the elephant.

"Upon the beasts backs was a litter. Encrusted in jewels, solid gold and with curtains of crimson silk as thick as a carpet tied back by gold cords. The litter was made of delicately carved black teak and white ivory. Red gold eyes started in all directions.

"Inside sat the man. Jewels adorned both hands and covered the entire front of his turban. Greatest of all, a ruby decorated his turban." Kazi held his hands a few inches apart to indicate the size of the great stone.

"He sat arrogantly. Proud as the mountains, he stared. Wealthy as a Rajah, he surveyed all before him. Master of the beasts. Master of the great warriors who guarded him. Master of the woman. And he, it was he who was worth looking at."

Kazi sat like a Raja as he told stories about life by the brown river. He recited stories of Hong Kong that his father described to him. Many ships, floated on the seas, more than the flocks of sea birds that hovered over the harbour. They brought rare treasures from so far away that a bird may die before it reached those lands.

Ayan liked best the stories of sea monsters. Huge beasts that spouted water from the ocean and were hunted by small fierce men.

After the mission teachers arrived, the caretakers panicked whenever anyone touched Kazi. One boy poked one of Kazi's fat cheeks when he sat in the courtyard telling stories. The mission teacher beat him terribly. The caretaker took him to sleep in the room behind the kitchen for a week. The punishment for touching Kazi grew so severe that Ayan feared touching him in the presence of a caretaker. But, there were no caretakers around now.

Ayan slapped Kazi's belly harder, feeling a static vibration shoot through the rolling fat belly.

Kazi sprang to life, bolting upright, "Late! Am I late?"

Bleary eyes blinked. A fist rubbed his eye as his lip dropped into a pout.

"Brother," Ayan whispered. He stared hard at his brother, willing him to wake up. "I saw father in a dream."

Kazi's body plopped back onto the thin sheet of cloth covering the rope-mattress bed. An impatient groan emitted from his lips, followed by a bored reply, "For this you wake me up, Ayan? Fantasies and imaginations?"

"No, no, no, brother. Not imagination, I promise. I looked right into his eyes and I could see their whiteness. He is very real to me."

Kazi rolled his eyes. "You are trying to be important."

Ayan felt a knot in his stomach.

Kazi sighed a big breath and rolled onto his side. Their eyes meet for several seconds before Kazi asked, "Where were you?"

Ayan swallowed the lump in his throat and talked as fast as his tongue would allow:

"It was a ship, Kazi. I swear, a great big ship. It was darkness, but not night. The dark moved. It was heavy. My feet burned and were broken open. At first I thought I was lost. I felt the ship bobbing up and down. I fell and hurt myself. Water filled the darkness. And father was there, in the door, only there was water coming out of his mouth."

Kazi's eyes changed from receptive to mortified. "Bite your tongue, little brother. You're talking about dark places. Where you dreamed of sounds more hellish than peaceful."

Ayan recoiled at Kazi's use of the mission teacher's word for that place. It just didn't seem right to talk about the white people's death and their father at the same time.

"Father would not be in such a place," Kazi continued, "I know."

"But it was . . . him," the angry words exploded from his

mouth.

A slew of orphans put fingers to their mouths and hissed, "Sssshhhhhhhh!"

Ayan lowered his voice. "He was trying to talk. It looked like he had something on his mind."

Kazi lowered his voice to a whisper, forcing Ayan to move closer. "People who've passed from this life do not have things on their minds. Do you know why?"

Ayan shook his head.

"Because they don't have minds!" Kazi hissed, his sour breath nearly blowing Ayan back onto his bed. "Father's body is white and fat at the bottom of the ocean."

Ayan ignored his brother.

"Do you think one day I will work on a ship? I'm sure if I did, I would not drown, and father would be proud."

"When are you going to understand?" Kazi groaned. "It's not a good life being a shipman. You will work from the moment your eyes open to the moment they close. You get blisters on your hands from shovelling coal into the fire. The white men sneer at you and call you a "Lascar". This is what father's life was like, and then it ended in a most terrible way."

"But I heard that the ships dock at all kinds of exotic places. And that you get to stand up top and look out at things you've never seen before."

"You will not be respectable."

"Father was a respected man."

"Becoming a Lascar is not respectable."

Kazi thought for a moment. "We can become respectable."

"Why?" Ayan spat the words. "Because white people tell you so? Is it better to be respectable than to be like father?"

"More likely you'd be working too hard to see anything."

Ayan wanted to end the conversation. He turned his back and flopped on the bed. "Better than being in here," he muttered.

"Don't speak too soon. The word is that you and I will be

leaving tomorrow."

His eyes flew open. Sweat soaked his body. "What?"

"We're getting older, Ayan. I'm almost twelve, and there are plenty of babies on the street who'll need these beds. Tomorrow, your dream of being a worker will start to come true." Kazi's voice quavered beneath his important facade.

"Why didn't you tell me?"

"I wanted you to get a good night's sleep."

"Who told you?"

"Go to sleep."

"Kazi"

"Sleep."

Ayan lay back, but he could not sleep. It was important news that no one told Ayan, so his father came to tell him, like any good father would.

He knew what he would do first. Get a drink of water, all by himself, without asking a caretaker, or worrying about the mission teacher narrowing his eyes and telling him how ungratefully he behaved.

CHAPTER 2

Rain blinded Ayan. It blackened the sky as it pelted his skin mercilessly. He should return to Kazi, but he waited in the courtyard outside the temple. The soft glow of candles danced across the glossy stone floor as two Devadasi danced before their God and before several British officers.

Ayan pushed down the guilt. He should not be looking at foreign gods, or the women who married and served them. Ayan did not approve of women displaying themselves in public. Yet these young girls did not appear to be evil. They were dark skinned, unlike the unchaste women brought to the brothel. They were lighter skinned, slaves from over the mountains.

Ayan breathed in their sweet perfumed scent and closed his eyes. The first night was always the worst. They were beaten. They screamed. Theirs was not the world of a courtesan.

A snap woke Ayan from his daydream. He gasped and scrambled to the side of the road as a row of dark horses emerged from the night. He squatted as sipai, private soldiers, bearing the insignia of the East India Company rode past. They were the new rulers of India. He stared in awe as the Muslim and Hindu soldiers rode by, oblivious to the torrent around them. These were high-caste men who would have been rulers in their own small territories, if the East India Company had not divided their lands into "presidencies".

The orphanage strictly taught the new organised government. The street taught Ayan that much happened that historians did not understand. At least, they did not understand that the sipai did not like the new British princes of India.

For the sipai to be out at night in the rain meant only one thing. Another rebellious uprising. Ayan did not know what a rebellious uprising was, but was aware that it was not a good thing. The gutters filled with blood. People died.

No one would think twice about a beggar boy's death. Ayan waited a while. Then he ran, following the black, slick stones to the alley where Kazi waited beneath the broken wall.

The night popped with the sound of muskets. The sound echoed down the empty alleys. Ayan ran faster, disregarding the risk of slipping in the gutter slime, or cold stones. His heart pounded in his chest as he climbed over the concrete wall that separated the brothel from the rest of the village.

He squatted in the darkness of the quiet garden and waited. The rain stopped as suddenly as it started.

The slavers' horses stood under cover on the edge of the stable. A man of considerable wealth came out into the garden. A Bengali from the Bhadralok caste, he would visit this hovel to derive a pleasure too debase or cruel for a courtesan or more valuable concubine to sate.

Ayan held his breath as the man crossed the sodden garden and left through the side gate. His breath left his body in a long, silent hiss. He ran across the yard, his body so low it brushed the weed tops. A moment later, he ducked into a dark hole in the stable wall and felt past the rubble to the crumbled feed room where the boys slept.

"Kazi?"

Ayan froze. Kazi's rapid breathing alerted him that something was not right. The only sound he heard for several moments was the thumping of his own heart. Ayan could tell that Kazi had crawled into the farthest corner of the room, under what had once been a feed bin.

As Ayan lay in the dark he noticed other sounds. At first he dismissed them as the sounds of the slavers' horses. Now he noticed that they were much closer. He listened hard and realised that someone was on the other side of the wall. He could make out the soft breathing of several young women. Their scent permeated the stable.

"Ayan, let's leave this place."

"Quiet," Ayan hissed. "They will hear."

"I want to get far away."

"I do too," Ayan admitted. He saw the blue shadows of mountains to the north, and the blue sea to the south. Both promised a better life than the one they had etched out here, living in holes like animals, living among the people, but unseen.

The musket shots sounded closer. Kazi shivered. Ayan dragged a ragged blanket over them, blocking them from the night.

"There are British in the brothel."

"I know," Ayan whispered.

"It isn't safe here anymore. We need to get away before something bad happens."

"Shhh," Ayan whispered, as someone shouted something indecipherable from the other side of the wall, and then ran down the alley beyond the stable.

"They're coming," Kazi's voice cracked under the strain.

"Whatever happens, do not make a sound." Ayan tilted his head slightly, trying to see into the moonlit courtyard. "Be quiet and tomorrow we will leave."

"Where will we go?"

"The mountains. Toward the forests. We will make a life for ourselves in another village."

"Merchants?"

Ayan nodded.

"No. Farmers. I want to grow rice."

"Rice then." Ayan's breath caught in his throat. "Now be quiet Kazi."

Ayan listened hard. The soldiers were still outside. One girl started to cry aloud. Ayan held his breath and willed the girl to be quiet. Another whispered in a language he did not understand. The words did not calm the rest of the girls, instead the crying increased.

Ayan lowered his head. He knew what would happen. The

slavers would come in and silence the girls. The stable door opened. Light flooded into the room beyond the hole that Ayan and Kazi hid in. Kazi buried his head. Ayan felt his eyes being drawn to the light that came through the broken slats and boards. He could see the silhouettes of girls tied to the stable wall, not three feet away from him.

Men's voices hissed. Fear tinged their voices.

"Keep them quiet," another voice hissed. Ayan recognised the voice as one of the men who worked in the house. "Keep them quiet or we will all die."

"No!" another voice from inside the brothel hissed. "We paid for them."

"No good if we are all dead," a gruff voice said.

"Be done," a slurred voice hissed.

"Get her out of there," one of the brothel workers snarled.

The rapport of a pistol echoed through the stable, silencing everyone.

Ayan held his breath, hoping the girls would remain quiet. One girl whimpered. Another screamed. The scream died in a sudden gurgled gasp. Startled, Ayan's head lifted. Another girl was half lifted against the boards. Ayan saw her body lurch, then fall. He waited as another screamed. Ayan saw the glint of steel flash downward towards another girl. He watched in horror as her cries drowned in a strangled choke.

"Quickly!" a man spat the order. Two other men ran forward and grabbed at the girl closest to Ayan. He watched them lift her, screaming, from the floor. Her body lurched under their hands as one covered her mouth. The other plunged a knife into her side.

"Not them all!" the brothel owner wheezed. His efforts were useless. "Not everyone!"

"Next time pay your bribe, old man," one of the slavers snapped. "It is bad for business to damage the goods."

"I paid my bribe," the brothel owner whined. "I paid."

"British!" The word was screamed into the night as an insult.

Ayan thought the same. The girls died because of the British. His father died because of the British. They were thrown from the orphanage, onto the harsh streets because of the British.

Flashes of lightning broke the darkness. Blood spurt out of the mouth of the slaver closest to the stable wall. He crumbled onto the girl he held. Lightning flashes, mixed with the report of pistols. Kazi screamed. Ayan scrambled to cover his mouth. Behind them blood-curdling cries mixed with the screams of the girls. Then silence.

"What's this?"

"Looks to be whores, Major."

A man sniffed with disgust. "Any alive?"

"Two or three, Major."

"Just what this cesspool needs, more whores."

"Do we take them?"

A small flair of fire illuminated the major's face as he lit a cigarette. He dragged long and exhaled a thick plume of smoke.

"Leave them. Let God sort them out."

Kazi shook. His body trembled violently. "We must go." He repeated the words over and over.

Suddenly flames leapt into the darkness. The cigarette had been thrown into the stable like a final insult. Ayan crawled out of the hole.

"Get out." He hissed at Kazi. His brother paused only a moment before gathering his senses and following behind. The roar of the flames mixed with the screams of two girls, still tied up inside the stable.

Ayan ran over to the stable wall and pulled on the ropes. They twisted in his hand as the girls fought to free themselves. He pulled and yanked at the knots, but they refused to come loose. Flames crawled up the stable wall.

"Ayan!"

He turned to see Kazi outside the stable, a look of horror on his face. Ayan turned back to the girl. She did not scream anymore. The stench of burning hair was almost overwhelming. It was too late.

"Ayan! Come on! "

Ayan left the stable, and together the brothers cleared the garden wall. They ran and ran until they could run no more.

* * *

Ayan stretched his long legs out as far as they would go, and still he remained in the shade of his betel nut tree. Their tree. Kazi had succeeded in growing this tree, when men who grew up on the land had struggled to raise crops in the merciless soil of Sylhet, Eastern India.

Ayan smiled.

"What are you grinning at?" Kazi grimaced.

"I admire what we built for ourselves," Ayan replied.

"We have not done so badly. The melons are almost ready."

"There is no money in melons!"

"I have been told my rice is very good my dear brother Kazi."

"I must tell you many times. There is no money in rice. Have you made any wealth? Does your rice do more than keep hunger from tormenting you?" Kazi seemed frustrated.

Kazi carefully folded a tobacco leaf over a betel nut. His hands deftly wound the packet together in the manner that would produce a powerful high.

Ayan watched Kazi pop the small nut pieces into his mouth and start chewing.

"There is much money to be made growing betel nuts," Kazi grinned showing red stained teeth. Kazi walked away from Ayan and into the house. Moments later he reappeared as he sat by the window and laughed at his younger brother.

"You do not know what you miss, brother." Kazi leaned out the window. "You are a foolish man, denying yourself the betel nut when we own the whole tree."

Ayan waved and pretended to laugh. He drove the hoe into the crumbling earth. He stabbed again and again, burying the growing anger and guilt. He almost wished Kazi was not special. Then Ayan could wish for a bug to kill the betel tree without feeling guilty.

"The tree will make us rich!" Kazi yelled.

"You have a buzz," Ayan called back.

"I am happy," Kazi pouted. "You are a cruel man to deny me a simple pleasure."

"I deny you nothing," Ayan sighed and stretched.

"Why don't you share the betel nut with me?"

"One of us must work," Ayan bit his tongue the moment the words were out. A clay jar smashed in the house.

"Ayan, why do you struggle in the soil? You know it will not produce many beans."

"It will produce some," Ayan called back. He turned, surprised to see Kazi under the shade of his tree.

"You understand the ways of business now?"

Ayan leaned on the hoe and lowered his head. "I understand some things."

Kazi laughed. "Tell me brother what you know."

Ayan wet his lips. He sensed Kazi only wanted to mock him, to laugh at his ignorance.

"I worked hard this morning. I thought about the betel tree and the rice business."

"Yes," Kazi laughed. "How many of our neighbours enjoy two businesses. We are indeed good merchants."

Ayan resisted the urge to ask his brother that, if they were so special, why did hunger still sting their bellies. He let the hoe drop and sat on a rock by the betel tree.

"I do not believe that these two businesses belong together." Kazi laughed, his grotesque red tongue lapping his lip.

"Listen to what I have to say. Only certain customers buy betel nut."

"Good customers. They return again and again."

"Yes," Ayan lowered his head and spoke slowly so he would

not confuse his thoughts. "They do, but they do not buy rice. They buy enough betel nut to get high for the rest of the day and then leave. Two old men who bought betel from us died last year. If one more customer dies of betel nut disease then we will not earn enough money to eat. It may take months for another customer to find our tree. It is not like we can go out and tell everyone that we have the tree, or ask them to come try our nuts. I am torn, my brother, because I know that the betel nut sometimes makes enough money for us to buy beans for dinner."

Ayan took a deep breath and hurried on before his brother interrupted. "The women fear the betel nut customers. They refuse to come anymore. Many will not even let me sell rice to them from the back of the property. Instead, they walk down the hill to the village and buy something else to feed their families. We have good rice. I have often heard them praise our rice. They are quiet women, who are afraid of men who are high."

Ayan stopped short of saying; they feared Kazi when he was high.

"Ayan," Kazi's words slurred. "What are you saying? You know I only allowed you to start the rice business to humour you. It was as much as any good brother would do, but you waste your time sludging through the muck and water growing rice that no one wants."

"That is not true. The first years, before the betel tree grew tall, we sold enough rice to eat well. Women came to buy rice every day, until . . ." Ayan didn't know how to remind his brother why the women now avoided them without sounding spiteful and jealous. Instead, he tried to turn the subject.

"You know things. The mission teacher taught you many things. You are special. But not when you chew the betel nut. It makes people afraid of you. You do things to frighten the women."

"Why worry myself over common women?" Kazi chuckled.

Ayan sighed. "Kazi, you now eat more nuts than we sell."

"So, what? We have no buyers right now anyway! By the time a new buyer shows up, new nuts will have grown. When they grow, we will have money again. Until then, we will eat your rice."

"Maybe we will earn enough money to become respected if you stop eating the nuts."

Kazi grunted and struggled to his feet and stumbled toward the house. Ayan didn't look at the house this time, knowing that Kazi waited to show his tongue again. Instead, he returned to his work, ignoring his brother's inevitable mocking.

Ayan worked under the scorching sun, loosening the soil so it would drink the rains when they came, instead of running down the hill. He dug deep, wishing it was as easy to dig the weeds and rocks that burdened his heart.

No matter what Kazi said, they were happy when they first arrived here. They sat at their front door and laughed into the night, talking about their good fortune.

Ayan started to notice a change in Kazi after the first year. The women started to look for Ayan alone. At first Kazi laughed that they sought the younger brother's handsome face and muscular build. Ayan laughed too, not understanding until much later that jealousy grew in his brother's heart. Kazi never said anything, but it was obvious to them both that Ayan had grown to resemble their father, with his strong muscular build and rugged handsome looks.

Kazi had changed too. The flesh on his cheeks and arms sagged. His once round belly hung limp over the rim of his sarong. Ample flesh covered the top of his body, but his legs were thin and gaunt like those of an orphan boy. The women never smiled at Kazi.

Kazi always paid special attention to a particular young woman with soft skin and dark eyes. Her pale gold sari flowed gracefully from her slender arms. She laughed lightly when the brother's complimented her. Kazi often found reasons to stay in the lower corner of the property where she appeared. One day she followed a group of other women from the village. Their laughter caught Ayan's attention and he dropped the hoe anticipating a large sale. Kazi greeted the young women amiably.

Her friends turned and laughed at her, making jokes about Kazi's belly. Flustered, she ordered Kazi away as if he were merely a servant. Kazi froze on the spot for a moment and then headed to the house. That night he chewed betel nut until he couldn't stand. After that day he lost all interest in the rice buyers.

Ayan wondered at the power of a woman's laughter. It could make a man feel strong enough to fight a bull. Or, in Kazi's case, make him ruin everything he spent so many years struggling to build.

After that day Kazi went out of his way to drive women away. On hot days he removed his shirt just when Ayan was complimenting a potential customer. He would walk forward, his belly flopping over the rim of his sarong, all but begging patrons to look at it. And then the round shiny ball started to grow on his lower lip. Tiny at first, it seemed to grow almost daily, until it was the first thing that drew a gaze from Ayan, or indeed any customer. Ayan almost welcomed the day Kazi grew so lazy that he refused to leave the house. Late at night he closed his eyes and saw wise, special, Kazi who prevented them from starving on the streets.

Ayan thought back to the time on the streets, when they found a dead boy under a pile of garbage.

"This is what happens to people who turn away from Allah," Kazi said with an air of importance.

"Allah is our protection and our wisdom. Father taught me this."

"Will we end up like this?" Ayan poked the body with a stick.

"Do not defile the dead. Show some respect." Kazi put his hand on Ayan's shoulder in the way a father would. "This boy lost his way. A boy who loses his way will not live to grow."

"How does a boy lose his way?"

Kazi pointed down a dark alley. A group of boys huddled at the far end. "They lost their way."

Ayan stared for a long time down the alley. He did not understand how they lost their way. He saw them. They were right there. All they needed to do was walk out of the alley and they could find the road.

After the gruesome find, and Kazi's speech, Ayan did not feel comfortable in the dark holes of the city. He did not like to share the fires with other boys and the dark men who drank until they fell down.

He preferred to wander around the docks, watching the sailors work. Kazi kept them deep in the city looking for work and begging. They slept in alleys so narrow they were forced to sleep back to back between the high solid walls. One night, some men entered their alley and threatened the boys. Kazi screamed at the men with a fierceness Ayan had never seen. The men ran in fear. Ayan desperately yearned for that Kazi to return. He understood now. Kazi lost his way.

Ayan wasn't Kazi, never would be. Kazi's skin was thin and smooth. Ayan looked at his hands. They were covered in dark hair and tanned from the sun. Women favoured Ayan's face, while they feared Kazi. Then, there was the little ball, the growth hanging from Kazi's lower lip.

Ayan tilted his head and looked at the growth. Kazi never talked about it.

It amazed him how something so small created such a huge rift between brothers as close as they once were. He held up his thumb and squinted his eyes. It seemed strange that the betel nut sickness hit Kazi so young. Everyone agreed, only old men had lip cancer from the addictive nut. Ayan moved his thumb a few inches. The growth was larger.

Now, he had no choice. Something would happen today, but he didn't know what. His father had visited in his sleep. That always meant something important would happen soon. Ayan saw his father's sad eyes, as real as the night in the orphanage. That day, their lives had changed forever. Ayan's mouth grew dry. Realisation dawned that his father wanted him to take charge. Today they would discuss Kazi's health.

Stood in the doorway, he looked around the fine house the brothers built with their own hands The cool darkness invited him in, but he hesitated, afraid of seeing Kazi already slumped in a buzz. Ayan filled a clay cup with cool water from the pitcher. He drained the cup before making eye contact with his brother. He simply said, "I don't like the looks of your lip, brother."

He waited. The sounds of Kazi's chewing, breathing and chewing continued. The breaths gurgled in muddy bursts. Each one shuddered through Ayan's body.

"Sometimes it gets smaller," Kazi said. He looked at the ground, busy rubbing his thumb on the edge of his bowl.

"No it does not grow smaller. I've been watching it."

Kazi looked out the window. "Not growing bigger, though. I'll say that much."

"Not yet." Ayan pushed his brother, tempting his brother's anger.

Ayan's heart leapt to his throat as Kazi's fist struck the table top. Kazi rose, his eyes wild as the shrill in his voice.

"What are you doing to me? I set apart today to chew on some good nut and you use it as an opportunity to upset me. My mind is not in the place for this kind of conversation, Ayan. Perhaps you might have waited till …"

"Till when? Till you are in the hospital, costing us every bit of money we have? No longer able to walk or talk, not even able to breathe?" Ayan let his voice rise. "Do you want to destroy everything?"

The tight bands around his chest loosened as he let his anger vent. For the first time in his life, he drew a full breath, filling his lungs. "Kazi, the betel nut is killing you."

Kazi rose to his feet, trying to regain the 'important stance' he used in their childhood to intimidate other children. It no longer held any power over Ayan. He stood tall, looking down on his brother. Although Kazi wore a shirt on this day, his belly protruded through the fabric.

Kazi veered left, heading straight toward the mirror. He fingered the fleshy bulb hanging down from his lower lip.

"Does it hurt?" Ayan asked.

"Tender," said Kazi, squeezing the tumour gently. "Like when a bug bites."

"Let me see." Ayan stood behind his brother and looked down over his shoulder. Kazi stood as quietly as a child waiting for a father's inspection. He suddenly realised that the order changed in that moment, forever. Ayan stepped back, unsure if he wanted to take on the role of caretaker. He put a finger on Kazi's lower lip and bent it downward so he could take a better look. Its texture reminded him of a damaged piece of fruit. It started to swell from the inside and grew out. There were now wrinkles on its surface. He withdrew his finger and flicked it against his sarong

"Should we cut it?" Kazi asked.

Ayan laughed falsely, "That's what doctors are for. We'd take off your head."

Kazi looked thoughtful as he replied, "That wouldn't be any good. I need my head to get buzzed."

"We can start over."

"Start over?"

"Without the tree. We could move somewhere else. Start over."

"No," Kazi sighed. "It is too late for me."

"We can cut down the tree."

Kazi's face blanched and he swayed on his feet. His mouth opened, and closed.

"The rice will feed us."

"It will not pay for doctors."
"We will make do." Ayan whispered.
"I cannot do it."
"I can."

CHAPTER 3

Ayan stepped over a rock in the narrow trail. Trees crowded the trail as it snaked down the side of a steep hill. Through the trees, Ayan could make out the muddy river below. His rice fields were now in view. He should check the rice, but didn't want to endure the swarming bugs, or the heavy heat trapped in the river valley.

Ayan avoided the clear path that lead from the river. Women often spent their afternoons washing clothing in the river and caring for babies. He didn't want to interrupt their chatter and laughter.

He cut his own trail through the bush, making enough noise to warn animals of his approach. A snake slithered from the ferns under his feet. Tall rice spikes lined the river and edged back into a small marshy area. He wandered between the plants, careful not to trample any. The plants grew heavier than he might have liked, the result of not being thinned properly. The water barely reached his ankles in some places.

Ayan picked up a big stick and used it to dig away at the river bank. A trickle flowed into the lower ground. It took several hours to dig away enough mud to create a few puddles in the middle of the rice field. He bit off a few hard kernels and chewed them, spitting them out in frustration. He left the rice field and followed the village path to the most populated section of Sylhet.

The previous day's conversation had changed things between the brothers. Some of the old Kazi returned. Ayan intended to buy two cups of thick beans to make Kazi smile when he returned. Women used food as medicine. He hoped the nourishment would calm Kazi's lip.

A long line led from the bean tent. He recognised most of the villagers. Many women stood in the line, saris wrapped tightly around their slender forms, yelling at their children. Several men stood in the line, most waiting impatiently for their turn. Ayan watched a couple of children play in the dirt.

"Miah."

Ayan did not turn at the sound of his surname. The whispered tone warned him the men did not mean his name as a salutation. He lifted his eyes, meeting the glance of an old man who provided much of the boys' earnings. Everyone knew the old man frequented the betel nut sellers, but in town, the man would not acknowledge their relationship.

The tree. Their lives tangled around that tree. It made his brother sick. Then, it became their only hope. Some men were tangled in the responsibility of wives and children. Kazi and Ayan's lives were tangled into the life of the betel nut tree.

Whispers and muffled grunts behind him caught his attention.

"A man should have some shame . . ."

"Miah, a name that will not bear any sons . . ."

Ayan turned and looked down at two men. His glare silenced them for a moment then the whispering continued in sinister tones. Ayan flashed a last irritated glare and returned to the queue, which rolled forward as sluggish as a fat-bellied snake.

With its intrusive coarseness, a scabby toe stubbed the back of Ayan's left heel. Ayan moved a tiny step forward. An inch or so, hoping that the contact had been accidental. A few moments passed before the intrusion repeated itself. The man's toe licked Ayan's heel with all the smoothness of gritty sand. Ayan turned, his forearm muscles tightening in mute threat.

"I've always made it a point," he said, "to keep both my feet on the ground."

The two men stared up from hideous faces, their complexion so darkened he wondered if a coat of grime covered their skin. Their dim eyes didn't surprise him. There were many in this area who could never grasp the wit in Ayan's statement. To mend the misunderstanding, Ayan spoke as if to a child.

"Can we stand here without you touching my foot?"

"A feisty sort you are. Must have hunger in your belly."

"Don't we all, sir," Ayan said, phrasing the sentence more as a statement than a question.

"Oh," laughed the old man, "indeed we do."

"Some of us more than others," he said.

The hairs on the back of Ayan's neck stood up. Not so much from the man's words, as his incendiary tone.

A hard pause followed. Ayan turned toward the tent. The jolly bean seller and his wife chattered with their customers, fawning over them and complimenting them. Ayan's irritation numbed when he remembered that he had done the same thing to win a sale and earn a loyal customer.

Five women stood in front of him, not one of them eager to return to the solitude of their own home and the burden of hungry mouths and dirty faces that demanded attention. The women laughed and flirted with unabashed humour as they enjoyed their few moments of peace before returning to the duty of wife and mother.

Two women collected their pots of beans and left, moving the line a few feet forward. Ayan covered the distance in a single step and settled in to wait, not begrudging the women their reprieve. A stiff toe jabbed into his heel, hard.

Ayan rubbed the back of his heel with his opposite toe, but didn't turn around. The men sniggered like beggar boys and resumed whispering loud enough for him to make out most of the words.

"We're both in the same line," Ayan said, hoping to imply that all people are children in a single universe.

The two men fell silent for a moment and then laughed outright. The older man said, "But you're in front of us."

Ayan's eyes flicked, studying whether they could be serious. Were they threatening him?

"I came here for food." Ayan hoped that feigning ignorance of their threat would avoid a confrontation, "Not to engage in a conversation that can go nowhere."

"Most assuredly," smiled the old man, flashing darkened teeth, "a man like you is always going places."

"I have no plans to travel."

"An important man like you?" Both men laughed at the slight.

"Do you have something to say?"

"I would not lower myself to talk to you."

Ayan smiled at the irony. "Of course not." He replied with quiet authority, hoping to end the conversation. As time dragged, the line moved forward, until finally Ayan was at the head of the queue.

"Two bowls of beans."

"Most excellent sir." The bean seller smiled. "I hope Allah blesses you."

"And you, also."

"All is well?"

"Yes," Ayan replied cordially, but noticed the distinct absence of jovial humour that the bean seller had shared with his other patrons.

Ayan watched as the man quickly poured the beans. To his credit, he filled them to the brim. The bean seller turned a critical eye on the two men waiting to be served next. "Go inside, dear."

The soft-spoken words rung with authority. The bean seller's wife slipped into the tent without looking up. Ayan wondered who the men were to make the bean seller so upset to see them in his line. Ayan paid with several coins and nodded politely. The bean seller flushed embarrassed. The insult that Ayan had repeatedly visited the bean tent, while they had not bought rice in more than two years, remained unspoken.

Ayan stepped to the side and walked a couple steps. He turned to watch the bean seller nervously address the two men.

"Two bowls of beans and do not fill the bowls with broth," one of the surly men ordered.

"Fill them to the top if you want to be paid," the other man threatened.

"Most assuredly, gentlemen, you will find my servings fair." His voice quavered slightly

The wife remained behind the tent flap. Ayan watched the bean seller suggest that coins be laid on the table before he filled the bowls. The men scowled at the bean seller and then grabbed their bowls, wolfing their food down before they moved three steps from the table.

The older man lifted his head. Bean juice dripped down his chin. Their eyes met for a moment. A sly grin split the man's grimy face. The skin crawled on the back of his neck. Ayan felt sure they would meet again.

* * *

The heat pressed down like heavy weights making it difficult to breath and Ayan struggled to sleep. A moonbeam shone through the window and he measured the night by the moonlight moving across the floor. It moved only a foot or two between the times he woke.

He gave up trying to sleep and left the house. He lay on the ground staring at the stars. The air washed over his body cooling him, making it easier to think. This time of the night made life bearable. It reminded him of the last time he'd truly been happy. The night of the good dream when Kazi told him they would soon live on their own. They ate breakfast and stood before the mission teacher and listened to a long talk about their soul and not breaking the law. Ayan stood patiently staring up at the mission teacher wondering what any of that had to do with their escaping the orphanage.

They spent most of the morning running around the streets, laughing and chasing each other. Kazi stood for a long time watching a monkey dance. The beggar finally chased them off, saying they were scaring people away. Ayan begged to see a real ship. Kazi finally gave in and they walked down through the narrow streets until they turned around a crumbling wall and came into full view of the harbour.

Ayan stopped breathing. Great ships filled the harbour. Some towered higher than the orphanage and floated on bright blue water. The salty smell tinged his nose, far more pleasant than in his dream. There was so much movement that Ayan didn't know where to look at once. He turned back and forth, one moment watching large wooden boxes being lowered off a ship on chains, the next, watching a blindfolded horse being led down a swaying wooden plank.

His father's face returned to his dream, beckoning him once again. Even in his sleep, Ayan fought between the idea of following in his father's footsteps to the sea, and the sadness he would feel at leaving Kazi.

* * *

Ayan woke with a jerk. The moonlight washed the room in pale grey shadows. The shadows did not move. The night animals remained silent. Only Kazi's gurgling snore broke the night's stillness as he struggled for breath in painful gasps.

Ayan's heart pounded against his chest for several minutes before he relaxed. Kazi lived. What had awakened him?

A chill swept his body. Muffled laughter rippled through the night. Ayan reached under the bed and felt for a blade he kept there. He slipped silently across the room, lowering his body behind the door. Cat-like movements, practiced from years surviving on the street, brought him to the door without producing a sound. He slipped through the front door.

The moonlight made the shadows take form in the pale light. Two black silhouettes moved beneath the betel nut tree. A tree branch bent down and sprang back up. Another dark branch lay on the ground, broken. The forms moved clumsily, struggling with a large bulky shape. Ayan breathed slowly from his mouth, silently watching.

Thieves. Their laughter would cease before the sun rose. Moving with feline grace he crawled barefoot across the grassy dirt. He travelled low, becoming nothing more than a shadow on the ground. The men remained too intent on their harvest to pay attention to their surroundings.

Ayan sank lower. Each movement, each sound, became a part of the night. The temptation to rush in and save the betel nuts almost overrode the fear that the intruders were high, and therefore dangerous.

A few more feet and the pale light outlined the thieves. The older man from the bean line crouched low, exhausted from his night's work. The younger greedily plucked another bean from the tree. The bag looked like it already held half the tree's harvest. Ayan adjusted the knife, the sudden glint catching the older man's attention. In one startled movement, the old man pulled a knife from his belt, and turned to confront Ayan.

"Leave," growled the older man. The younger man's wicked grin widened, despite the look of fear that he struggled to conceal.

"Drop the bag."

"It is not you," said the old one, "who is in charge?"

Ayan readied for an attack. He flipped the blade easily and held it ready to attack. "I will never forget this insult. My brother and I will track you to the ends of Bengal. Your hearts will lie on the ground. Your thieving hands removed. Then, the world will know what you've done!"

The men withdrew and cast sidelong glances at each other. They obviously didn't know about a brother.

"Leave now, before we make you pay for this insult!" spat Ayan. The younger man was shifting nervously from one foot to the other, obviously unsure what to do next. He kept looking to his older companion and then back to Ayan, waiting for someone to make the next move. Suddenly the old man dropped the bag of nuts on the ground and backed slowly away from Ayan, not dropping his gaze until he was fully back among the shadows of the night.

A pain filled Ayan's heart. Kazi's operation lay in a pile by his feet. To Ayan this was the same as a pile of coins lying on the ground. Gold coins that would rot within days if not sold. Only weeks ago anger turned into threats to cut the tree down. At first, the tree's death meant Kazi's life. Then, the tree became Kazi's only hope. Now, even with all their efforts, time may run out before enough nuts grew to send Kazi to a doctor.

"What was it? Prowlers?" Kazi's sleepy voice called from the house.

"Yes, brother."

CHAPTER 4

Ayan paced. The gnawing in his stomach returned shortly after sunrise.

"Eat," Kazi said absently.

"Not hungry."

"You did not eat yesterday."

"I will not eat today, either."

For most of the day he avoided Kazi, afraid of finding him chewing the betel nut. Kazi accepted fate without a whimper. The betel nut numbed fear, but at the same time, it left his brother useless. All the burden of grieving and finding money fell on Ayan's shoulders.

Ayan sat for hours, aimlessly staring at the weed-covered field. Small plants struggled for survival, but Ayan found it hard to pull the weeds that choked the tender shoots. Each day the chore took more effort.

A green object caught his attention. He stared at the discarded betel nut already wrapped in a tobacco leaf. Ayan reached for it without thinking. The nut rolled in the palm of his hand, smooth and cool. The bean offered freedom, if only for a moment. Ayan simply needed to pop the betel nut in his mouth, chew and troubles vanished. The nut played between his fingers. Ayan wanted peace. He wanted relief.

"Lost."

Ayan swung expecting to see someone behind him. The field remained empty. He heard the voice. Heard the word "lost" uttered just behind him. Did his mind play tricks?

"Lost," Ayan repeated the word. That is what the betel nut promised, to steal his soul. The image of the dead boy floated before him. Except this time Ayan did not look on the bloated corpse with the eyes of a boy, but the eyes of a man. "He is lost," Kazi said that day, and Ayan knew now how a boy could be in plain view and still be lost.

Ayan stood and threw the bean as far as he could. He scanned the world around him.

A couple of women walked up the path. They hid behind their saris as he approached. Ayan nodded and held up a bag of rice. One woman shook her head and hurried on. The woman in a bright yellow and orange sari hesitated.

Ayan heard their arguments as he crossed the field. The woman in the bright sari sounded pleading. The other woman finally shook her head.

Ayan hurried across the field.

"Rice, please," the woman in the bright sari whispered. "It is for a special meal for my husband."

Ayan pulled a bag of rice from its storage place under a rock. "It is a good day," he said politely. "Your friend does not need rice?"

The woman's eyes fluttered with embarrassment. Her head shook, no. Ayan held out his palm to accept the coins. "Your husband is a lucky man to have found a good woman."

The woman blushed. "Thank you," and then rushed to rejoin her friend. Ayan watched them walk away, their heads turned toward each other as they whispered.

The hours dragged. Ayan stood on the edge of the field until the sun dropped low enough in the sky and he could close the shop. He approached the house, carefully avoiding the torn and bare spot on the betel nut tree.

It took only a moment to close the shop. He closed the shutters as an argument raged in his head. Kazi sat alone, lost in the buzz from the betel nut. A half-finished bowl of rice lay spilled on the floor. Ayan cleaned up the rice quickly and then turned to Kazi.

Ayan stared at his brother. He ached to comfort him, to sit beside him as the sun sank. They could talk like in the old days when they shared dreams of wealth and home. An eternity passed in the darkening room before Ayan turned to leave. He wondered why he stood, every night, debating whether to stay with Kazi's snoring body. Or walk to the village, where people still hoped for a good life and worked hard to fulfil their dreams.

He wandered down the path, aimlessly kicking a rock. Tear stained cheeks were the only indication that he grieved. Ayan feared that nothing remained in his life except tears and anger. He followed the same path he'd followed for weeks. It led past the unused path to the area where women washed clothing on the rocks. He passed through the ferns and undergrowth past the trail that lead to the neglected rice paddy. The path hardened here, and widened, grooved by heavy wagons.

Ayan followed a rut to the edge of town. A thin path cut around the houses and through tall stands of coarse grass. Ayan emerged near the market.

A group of elders already gathered under the shade of trees. Dark eyes watched him intently from leathered faces. They unwrapped various packets of barks and leaves. A few packets of foul smelling pastes already lay on the ground waiting to be stirred into a tea. Ayan strode on, until he entered the market and walked into the first booth. The merchant smiled and continued tending his wares, as Ayan studied the collection of porcelain cups. Pale white and red flowers danced on the translucent white surface. With a short nod, Ayan moved to the next booth.

This merchant sold silks. A selection of the red, orange, and yellow cloth hung over a beam and gently fluttered in the warm evening air. The merchant, like all of them, ignored Ayan. They knew of Ayan's misfortune and accepted Ayan as a merchant in his own right. They afforded him the respite of wandering the stalls, dreaming of better days. However, Ayan never dreamed of better days. He just forgot the pain of existence.

One silk caught in a stray breeze. The silk undulated, reflecting light back in the green and blue shades of the ocean. The silk rolled like the waves on the Surma River.

The silk moved under the touch of a hand and then dropped to reveal dark eyes. Lady Achala. Her eyes narrowed in laughter at Ayan's fright. A smile parted her full lips. She tilted her head to display the beauty of her skin and translucent eyes before disappearing behind another layer of silks.

Ayan sucked in a breath and stepped back. He rushed around the back of the silk stall and hurried to the bean tent. Ayan had enough money to buy supper tonight. The bean tent provided a safe refuge from Lady Achala. Shame washed over his fear of a woman. It took several moments before his breathing calmed. Of all women, she was the only one he held no respect for.

Lady Achala lived with her two sons at the fringes of Sylhet, on the edge of the merchant's area. She would sit on a pile of silks before the doorway of her hut. Few knew whether she really knew the future, or used gossip and fear to torment those who passed.

Some people liked the attention. She played on their vanity and dreams. For some she called out promises of wealth and pleasure. Ayan had once watched her as she teased a young woman about her future husband. Then, as the woman blushed with delight, the vision changed. It always did. The beautiful man in her future demanded too many sons and beat her for the birth of a daughter. He then threw her out in disgust. Ayan's lips tightened as he watched the poor child run away in tears. Lady Achala chuckled to herself.

Ayan soon learned that conversing with the psychic held only two types of visions. Whether positive or negative the outcome of the vision depended on the amount of gold in the client's pocket. As far as Ayan believed, any person who claimed to see the future mingled their soul with dark spirits and should be avoided. It was wrong. Psychic predictions seemed frighteningly unnatural to him, like the religion of the mission teachers. Their teaching told that men must work as slaves to be good, and if they succeeded, their reward would be a place in the sky. Ayan's insides felt wormy as the mission teachers talked. He felt the same sensation when Lady Achala looked at him.

Ayan stood in the bean line and watched the drama unfold before him. Nothing ever changed. He stood behind the same group of women who were in the line the day when he met the thieves. The women chattered and laughed with the bean merchant. Ayan smiled. They not only went through the same motions, but they even talked about the same things they did that day.

The bean merchant smiled nicely over the woman's shoulder. He filled Ayan's bowl to the brim and nodded. Ayan smiled back and nodded with respect. The respect he earned for caring for Kazi offered little comfort. Men no longer remained aloof, treating him with the disdain with which they treated all other betel nut merchants. Now, Ayan was simply a young man helping his unfortunate brother.

The respect he once hungered for did not fill the void growing in his heart. He found a space under a tree and slowly chewed the beans. He noticed that the merchant added a little meat to his broth. Ayan congratulated himself on the foresight to treat the merchant with extra respect tonight.

Lady Achala moved between the houses. Ayan imagined that he heard a rustle of silks mixed with the tinkle of chimes at her waist, wrists, and ankles. He munched a piece of meat and watched her settle in front of her home for the parade of evening clients. Several people dropped coins on her silk pillows and waited for her to sway gently. Her voice sang in melodic chorus with the words she chanted. Some clients rocked in time with her, while others stood mute.

Ayan sat by the tree finishing his meal. He closed his eyes and let himself get lost in the music that played seductively on the breeze. At first, he heard flutes, then he realised that a woman's voice called.

"Come talk to me, boy," the voice said loudly.

Ayan startled, his eyes opened, and he looked around for the source of the invitation. Was the voice directed at him?

"Boy. Come talk to me." Lady Achala looked straight at him. There was no mistaking who she was addressing. Ayan stood up and walked over to the psychic.

"Why do you call me 'boy'?" he asked. "Do you not have sight of my true name?"

The corner of her mouth turned up and she waved away the onlookers with a flick of her jewelled hand.

Lady Achala looked up and smiled. Ayan was taken aback by her deep green pupils. He had assumed they were brown like the other woman's. The contrast both frightened and attracted him. Only twice before had he seen that particular shade of green. Once in the jewel of a rich lady who was being carried through the streets in a litter. She had opened the curtains so everyone could see the expensive jewels she wore to a party. The other time was on rugs imported from Persia, a country dry as salt, where no ferns or great trees lived.

"It does not work that way," she said matter-of-factly. "If I saw all things, my mind would be too big for my skull."

Her tone laughed at him, but the logic made sense. Ayan laughed. It refreshed him to hear a woman use the colourful language he grew up hearing as merchants bantered to each other, and noble people used when talking loud enough to attract everyone's attention.

Ayan dismissed her psychic's gift. She possessed a poet's soul.

"So what do you see?" he asked quietly.

They waited. Ayan grew uncomfortable, wondering if she waited for him to toss a coin on her pillow. The single coin tucked in his clothing grew heavy. His fingers twitched. A moment later, he wet his lips and reached beneath his clothing.

She spoke the moment he touched the coin. "Water," she said, drawing out the first syllable, her lips forming a perfect O.

Ayan fingered the coin. Her feet moved forward to cover the silk pillow. Her eyelids drooped slightly as she stared into the distance beyond Ayan, toward an invisible horizon.

"You belong there," she said. "They take men like you."

"As a Lascar?" he asked, cursing himself for the ease with which she had trapped him. Now she could manipulate this bogus discussion. She saw nothing. Any beautiful woman held the power to manipulate and deceive a man. They did not need evil spirits to help them.

"One does not expect that you own a ship."

Ayan laughed, relieved now that he uncovered her ruse. Now, he could play the game out without fear of attracting Allah's displeasure or ruining his soul.

"You do not convince me. Water, ships. You can say such things to any person with as much conviction as you would mention food and rivers. Why apply these matters so directly to me?"

Lady Achala feigned patience. The game did not surprise her, or frighten her. In fact, she appeared comfortable dealing with sceptics Ayan waited for her to tip his balance in one direction or the other. The logical part wanted him to prove her deception and return to the responsibility of caring for Kazi. The heart, his imagination, wanted her to prove that it was time to head to the sea. The desire to hear that the time to find freedom grew near, so near, that the taste of salt coated his mouth.

"Do you have a parent…?" she asked

"Every person," he grinned, "has a parent."

Her smile widened to show white teeth. Green eyes rolled as she continued, "…who knew the sea?"

Ayan leaned from scepticism toward belief. "You mean," he asked, "was on the sea?"

"Yes," she replied. "I do not see the sea, not as I have been told it looks like. I see blackness, a dark hole. A man."

"Yes," Ayan sighed.

"I see the colour red."

"Yes," Ayan nodded.

"He wants you to follow him. Go find him. It is where you will find manhood. Go now."

"Wait," Ayan, regained his balance, "I gave myself away. When I said 'on the sea', I handed you that information."

"You go now," she repeated, fanning herself with a rag despite the growing coldness.

"Until you go, you will be merely a boy."

"I..."

She stood, her perfumed hair inches below his nose. She never looked up, but examined the expanse of his chest. "You will become as strong as him. You too will be able to lift incredible weights without struggle." She sagged wearily to her chair.

"Anyone can see I am strong."

"Strength does not prevent a man from losing his way."

"I am not lost," Ayan said sternly.

"No?" Her laugh rang soft as the evening breeze. "A man who is lost rarely understands that he is lost."

"This does not make sense."

"Words of wisdom do not make sense to a man who is lost. That is the nature of being lost."

"Will I find my way on the sea?"

"No."

"Then when will I find myself?"

"You will find your own path by helping others find their way. It is your destiny to touch several souls before you understand what it means to be a man."

"And if I do not help others?" Ayan did not like the intent behind her words. He wanted to help Kazi by earning enough coin to hire a surgeon. He wanted to make their shop flourish. He did not want to waste time helping others.

"Then your destiny will be lost forever. And, you will lose the greatest gift a man can have."

“This gift? What is it?”

“The love of a woman.”

“Ah,” Ayan smiled. “I will be wealthy enough to marry a wife?”

“No. When you own nothing, and there is nothing more to lose, then love will find you.”

“How can I marry if I do not have money?”

“That,” she whispered, “you must learn on your own.”

“How will I know when this comes to pass?”

“You will know.”

“And I am to trust you?” Ayan’s brows shot up as he watched for any sign of jest or deceit in her voice or manner. A waft of jasmine filled the air as she fell back to her pillows.

“Go, my boy. I never tell lies.

* * *

Stars blanketed a blue-black sky. The black path snaked up the hill into the darkness. Moonlit grass and trees painted the night in various shades of greys and blues. A silver moon stream cut a path down the hill. Ayan saw none of this. His mind wrestled with the argument, do psychics exist, or do only liars claim to never tell lies.

The moon peeked through rain clouds as they sped across the sky. Ayan sat on a chair and etched another mark into the table, thirty. One month passed since he met her. That meeting ruined the pleasure of the village.

He felt the burden of Kazi’s pain. He worked in the shop through the day, and at night, the dreams of the sea returned. He learned the hard way the truth about Lady Achala’s torment. He went back to working in the rice paddy and his field. The field lay harrowed, the earth turned, waiting patiently for the storm season to saturate the thirsty earth. The young plants grew lustily, freed from the nettles and choking weeds.

He deepened the rice paddy and extended it. He dug for days, leaving deep piles of wet mud at the side of the paddy. The next rain would wash it away and bring needed nutrients from the surrounding forest into his paddy. He worked hard. His chest expanded again. A mute reminder, that he ignored her vision.

The night beckoned him to bed, but sleep eluded him. The dreams returned with vivid clarity. Great waves swamped the boat, filling the dark cavern with green water. Ayan looked at the door, but his father never appeared. Now, Lady Achala stood there in a green sari. Her eyes looked past him. Her voice whispered, "Go now boy." He woke in a cold sweat, too early to start work, too late to find comfort in sleep. The dream became a nightmare. The nightmare became a living hell.

The days dragged. Kazi failed to regain weight despite the extra food. When Ayan became depressed, Kazi starved. He did not lose much weight, but his skin sagged. Folds of skin hung from under his arms and around his belly. The extra food did not fill the folds; instead it made other parts of his body stretch.

Ayan stared out the window. Two people approached across the field. He frowned. The shop closed hours ago. He stood and watched, wondering who would visit at this hour of the evening. One woman laughed a sound that he could recognise in the depths of a fever. Ayan leapt from his chair and ran out of the door to greet the visitors.

"Hello cousins," Ayan said, barely able to contain his excitement. "I am so pleased to see you," he said as he grabbed the women and hugged them tightly. "Come. Come inside."Ayan ushered the women towards his home.

"Kazi! Kazi! Come see who is here! It is Faiza and Mirvat come to visit us."

"I see you are all dressed up," Faiza said, aiming her palms upward while pointing at Ayan's clothing.

Ayan blushed. Not so much in the fact that he'd recently replaced his dirty, worn, clothing with a new Punjabi suit, complete with long shirt, baggy trousers, and strapped sandals, but he also purchased a nice tatty shawl for his shoulders.

Though the material was thin, and lacked ornaments, it looked striking when placed across his broad shoulders.

He had worked for another man for an entire day, doing the work of two men, to earn the money for the Punjabi suit. He did not measure the suit by its ornamentation or colours, but by the satisfaction, he experienced when working hard for an honest day's pay.

"I waited half a month for your arrival," he teased.

"It takes time for two women to prepare for such a challenge," Mirvat teased back.

"I am sorry, but I needed to arrange for my household to be cared for."

Ayan reached down and startled her by kissing her innocent, sincere cheek. He didn't know which one he liked best. Mirvat, with her saucy eyes and sharp tongue, or Faiza who was innocent and honest as a child.

"I am getting ready for Calcutta," Ayan replied, holding out the shawl for their examination.

"Sandals aboard a steamship?" asked Mirvat, her eyebrows raising, taking the top part of her headdress with them.

Ayan smiled. "Who knows if I'll secure a job," he said gently. He frowned. Trust Mirvat's insightfulness to realise he'd made a foolish purchase. The merchant grew excited at the size of Ayan's purchase and he then brought out the stylish shoes and even a few gilded belts. Ayan, unaccustomed to spending so much money on himself grew flushed and forgot that stylish shoes were not practical on a ship.

Taking advantage of the pause, Faiza veered away from her sister's comment. "Is Kazi here?"

"Yes." Ayan glanced toward the hut. He lowered his voice despite their distance from his brother. "Don't say anything about his lip. I'm sure Aunt Fatma told you."

"But if we're to care for him…" Faiza began.

Mirvat's exasperated sigh was interrupted by Kazi bursting

from the house.

"Cousins," he shouted, stretching out his fleshy arms.

Each of the women took an arm, and they hugged for a moment.

Mirvat patted Kazi's belly. "We're here to take care of you, Kazi."

"Just keep you company," Ayan interjected, turning the conversation away from graver subjects.

Mirvat's eye caught Ayan's. They shared an invisible nod."Yes, you'll need someone to talk to."

"But I can talk to myself!" Kazi declared. "Been doing it my whole life."

Everyone laughed. Ayan smiled in pride. Kazi rarely pretended to be important anymore.

"Doesn't he speak with you?" Faiza inquired, aiming a quick thumb at Ayan.

"Yes, but I listen to myself more," Kazi chuckled, patting Ayan on the shoulder.

"Are your parents good?"

"Yes," Faiza replied politely.

"They do not need our care." Mirvat laughed.

"We walked across a large field," Faiza said. "I do not know much about tending fields."

"The field is ready," Kazi said. "Ayan has it ready, and I can help harvest."

"There should be a fair harvest this year, but I have hired someone to harvest the rice."

"And," Mirvat glanced slyly at her cousin. "I can sell it for a high price."

Faiza laughed, "No doubt. My sister could entice a Raja to part with a gold-and-jewel encrusted elephant in exchange for a simple loaf of bread."

Ayan smiled approvingly. Mirvat tossed her head at the slight, but her eyes beamed with the intended compliment.

Ayan stepped aside to let his cousins enter the house first.

"When do you leave?" Faiza asked as she looked around the dirty room.

"Two days hence." Ayan wiped the table with a rag.

Mirvat grabbed the rag with a laugh. "How you two have lived alone this long is a wonder." She wet the rag and wiped the table. Faiza drew some spices and a loaf from her bag and stirred rice on the fire. Within moments, a savoury meal sat on the table.

Ayan watched the warm scene unfold as the women wiped and lit the lamp. Their laughter filled the room with warmth, as the jasmine in their saris and hair permeated the air.

"I cannot believe you are heading to the ocean." Faiza broke into Ayan's thoughts.

Mirvat flashed her sister with a frown. "Faiza! It is not our place to judge Ayan."

"I didn't mean disrespect. I just wondered why he would leave this fine business to slave on a ship."

Kazi rolled his eyes dramatically. "I have told him about the life in the belly of a ship." Kazi threw his hands up dramatically. "But, who can reason with a dreamer. He believes father is calling him to the sea."

"I thought your father was dead?" Faiza put a hand on her chest.

"He is," Kazi sighed. "Ayan has dreams where father tells him to go to sea."

Both women nodded knowingly.

Ayan sighed. "The money will help pay for . . . expenses, Kazi. We have been over this several times."

"Yes, but there is other work where a man is not driven from bed in the morning and works until he falls into an exhausted heap at the end of the day. Where men are treated worse than dogs, and if they die, one tries to give them a proper burial." Bitterness tainted his tone. Even Mirvat looked down, uncertain what to do after the angry outburst. Ayan held his tongue, familiar with Kazi's outburst. Kazi never showed any emotion at Ayan's decision to leave. He never ranted when Ayan shared his plans. Ayan never realised how much his leaving hurt Kazi. In fact, Ayan never thought about anything but his fear of losing Kazi and living alone for the rest of his life.

Mirvat and Faiza started talking between themselves. Within minutes the friendly ambiance returned to the room. Laughter echoed across the field well into the night. Ayan felt disassociated. Kazi and the girls hit it off, chattering endlessly as he watched.

This was now a strange place. The women brought an unfamiliar element into the house. Even Kazi behaved differently. The man laughing with the women was not the betel nut addicted brother of the last few months who needed to be dressed, or to be reminded to eat. Kazi's eyes danced with laughter as the women told stories. Ayan sighed. It was time to leave.

CHAPTER 5

The wind blew dust clouds up off the road, yet offered little respite from the merciless sun. Ayan stopped walking and rested his palms on his knees, his mouth parched. Cramps tightened the muscles in his calves. He took several deep breaths, startled at how quickly his body lost its true strength.

"You can't be tired," he said to himself. He glanced around to make sure no one saw him resting on the three-mile hike from his home to the train station. He shielded his eyes with his hands and looked both ways. The road stretched endlessly in both directions.

"Things will get harder from here on in."

He stood upright and told his body that it was not tired. It was just the tension of leaving Kazi in the care of two young girls, mixed with the nervousness of finally heading for the sea. His worries had been eased slightly by the caring nature of his cousins, but his fears for his brother's health had been replaced by the fear of the unknown.

Ayan forced himself to move forward. The warmth of Kazi's hug still tattooed his shoulders. They held tight for several moments. They parted without a word. Ayan wondered where fate planned to take them. He realised that in the month of preparation Kazi had never asked the one important question: When did he plan to return? It occurred to him that he never made plans with his cousins, or his brother, for a return. He realised why his uncle let the girls come. Of course, they expected Kazi to die and Ayan to disappear. The house and business would give the girls enough wealth to earn them a husband. The way fate wove everything together amazed him. His heart fell. This is not the destiny he wanted; to choose between his brother and the sea. He wanted both.

* * *

Sharp pain shot up Ayan's shoulders. The ground rocked. His head jerked off the seat and slammed back. He opened his eyes. Bright light flooded the tightly packed train car. He blinked against the light and tried to adjust his body more comfortably between a large man and the window.

"Are you from Fenchugonj?" A man of similar age, or maybe just a little bit older, asked the question. A boy in his late teens sat beside him.

"Yes, I am," Ayan smiled. "And you?"

"Just on the fringes," the older one replied. "Where the trees get thick."

Ayan realised that this pair came from an even poorer section of the village than he did. He wondered how they afforded a spot in the coach, instead of being crammed like cattle in the boxcar, or riding on top of the last car.

"You've got strong arms. I reckon you wish to find work as a shipman. I have wanted to do so myself for years, but I had to wait for my brother to grow older. In my opinion, he was old enough years ago, but our mother worries." He laughed indulgently and shouldered his younger brother playfully. "She wanted him to grow strong, grow as many inches as he'll ever grow."

The boy smiled shyly, "I'll grow taller. I will be the strongest shipman."

"You will make a fine shipman." Ayan nodded. Emotion cut his heart. He missed Kazi with all his soul. He envied the brothers. He never entertained the dream of sharing his dream of the ocean with Kazi. Ships never took men with Kazi's stature. How terrific it would be if they could go to sea together. Life without the betel nut tree and no disease, that needed money and operations. The brothers could simply make a good living and explore the world. He sighed. No such thing would happen in this lifetime.

Ayan embraced the conversation, hoping to distract his

emotions with chatter. "I am Ayan. What are your names?"

"I am Akbar," said the talkative one, aiming a finger at his chest. He pointed to his brother. "This is Emran. He doesn't talk much."

"Have you ever asked him anything?" Ayan grinned, checking to see if his fellow travellers had a sense of humour.

"What could he tell me that I don't already know?" Akbar smiled. Emran smiled too; a shy withdrawn grin. He bent his head and grinned toward his lap.

"I don't suppose you have any connections aboard the ships?" Ayan asked. "The only thing I knew was to go to Calcutta."

"When you live on the fringes," Akbar replied, "you don't have connections. You're lucky if you have food." Akbar leaned forward and winked. "We do, however, know of a lodge where shipmen gather. In my experience, if you're friendly, doors open for you."

Ayan smiled. "That doesn't quite explain why so many unfriendly men have power, does it?"

An uproarious laugh escaped Akbar. Ayan was pleased to see the joke hit its target. He expected that, like most poor people, the brothers enjoyed a good poke at the rich and powerful. And then Emran laughed. And that set Ayan off.

The three shared a big laugh that drew the attention of others travelling in the train car. Ayan realised that this was his first real laugh in a very long time. The knots in his stomach loosened as the laughter spread through the carriage.

Today was a good day. He had laughed, and he made his first real friends.

* * *

Ayan woke with a start. "Wake up! Wake up!"

Ayan jumped up and brandished his knife, expecting a thief, or worse. It took a moment to recognise Akbar.

"I was having a good dream."

Akbar grinned back and slapped at the knife.

Ayan slipped it back under the mattress and dropped on the bed.

"It was a good dream," he sulked. In his dream, a snake with a markedly green body crawled toward him upon a stone mattress carved in a circle. The snake kept displaying its tongue. Ayan sighed. Like most dreams, he would forget it within minutes.

"Well your dreams are about to come true, my friend," Akbar laughed and flopped on the mattress beside him. He waited until Ayan looked at him. "We have work."

Emran stood quietly by his older brother's side with a flushed grin. He only knew the brothers for four days, but it was enough to learn that Emran's emotions played on his face. Ayan took a second look at Emran, something disturbing shadowed his expression.

"What's wrong with him?" Ayan sat up in bed and pointed at Emran. He crossed their shared room. The rooms in the inn were small and filthy, but they were better than the street.

"Do not mind him," said Akbar, avoiding his brother's eyes. "He feels nervous about the idea of being on the waves. The boy doesn't know a good opportunity when fate offers it to him." Akbar looked at Emran, levelling a fatherly look of irritation.

Ayan pulled his shirt over his head and let his brows arch as he watched Emran intently.

Emran spoke softly. "Brother, you should listen to mother more. You talk of this as if it is a prize. Those men treated us like a pair of gutter rats."

"Emran, you didn't even know what a gutter looked like till we arrived here."

"Which men?" Ayan interrupted.

"Put your shoes on and come with us," Akbar said. "They want to meet you. We've told them all about you."

"You talked mostly about yourself," Emran corrected with a hint of disdain.

"I told them that we were hard workers who would not cause

any trouble."

"As long as they can secure employment for us, on a ship," Ayan countered.

"Of course on a ship," Ayan laughed. "Do you think they are fine merchants who ask me and my brother to be house servants?"

Emran chuckled audibly at the idea. Ayan did not worry how other men treated him. His joy of being on a ship that very night hurried his dressing.

* * *

Ayan followed the brothers through the inn. They descended a narrow staircase at the rear of the building and peered into the kitchen, which hummed with activity. Dirty women with large eyes plucked chickens in one corner. A small boy lugged a heavy bucket from the well outside. Ayan stopped to let the boy pass. For a moment, Ayan saw himself in the filthy scraps of rags covering the gaunt body. Sweat trickled through the grime on the boy's neck. Ayan looked at the fat cook. Soup splattered from the spoon he waved at a young girl. Ayan doubted the boy would fill his belly from the scraps earned from the day's labour.

The previous morning, Ayan had noticed two European steamers moored at the nearby docks: The Victoria and the Bengal. The Victoria bustled with activity as well-dressed servants ran to fetch for fine ladies. Black boys stared off the side of the ship with white eyes. Ladies chided them and teased in the same manner they would with a lap dog. A black man walked a tall skinny dog. The animal stood waist high, but Ayan may have easily spanned the animal's gaunt waist with his hand. The dog wore a heavy gold-and-jewel encrusted collar. The black man noticed Ayan watching and yanked the dog around. They walked the length of the dock and up the Bengal's gangplank. A couple of servants followed their masters across the deck. The Lascars' faces were torn with strain as they loaded bundles onto the ship.

"Ayan?"

Ayan snapped out of his daydream, nodded to Akbar and followed the brothers past the kitchen and down a crumbling set of stone stairs toward the basement. He stopped halfway down to glance over his shoulder. A group of Bengali men wearing bright coloured sarongs followed. Ayan moved forward, listening to bits of conversation while the men whispered among themselves.

Ayan wondered which ship these recruiters worked for. He eyed their bright sarongs, the bold colours almost glowing from the richly dyed cloth. Ayan thought that these men must work for a benevolent ship. The ability to dye clothing remained restricted to people who earned more money than they needed to live on. It was hard for Ayan tried to imagine owning enough coins to do such things.

When they reached the cool basement, the brothers stopped and allowed Ayan to step in front of them. Ayan glanced behind and noticed that Akbar and Emran pressed together, hiding behind Ayan's girth. Akbar grinned and motioned forward. Ayan looked up at the group of wealthy men sat at a table near the far wall. He remembered being close to men such as these, as a child, when begging for work, but Kazi did the talking. Ayan rarely paid attention to the rich men, all that concerned him was the end of the day when Kazi ran back to show him the food they earned in trade for a day's work. They often worked for an entire day in exchange for two melons or a small loaf of bread.

His past experience hardly qualified him to take the lead when dealing with wealthy men in dyed sarongs. Ayan nodded humbly at the group. As far as he recalled, he never stood this close to men of means.

The men examined him and talked among themselves as if they were examining livestock. None of the wealthy men volunteered their names. Some stood, while others lounged behind the greyish, splintery table.

After a moment's pause, one man stood above the rest. His sarong glowed scarlet with blue trimmed cuffs. The way other men moved to avoid his touch, or bowed their head when he looked their way, spoke more than words could ever. This innate power made him the leader.

Their eyes met. Ayan held the man's gaze for only a moment before turning away. The depths of the leader's eyes held secrets. Murder. The word rippled through Ayan's spirit like a premonition.

"Kind of small, no?" the leader said with disgust, loud enough for them to hear.

Akbar and Emran held their hands up. They began studying themselves. Akbar ran his fingers through his shaggy black hair. Emran just stood quietly, flexing his fingers.

Ayan overheard a single whispered word, "Dirt." He looked up to catch two men staring directly at him. He did not understand whether they pegged him as a farmer, or whether they used the term as an insult.

The boy started to shift from one foot to the other. Ayan was worried that Emran would flee, ruining all their chances of being employed. He looked at the half-completed ledger on the desk. The papers formed a list. If only he knew how many spaces had to be filled. Weeks may pass before another ship needing Lascars sailed into the harbour. If they didn't land a berth on this ship, the harsh reality of life in Calcutta without money would become all too real. Ayan needed to protect Emran from that fate.

Ayan held his shoulders straight and stepped forward.

"How do you mean?"

All heads turned toward him. Akbar and Emran fell silent. Emran scrunched even smaller. Ayan swallowed.

"You mentioned being small . . ."

The leader swung his hand around, knocking over a blue jug. He pointed a fat finger at Emran.

"The boy is small. Is he strong?"

"You met him last time we . . . came down," Akbar croaked.

The leader did not look up from the ledgers. His fingers laced through his glossy beard.

"That was before you brought him." He stuck his finger stuck out at Ayan, and paused.

What would happen if Emran prevented Akbar from securing a spot on a ship? Ayan knew. They would part and the streets would swallow the quiet boy within a few short days.

"I will not take the boy's job."

The raw pain of leaving Kazi left his spirit feeling lost. It would be impossible, for reasons both practical and emotional, for the brothers to part without one, or both, facing disaster.

The man's eyes rose slowly. The leader placed large hands on the table. "You like to think of yourself as honest?"

"Yes," Ayan replied, embarrassed that his voice quivered.

"Then," said the man, "can you honestly tell me that this boy will work harder than you?"

Every man in the room turned expectantly. All eyes focused on Ayan. He turned to Akbar. The older brother's eyes shone with fear. Emran's head hung in shame.

He turned to the leader. "Yes," he nodded, their eyes meeting, holding, for a long moment. Emran's shoulders started to shake violently.

The Sylheti men snickered. Their leader's face shaded, hot with anger. He rose to his full height and kicked the chair back, slamming it against the wall. The man folded big hands into fists with the smooth grace of a predator. Ayan worried that he prepared to beat them. He shifted, ready to step between the man and boy.

A growl drifted from his throat. "Explain yourself."

Ayan started to turn to Akbar, then realised the leader expected Ayan to answer for the boy. He explained that he only met the brothers five days ago, on a train. A breath caught in his throat. The leader stared like a snake. Ayan remembered the dream. As long as he didn't move the snake remained motionless.

He took another step forward.

"It's not that a child can work better than a man of my size. It is that he would draw strength from a family member on board. Somebody to speak to, somebody to keep him from becoming homesick and to keep his focus up." Ayan surprised himself. "There is strength in brothers that cannot be measured in muscle, or gold. It is something that Allah himself put in their spirits. Brothers share a bond that gives them strength when many, stronger . . . more worthy, men have given up and shed their spirit."

Ayan mimicked the mission teachers' expressions and tones as they talked to children about respectability, though the words came from Ayan's love for Kazi.

The leader returned to the table and sat down. He leaned back and folded his hands together while he contemplated Ayan. The leader hissed, "Will you," his eyes narrowed, "become homesick if we take you? You who have no family on board."

"Yes. No," said Ayan, "I am older. I am a man."

The leader's brows knit together in a deep frown. "An honest man? Then what is the answer, yes or no?"

"No," Ayan shook his head.

The leader tilted his head and sneered. "You did answer, yes."

Ayan took a deep breath. "My father was a Lascar. . . . he died at sea."

The leader's hands lowered. The fact that Ayan's father worked as a Lascar appeased his temper. Finally, as if heaven intervened, the big man smiled.

"My boy," he pointed at Ayan, "You may be strapped with muscle, but you are no man. No one is, until he has worked on a ship."

Everyone openly mocked Ayan, except the leader. He stared evenly at the men. "I wonder." He paused until the others grew quiet. "I wonder if you will not regret your arrogance within a fortnight?"

"Does that mean we're going?" Akbar whimpered, his hands

twisting together.

The leader levelled him with a cold stare.

"Yes, I suppose," the leader muttered.

Several of the wealthy men leaned over the legers and pointed, arguing openly. The leader scowled and barked in anger. He slashed a thick line through a random name on the ledger and leaned forward, daring the others to oppose him.

The leader looked at Ayan and a wide grin split his face. "I am not worried. If you fail me, we can feed you to the sharks."

Laughter rippled through the group. Ayan looked at Akbar. The smaller man pursed his lips to hide the smile. Emran lifted his eyes to meet Ayan. His soft eyes full of sympathy. The others laughed as the trio exchanged startled glances.

"Now," the big man rose from the stool and slammed the book shut. "Turn out your pockets," he ordered. "Nobody earns a job without paying for it."

Ayan choked on his laugh. He knew without question that the man did not pose a joke. The leader placed the blue jug upright. He carefully centred it by the corner of the table. One of the others filled it with water.

Despite the overt absurdity, Ayan watched Akbar and Emran pour coins on the table. Their hands trembled as they handed over every coin they owned. The fear bit in the back of his mind that the entire interview may have been set up to cover a robbery. A hand moved to cover his purse. The brothers' coins jangled as they hit the table and as the men scrounged to collect them. Ayan felt, more than saw, the leader's eyes drift across the other men's heads to rest on him. He pulled out the eight coins hidden within the folds of the Punjabi suit and threw them on the table.

CHAPTER 6

"She weighs over 2,000 tons," Akbar gushed anxiously as they walked towards The Bengal. "She carries one hundred and fifty first-class travellers."

Ayan bit his tongue. This did not seem like the time to point out the fact that first-class did not necessarily mean Rajah-wealthy. He eyed the ship with understanding borne from spending most of his childhood begging and working on the docks. The hull had dulled with age. Only the deck of the steamer shone with care and concern. Anything that did not touch the whites fell into disrepair. Other ships blocked his view. He hoped that when he saw the ship as a whole that she would shine with the glow that only British and American ships shared.

"She was born in 1840," Emran whispered.

"1850," Akbar corrected. "The Dutch owned her and then the Boers. Now, she is owned by an English industrialist."

Ayan listened to Akbar struggle to pronounce the word. The ownership of the vessel did not concern him.

"... Swamped off of Cape Horn in South America." Akbar's words broke through Ayan's thoughts.

"I do not want the ship to be swamped while we are on board."

Ayan turned and looked at Emran. This was the first full sentence the boy had uttered since their meeting, a fortnight ago.

"I heard that The Bengal is owned by the New York, London & China Steamship Co. of London," Ayan corrected Akbar. He winked at Emran. The boy grinned back, their laughter lost in the cacophony of dock noises.

They waited for crews of Lascars to move several large crates to waiting ox carts. The men struggled under the weight of the crates and the abuse of the bosses. A moment later, a narrow path cleared and the three used it to escape the chaotic scene.

"We will see every corner of the globe," Akbar smiled.

They rounded a large pile of crates covered with a brown tarp, and The Bengal came into full view. The three stopped dead and stared. The hull needed cleaning, the brass railing was covered in black soot and black smoke puffed from the columns. Ladies rushed across the dock ordering servants to hurry with their luggage, or chiding children to remain close. Men in black suits and white shirts stepped out of coaches and hurried up the gangplank, ignoring everyone in their way. The European women hid under parasols and loudly complained of the heat.

Emran pointed to crates full of fruits being carried toward the ship. The fresh scent permeated the dock. Emran almost drooled when he asked if any of the multi-coloured delicacies were to eat. Ayan remembered the miserly way the servants handed out melons, even the overripe ones. He did not believe the owners planned to share the fruit with them, but he held his tongue.

They veered toward a crowd of men dressed in shabby Punjabi suits, similar to those that they were wearing. Some waited in silence, seemingly lost in their own thoughts, while others looked around, marvelling at the treasures and wealth surrounding them. Ayan moved deep in to the crowd and waited. Some held small bundles of clothing, but most brought only themselves.

A table sat on the dock. The men from the basement sat behind the table, minus the leader. They bickered over the ledgers, searching for men's names. Slowly the crowd thinned, moving one at a time into the ship.

Ayan heard the other Lascars talking above the crowd.

"We are privileged to work on such a fine ship."

"I paid twenty gold coins. I will make more than that before I arrive home."

"I hope the trip is short. I will work for one journey and then return home to marry."

The men laughed and jested among themselves.

"What do you think, Ayan?"

"I believe, Emran, that we are indeed lucky." Shivers of

excitement ran up Ayan's back. He shared the same sense of adventure that shone in the boy's eyes. But something did not fit. Something he couldn't quite put his finger on. He had watched Lascars and white merchant seamen load and unload ships for years. The quartermaster set a table for the men to sign up. The men dropped their sea kits and made their mark.

A group of old Lascars talked about a faraway place called the Caribbean where slave traders forced Lascars to bury the rotting bodies of slaves. Ayan worried that The Bengal may travel to such a place. He wondered if the Europeans knew, or even cared, that Allah imposed strict rules for the handling of a dead body.

"This Caribbean," Akbar interrupted, "sounds like an evil place."

The experienced Lascars exchanged glances.

"Evil places reside in men's hearts, not in places," one man answered.

"Do you fear evil, boy?" Another man looked straight at Emran.

"No," the boy said uncertainly. "No."

"Good," said the stranger, narrowing his eyes. "The world is full of evil. You will see evil close up; evil in all its glory."

The strangers laughed and turned their backs.

Ayan watched as the last few Europeans boarded the ship. He wondered what they would do if the ship swamped in an African storm. It wouldn't surprise him to learn that each traveller was matched by a crew member so that, if the boat sank, each passenger would desperately hold onto a crew member's back and be carried to safety. Ayan grinned at the image.

The sun scorched the dock before they found themselves at the table. The patience of the men at the table had worn thin. They snarled at Emran. Ayan gave them all of their names and waited for them to search the list. It amazed Ayan that these men, who mocked them in the basement only a day earlier, had forgotten their faces and names. The men searched through the scratches and marks on the ledger several times before putting a mark beside their names. They eyed Emran critically and then demanded more money.

"We have nothing more to give but ourselves," Ayan said in a low voice.

After a long pause, the men pointed towards the gangplank.

Ayan moved slowly up the rickety walkway. Akbar and Emran quickly followed. Ayan looked around the gleaming, polished deck before a harsh voice demanded he get into the hold of the ship.

As Ayan descended into the bowels of the ship, steel steps cut through his sandals. His hand recoiled from the touch of a sticky handrail. He gasped in his first mouthful of stale air. He'd never tasted air. He'd noticed scents in the air, but never been in a place where the air tasted like rotten vegetables, tainted with the odour of one-hundred-and-fifty working men, trapped in the hold of the ship for years. The smell of old cooking oil and sulphur mixed with the scent of the saltwater in the ship's ballast. Emran coughed at the stench.

A man's yell stopped the trio dead. They turned to see a soot-covered man yell in an unknown language. Ayan shook his head and signalled that he did not understand the words. The dirty man rolled his eyes and snarled, then flicked the tip of his whip towards a door. Ayan did not wait to see if this is what the man wanted. The trio only wanted to escape.

The clang of steel gears grinding and the scream of engines grew louder the lower they descended. Ayan paused. The man yelled louder and pointed down a long corridor. A group of men emerged from a long hall and headed down the stairs. Ayan followed them farther down the ship's tangle of stairs and halls. At each level, a man holding a paddle or whip forced them further into the belly of the ship. At one level several men looked up from their work and sadly shook their heads.

A large hand reached out and grabbed Ayan's shoulder,

yanking him off balance. Ayan had barely recovered when the man felt him over, squeezing his muscles and slapping his back hard. He never looked Ayan in the eye. He pointed towards a dark staircase. Ayan stopped at the top. No lamps or even candles burned below. Ayan felt into the darkness, unsure if the man really meant him to descend into the darkness. He turned to see the man shove Emran hard and point back up the stairs they had recently descended. Emran flashed a frightened look over his shoulder before disappearing. The man grunted and signalled for Akbar to follow his brother. Ayan opened his mouth to wish them well as the man turned and narrowed his eyes. Ayan decided to wish his friends well at another time.

Ayan descended the stairs, groping in the dark for each step. The engines throbbed louder, making it impossible to hear anything. A hand grabbed his shoulder and spun him around. Ayan yelled in the darkness, the sound drowned in the roar of engines. The hand shoved Ayan forward. The light ahead glowed red. A man pushed a wide-mouthed, long-handled shovel into his hand and pointed to the other side of the room. Ayan shuffled tentatively, afraid of tripping on something. A pale red glow filtered through a door. Another man stood beside a black pile of soft rock. Ayan watched for a moment and then started shovelling the coal towards the other side of the room. Ayan threw the black coal across the room until he lost track of time. His stomach growled and then knotted; still no one came to offer them supper. The muscles in his shoulders burned and his back weakened.

One shovelful was not heavy. Thousands became an impossible burden. No one spoke in the darkness. No one looked at the man beside them. Ayan paused once and the man behind him tapped his shoulder, and then shook his hand rapidly, motioning for Ayan to pick up another shovelful. Ayan tried to fill his lungs with the black, chalky air. His back protested violently when he bent to lift another shovelful of coal and when he paused to mop his brow, Ayan realised that his fist refused to unwind from the handle. He had to twist the shovel to release his grip. His entire body ached from the strain. Hours passed, but it was impossible to keep track of the days properly.

Sometimes a Muslim Lascar would come down the stairs and whisper that it was sunrise, or sunset. Men turned and looked at each other, but they could do nothing about the prayer times. They were unable to decide whether they had the right to alter the prayers to suit their shifts. After several weeks of arguments, Ayan decided to pray when he woke and before he slept. He prayed at the side of his bunk, touching his head to the floor.

"Do not let the English see you do that." He jumped; startled that someone would interrupt a prayer. A head poked in the door a bit further.

"A man knelt to pray on the back deck and a supervisor whipped him so hard that he fell into the water."

Ayan narrowed his eyes, unsure as to whether the intruder meant to insult him, or if the incident had really happened. The man nodded slightly and said, "Just watch your back," before disappearing from the doorway.

Ayan continued his prayer. When he finished, he gratefully flopped onto his bed. Why would the English object to prayer? How did a prayer harm anyone? It defied logic.

Life only changed for the few hours when his duty changed from shovelling coal to carrying garbage and sewage from the deck. The distaste of handling another man's sewage faded compared to the delight of seeing the sun, feeling the cool breeze against his back and breathing in clean, fresh air.

The third time the chance to work on deck was afforded to Ayan, he was happy to see Akbar. Ayan touched the cheek of his friend, and wondered if his own face looked as gaunt and hollow. Neither man spoke.

As he hurried across the deck, Ayan almost ran into a white servant with laced cuffs. The man gasped in alarm and wrinkled his nose. He threw Ayan an accusing glance and stomped away. The rudeness of the gesture did not alarm Ayan as much as realising that their eyes had met. Ayan glanced behind; making sure no one else had noticed the exchange. No one told him whether looking into a white person's eyes was a transgression of the rules, or whether the whites honestly did not see the Lascars. Either way, it did not seem reasonable. The Lascars worked hard. They did a respectable day's work and earned coins for their labour, yet, they were invisible to every white face. Some days, Ayan felt like a spirit moving across the deck, totally unnoticed by the European travellers.

What surprised Ayan more was that the Europeans looked at their black slaves and addressed them by their names. Not even the supervisors addressed the men who worked below the deck by their names. They rarely used any name, not even Lascar.

Ayan returned to the furnace. He held onto the hope that he would be on deck again soon, away from the burning red glow and dust-filled air.

Ayan worked quietly and diligently, shift after shift. To be considered a good worker was important. To Ayan's surprise, one night a supervisor pointed towards the stairs that lead to the upper deck.

The unfamiliar night sky filled Ayan with joy. He thought back to the times when on a hot night, he would lay near the betel tree and just look at the stars until he fell asleep. He did not recognise the stars tonight. Do the stars change as you sail across the ocean? On rare occasions Kazi would join Ayan under the tree. Maybe tonight they were staring at the same sky. The shift ended far too soon, leaving Ayan wondering why the shifts on deck seemed so much shorter than the shifts at the furnace.

One of the rare times the men had together was when it was time for their meal. It was not breakfast, lunch or dinner. It was just time to eat. The crew crouched to scoop the chunky broth mixed with rice from their bowls. One man thought they had been on ship for only thirty days, another argued that it was closer to six weeks. Ayan listened intently, hoping for some clue to exactly how long he had been on board.

Eventually, with no warning, the ship finally docked and the Lascars helped unload crates in an unknown port on the African coast. The men worked non-stop to empty the cargo, and then to load new crates of supplies. When everything had been checked and logged, the Lascars were herded back up the gang-plank and back below decks. Ayan was surprised that there was no opportunity to go ashore. He had often talked with Lascars in the Calcutta port and although no one said they would disembark at every port, Ayan had just assumed. At least the stop had been a change of routine, and the men had some time to chat below decks before the next round of labour started. Ayan listened to two men talking behind him. One of the men had been working near a supervisor, and had overheard that The Bengal was now headed for Spain.

To everyone's surprise, they lay in port overnight and the Lascars got an unexpected but welcome rest. Ayan lay in the darkness, focusing on the day when the furnace would lie idle and the men would go ashore. The Lascars had talked about visiting exotic ports where they browsed strange markets and ate strange foods. Had they lied?

During one meal time, Ayan finally had enough of the endless routine. Sick of being imprisoned in near darkness, he left his fellow workers and wandered up the corridor to the stairs. No one was guarding, so Ayan climbed upwards. Maybe at sea the supervisors felt no need to be so vigilant, because at the next landing, the next set of stairs lay unguarded too.

"You, man!"

Ayan jumped. It took a moment to understand that the superior had called him "man".

"You!" the supervisor shouted and lifted his whip.

Ayan bowed slightly, unfamiliar with the English word, but

recognising the whip. He tried desperately to remember the superior's name. His mind searched fruitlessly. Their names were not as important as memorising which ones preferred the paddle, which preferred the whip and who used their arm freely when a Lascar failed to obey fast enough.

"Eastern Indian?" The supervisor spat on the ground as if it were a crime that Ayan only spoke one language.

Ayan hung his head.

"Follow me."

The rift between whites, supervisors and Lascars, ran as deep as the colour of their skin. The white men believed that the blacks were animals who merely looked more like people than monkeys and Lascars were only things to be valued for the strength in their backs and shoulders, void of a mind or spirit. The supervisors used harsh words and whips to teach the Lascars where their place was.

Ayan followed the supervisor without a word to an unfamiliar part of the deck. He realised that the superior had mistaken him for someone else, which shook some of the fog from his mind. Ayan must have wandered far beyond the ship's belly.

He bit his tongue, hoping no one would notice that he was there. The idea of doing something different woke him from his stupor and the delight of doing something different refreshed him more than sleep.

He fell into line with a row of men, each selecting a mop and bucket from the pile. Akbar and Emran stood in the line further ahead. Ayan's spirit lightened at the thought of them landing the more desirable positions in the cleaning crew. He had seen them several times below as they slept, and had briefly bumped into Akbar, but never found the chance to talk to them since they had embarked The Bengal.

The line moved slowly in the pre-dawn dimness, mopping the decks while the Europeans slept. This was the first time that Ayan had worked with the men from the deck crews. Their outlook, while still that of the Lascar, was more amiable. They did not fear the Europeans, but simply resented them. This made them bold. Many of them mocked both the whites and the superiors.

Ayan listened as his fellow Lascars made snide jokes about The Cruel One, The Blonde One and The Laughing Hyena, among others. Ayan understood whom they talked about based on their descriptions. He could have told them stories about The Cruel One, but fear silenced him.

Ayan mopped the deck with the rest of the crew, pushing the dirty water overboard as they went. The man beside him glanced curiously but made no comment. Ayan smiled politely when the other man corrected a mistake he made. Ayan did not want to bow under this supervisor's whip. He expected to feel the whip later in the day and two beatings a day brought down the strongest of men. The loss of sleep would show as the day's work wore on.

As Ayan worked, tears tracked his cheeks. He tried to see everything; to remember the colours of the sea and the sunrise, to hear the clink of china as the Europeans ate their breakfast and the laughter of children. He stared unblinkingly at a tiny, squat-nosed dog that urinated on his mop. He wanted to remember everything about that morning when he was once again working in the red glow of the furnace.

A slow murmur rippled through the pre-dawn. Ayan shook his head in disbelief. He looked at the man to his right. He continued to scrub, but he knelt, head down. They prayed! He looked at the sky, realising that the dawn must be close.

"I Seek Protection of Allah," the voices around him whispered.

Ayan softly took up the chant. "The Cherisher and Sustainer of the Worlds, Most Gracious."

The whole line of men moved back as if one. Ayan slid farther down the deck and kneeled again. He bent low to touch the deck with his forehead. The man beside him gave a harsh hiss and shook his head, "No!" Ayan glanced back at the supervisor, who, not being Muslim, believed that the men were singing a sad song, not praying. Another tear trickled down Ayan's cheek as he realised that the prayer neared its end.

"May peace and blessings be upon all the Messengers of Allah and their companions."

A hush fell over the deck as the respectful silence hung heavy. The sun rose, waking everyone. The scrape of brushes on the decks increased in intensity as men struggled to make up the lost time. Ayan's soul soared. He wanted this memory to stay in his mind forever, but he would forget within moments of leaving the cleaning crew and finding a bed. If only the images of the morning followed him to the furnace room, they might make life bearable while he shovelled coal. The price of this memory more than compensated for suffering The Cruel One's whip; if he remembered.

Ayan did not mind the supervisors' curses. Any man might easily ignore curses uttered in a foreign tongue. However, the Cruel One's whip did not sting like the other supervisor's. It cut deep ribbons in a man's back that burned when sweat and dirt filled the bloody mess.

* * *

Ayan jerked awake and shoved a hand off his chest. An alarmed shout pierced the darkness as the other man stumbled and fell away.

Ayan sighed as the cleaning crew turned in for the night. He almost hated them, would have hated them, if Akbar and Emran did not belong to their crew. They started their day at sunrise and ended it at sunset. The setting sun promised a meal and a full night's sleep.

The Lascars working in the engine room toiled day in, day out, for many shifts before the sun's warmth touched their skin. Ayan stopped trying to track the days and nights. It was easier to let them melt into an endless darkness than to count how long he lived in this miasma of pain and hunger.

The cleaners continued to fumble around, blindly searching for a bed. They never learned to move around the cold steel rooms beneath the water level without needing their eyes. They stumbled through the darkness to find a berth, stepping on others and tripping over their own feet.

Ayan stretched his aching muscles. The red strips from the last beating still burned, infected from the filthy air and the damp ship's hold. That day, he welcomed the warmth of the furnace room to ease the seeping wounds on his body. Allah's mercy appeared in wonderful ways. The furnace room workers learned quickly that the furnace fire held healing powers that prevented their wounds from seeping; the sign of death for many. A fever followed the seeping, then the screams and delirium and finally, death.

The sleeping quarters chilled the men's muscles, cramping them, offering no comfort while they slept. The furnace eased the knots and made it easier to work. The cleaning men who returned from the decks brought the soft scent of the sea with them. Ayan closed his eyes and enjoyed the sensation of lying idle, if even for a moment.

The cleaning crew complained about their tasks. Ayan growled at the man closest to him, offering to trade places with him. The Lascars, who worked outdoors, mopping the decks and serving drinks to the passengers, did not realise how fortunate they were. They chattered for several minutes before they fell asleep. Ayan remembered how much comfort he derived from chatting with Kazi in the last few moments before the evening breeze soaked into his body and sleep overtook him.

A Lascar crawled through the total darkness and fell into the first empty bunk, falling asleep before he lay down. Ayan knew this signalled the shift change, but he remained still. He longed for one full day in the sun, to feel the afternoon heat burn into his skin and to enjoy a trickle of clean sweat slip down his spine, instead of the grimy, sticky sweat of the engine room.

Ayan tempted fate long enough. He pulled himself up, deciding to wait outside the engine room for his shift. The engine crew learned to wait at the door and start their shift quickly, to escape The Cruel One's attention.

Ayan squatted with a sigh. Dreams of working on the deck were futile. Dreams no longer gave him hope. They snuffed the remaining flame from his soul. Only the small, quiet Lascars worked on deck. In fact, much to Akbar's despair, Emran already worked inside the lounge. The young boy's quiet attitude, soft eyes and submissive nature earned him a place inside to work for the white servants. Ayan found it difficult not to envy the boy.

Few men were fortunate enough to have a gentle face like Emran. On a ship, a soft face became more desirable than hard muscle. Muscle forced a man inside the ship's bowels, to tend the kitchens, bathrooms, storage spaces and engine room. A soft disposition earned a man a place where they sipped water whenever they wanted, worked under canopies and chewed discarded fruit rinds when no one watched.

Ayan watched the next deck crew climb the stairs. His eyes narrowed at their arrogance. The pain of the whites treating him like an untouchable cut deep. The torment of having other Lascars look down and never meeting his eyes because he worked in the engine room, made him think evil thoughts.

A group of Lascars rushed up the steps, whispering that the belly was the very worst place aboard The Bengal. The Lascars stopped calling it the engine room and referred to it as the Bengal's belly, partly because the boiler room resided in the lowest part of the ship and partly because the Bengal had already digested three men on this trip. Ayan knew how easy it was to fall against the steel, hot enough to remove the flesh from one's bones, before the man's scream split the air. The men feared hot steel more than the fire itself.

Many of the Lascars whispered that the men in the engine room were already dead. A hush fell over the deck as the respectful silence hung heavy. The sun rose, waking everyone. The ship lurched, causing men to lose their balance. One day, fire rolled from the furnace making the room too hot to enter. Not even The Cruel One's whip drove the men back into the boiler room.

Ayan did not fear the fire or hot steel. What he feared most was drowning. If the ship swamped, the men in the engine room would not have time to navigate the labyrinth of stairs that led to the surface, meaning that they would be trapped in the ship's bowels when it flooded.

An older Lascar often told a story of a wreck he survived. The ship's propellers rose out of the water, the wheel's blades spun much too fast and the shafts, each one weighing a ton, spun at immense speed. He described the grinding of steel on steel and the sickening sound of gears breaking.

A young Lascar asked if he escaped through the hole in the ship's hull. The old man nodded and fell silent. The story always ended before anyone asked what happened to the other Lascars from the engine room.

Ayan looked up as a black shadow moved through the door, signalling the start of his shift. He took a shovel from a passing man and gave him a subtle look of dismay. The man's eyes sank low under closed lids, as if he were already in a deep slumber. Walking with open eyes was not necessary.

The faces of the Lascars who attended to the night shift chilled Ayan. He failed to understand why they were considered the night shift, as the boiler room shifts followed their own clock, dividing the day and night irregularly. Still, the men from the night shift looked like dead bodies from the streets of Calcutta, except that these corpses walked. They drifted toward the door, relinquishing shovels to the daytime shift.

Shovels lay scattered on the floor. Fresh blood and sweat still flecked the handle of some. Relief swept Ayan like a cool breeze; the night shift had endured a violent shift, meaning that their shift may be quiet. Ayan picked up a moist shovel and cursed silently.

Ayan was not aware that he had stopped to contemplate the men's fates until a hiss broke through his thoughts. A loud animal roar erupted from the engine room. Ayan jumped; startled that The Cruel One had caught him standing still. The man's haughty look and bitter tone spurred the other men to work double-time.

The Cruel One stepped into the engine room, his whip already flicking above Ayan's head like a snake's tongue. Even the boiler room's supervisors, The Fat Ones, cowered in a corner. Ayan focused on Kazi. It numbed the pain.

The Fat One's waist exceeded Kazi's. How did they survive? The idea of Kazi enduring the heat of the furnace room for an hour, let alone a whole morning, seemed absurd. The grotesquely fat men sweated profusely, intensifying their stench so that even the engine room, Lascars avoided standing near them for too long.

The Cruel One barked and Lascars scurried to their various positions. He left and the daily dance of feeding the furnaces started. Men scooped coal from along the room's wall and then swung it into the fire that fed the pipes. The fires flared, turning water to steam. The gears jumped and surged to life. The dance continued steadily, each man missing each other by inches when their shovels swung around, yet never missing their mark. The Lascars knew their moves well. No shovels clanged together; no coal was dropped. No one waited while another Lascar moved out of the way. The routine gave them strength, paced them and enabled them to endure the long hours ahead.

They poured tons of coal in the fires each day. The Fat Ones measured the diminishing pile against the wall to make sure they met their quota.

It amazed Ayan that his body could adapt so well. It shut down his brain to conserve energy, enabling his mind to rest while sleep eluded the body. His shoulders and legs worked unconsciously, making it possible to numb the pain. The months in complete darkness taught him to live without his eyes. The constant barrage of screams and shouts in a strange language from The Fat Ones trained his brain to shut down his ears. The real Ayan existed elsewhere; a creature somewhere in the spectrum between sleepwalkers, men who were neither alive nor dead and the wild animals who roamed the jungle around his rice paddy.

The phenomenon grew into an unnerving torment. Ayan awoke from the stupor to a burning sensation. It took a moment to realise that a supervisor's paddle was beating his back. His body slowed, pushed to exhaustion. Ayan swayed under the blows. Was this the second beating of the day? Or, had days passed since The Cruel One last beat him? His muscles screamed in rebuke when he tried to lift the shovel. He rocked a few times, using the momentum and the pain inflicted by the paddle, to restart his muscles. Ayan gasped beneath the combined pain of torn muscles and the relentless lashes from the supervisor's whip.

The pain of the whip stopped before Ayan realised that he had rejoined the dance. So much of Allah's teaching made sense to him at times like these. He understood the pain. His life before seemed like a shadow where a boy followed Allah. Now, he understood the intensity of holiness. The truth mocked him; to think that he believed himself to be holy before this moment. He had reached ground level, the absolute base of earthly existence, where mammalian functionality pertained not to the mind, heart, or spirit, but to the three-dimensional body, the tangible cavity in which all creatures dwell.

"Boring."

Ayan looked up, surprised to hear a word spoken in his language. The shock of being dragged back to the harshness of reality caused him physical pain. He turned around. The Fat Ones and The Cruel One were gone. Only Lascars remained. The

Lascar beside him stopped working and leaned on the shovel handles.

"Boring. This work is boring."

Ayan hefted up another shovel of coal and continued working. A moment later, the other Lascar did the same. He decided that this experience was rich and interesting, in the same way that burning nightmares were rich and interesting. Burning nightmares from which one's eyes can never open. Except, that after a while, everyone escaped burning nightmares. No one escaped the belly of The Bengal.

Ayan's vision cleared for a moment. The visualisation of the boiler room, black and red fusing together, tore a scream from his belly. It never escaped the constriction in his chest. Ayan shook as the last moments of consciousness faded into hallucination. He swatted the ribbons of perspiration in a vain attempt to retain his coherence. The perspiration did not move as he rubbed. It flowed down his body in deep, mud-choked rivers. The silver sweat alternately faded and grew bright as it undulated down his body, finally setting into pure gold, sparkling like the rings worn by white passengers. Ayan laughed. He became a buttery mass, a priceless magician from whom gold dripped in endless ribbons.

The golden rivulets vibrated into sweat again before each, one by one, transformed into sizzling beads of fire. Ayan tried to scream; the sound strangled him. His arms moved. The shovel moved. He turned and the dance continued. Flames licked up from the streams of gold, reaching toward the furnace, trying to join the hot coals that gave them birth. Ayan tried to beat out the flames.

A moment later, gold and flame disappeared. The roaring, clang of the engine penetrated and grew louder and louder, like an oncoming locomotive. The acrid smell of sulphur burned his nose.

Ayan whimpered, thankful to return to the land of the living where the heat of the shovel burned his hands. The dance of flames dried his eyes. The fear of burning to death kept him awake for the rest of the shift.

Ayan wondered again if this was the day he sat outside of the furnace room and The Cruel One whipped him and the Fat Ones yelled with urgency and beat him. Maybe or maybe not. It was entirely possible that a week or even a month had passed since that day. Ayan did not measure days anymore. Nothing existed before he walked onto the ship. He did not know if he had had a life before the ship.

CHAPTER 7

"Daydreaming?" screamed The Cruel One, his Adam's apple bulging obscenely from his skinny neck.

Ayan's mind jerked back to the present. It took a moment to realise that the Adam's apple was not the growth on Kazi's lip. Ayan had been shovelling coal into the steaming hot furnace when his mind wandered to thoughts of the growth on Kazi's lip. Ayan wondered what would happen if he simply pressed a piece of scorching coal against the growth? Ayan lowered his head, immediately embarrassed that his superior might read his mind.

"Saw-ree?" Ayan pronounced one of the few English words that all smart Lascars mastered in the hope of preventing a beating. It worked sometimes.

Unlike the other white men, The Cruel One rarely waited for lesions to heal before opening up fresh ones. Ayan dropped the shovel and fell to the floor, his belly landing on top of the shovel's wood handle. He silently thanked Allah that he missed the searing hot end. The metal would have seared and blistered the flesh on his stomach long before The Cruel One finished the beating.

The gratefulness in his heart withered like a young vine deprived of rain. The whip hissed as it slashed through his already torn skin. Ayan watched his blood splatter on the walls with fascination. He didn't need to turn around to visualise The Cruel One's expression. He knew the twisted mask of hate from watching other beatings. The Cruel One's face, normally a pale and tense assortment of ugly features, became a mottled white and deep pink as blood rose to the surface of his translucent skin. He never smiled. His face twisted into a dark scowl and his fist sought for a new hold in the whip butt with each blow.

The punishments never brought a smile to his face. He never displayed any signs of taking pleasure in the task; a pretence that did not fool Ayan. Somewhere deep within this man - if one could call him that – lived the desire to destroy.

"Are you trying to sabotage our beautiful ship?" The words permeated Ayan's pain, as the thin lash bit into flesh. "You'd like it if we stopped producing steam?"

Ayan heard the sound of shovels and the scrape of steel against steel accelerate as The Cruel One's voice rose to a howl.

"Saw-rye!" Ayan heard his own screams echoing far away. For a blissful, fleeting moment, Ayan entered the blackness, for a brief moment escaping into the holy sleep.

A hot nail pierced his skull. He opened his eyes, disappointed to be denied any respite. He moved his head, which renewed the agony. He stared at the grooved engine room floor. A thick sticky substance prevented one eye from opening. He wiped it away, smearing the blood through the dirt.

Ayan understood now. The Cruel One kicked him awake with his steel-tipped boot. From far above, a few English words he understood echoed in his mind. "Back to work!" Ayan covered his face to protect it from the next blow. He watched The Cruel One's boot heels as they crossed the room and disappeared into the hall.

"Back to work!" The Fat Ones continued the chorus.

CHAPTER 8

Akbar knelt down and pressed a wet towel against the swollen forehead. "It's not so bad," he said, dabbing the cloth around.

Ayan looked up from his cot. His throat tightened. He gulped, swallowing the anger boiling up from the pit of his stomach.

"You make me believe you don't know words," he whispered. Waves of fatigue enveloped him, then faded, each one threatening to push him back into sleep.

"Exhaustion is my enemy."

"Be strong. Be a good man. You are alive. Allah is kind."

He thought perhaps Allah had forgotten him. A surge of fear and hopelessness overwhelmed him.

"Allah has forgotten that I live."

"Allah never forgets! Remember your brother," Akbar whispered.

"Kazi," the word escaped in a sigh.

"Kazi needs you."

Ayan grabbed his friend's hand. A snarl twisted his lip. "Do you not know the meaning of words? What to say and when to say it? Does nobody aboard this ship, or in the world, know how to speak?"

Ayan's gaze hardened. Akbar glared back vehemently, examining his friend's face. Ayan's hollow eyes continued to hold Akbar's stare in defiance. He opened his mouth to emit a silent scream. He needed his friend to react. Anything to prove that they lived, to replace the shards of glass that pierced their souls. Akbar shook his head. "I think," he replied in slow measured tones, "you know too much about words. You say far too many of them. It's time to rest. It is not so bad."

"Not so bad?" Ayan mocked, "Not so bad? You know nothing of 'bad'."

"I know that sometimes it is better to be a poor man from a

poor village. We do not have words to make the supervisors swing their whips. Our minds do not wander from our work."

A tremble rippled through Ayan, depleting him of his remaining strength. He lay motionless, gasping for breath.

"Your scars run only surface deep."

Akbar rose. "You do not," he whispered, "see all my scars."

Akbar walked towards the door. "You make me thank Allah that I am only a simple man." His hand touched the handle. Fear swept through Ayan.

"Akbar," he whispered. Akbar paused.

Ayan did not want to be alone with the whip's song echoing in his mind. He did not want to visualise the Cruel One's twisted face sneering as it leaned closer to his prone body, or the blood-spattered boots that walked away as darkness stole his senses. He did not want to feel the burning welts that throbbed as they lured him to wakeful torment, the exposed flesh and nerves tortured by exposure to air and the softest brush of coarse fabric, nor see the blackened, rotting skin, filling the room with the odour of death. Ayan did not want to meet death alone.

Ayan calmed his voice. "Wait! I apologise to you, my friend. You know it's not in my nature to spear with my tongue."

Akbar looked at the floor, his head turned downward. "Perhaps you are poisoned by the whips."

A flicker of clarity lit Ayan's mind. His heart said that Akbar's words were not true. "A man should never take out his hardships on an innocent one."

"It's not true," Ayan croaked. "Poisoned men don't need companionship. Come back and speak to me for a while."

"What in your good life has taught you what poisoned men need?" snapped Akbar.

"Things are not always as they seem," replied Ayan softly.

Akbar laughed. "Where do you hear such foolish things?"

Ayan's mind stumbled on the words. "My mother; when I was young." Akbar nodded.

"Your mother? Would a good woman fill a young man's heart with such foolish thoughts?"

Ayan wondered if a woman could be a kind woman and a good woman. His mind clouded.

"You have endured the torture of The Cruel One's whip and you still speak these words as if they are truth," Akbar replied.

Ayan pictured the young woman who left scraps on the windowsill for them to eat. The one season when Kazi fell ill, she "threw away" the exact medicine he needed. Her soft voice begged, "Please; it is wrong to waste. I need to find someone who needs this medicine. Allah wants us to protect those who are innocent."

"Allah does not want men treated this way." Akbar said.

"Allah? How do you know what Allah wants?"

Ayan looked at the ceiling. "I refuse to let The Cruel One's dark heart enter my spirit."

"You can stop this?" Akbar replied.

"Yes."

Somewhere in Ayan's soul, a song played. Akbar took a space at the bedside. He settled down and touched Ayan's shoulder, a tiny gesture with healing power.

"Tell me," Ayan began, his lungs tearing with every breath, "of the scars I cannot see."

A flash of emotion rippled across Akbar's face.

Ayan sensed that a dam had burst inside his friend's mind.

"Friends share their pains with other friends," Ayan continued. He coughed and glanced sideways.

"More of your mother's wise words?" mocked Akbar.

Ayan liked the idea of having a mother. What was a mother? A woman who gave you food, who provided a warm blanket at night, who leaned out of the window and laughed at you and who taught you wisdom? This was a mother.

"Yes, my friend. My mother shared this wisdom with me."

"Just as you ache for Kazi," Akbar replied, "I bear scars for my brother."

"This is a hard place," said Ayan.

"Emran was not built for this kind of place."

"Only monsters are built for this kind of place."

"Yesterday was very bad for him. A white passenger complained that Emran looked at his wife," said Akbar.

Ayan's surprise revived his senses enough to blot out the pain for a moment. He answered Akbar with his eyes.

"Our superior, The Laughing One, let the man brutalise Emran for quite some time," confessed Akbar.

Ayan stumbled with the new word; brutalised. A white word. His soul cringed at the meaning. Did Akbar use the white word without thinking, or did the word have a dark meaning that held no equivalent in their language.

"Brutalised?" Ayan turned to ask and paused.

Akbar choked on a sob and his body trembled violently. Cold sweat mingled with tears. His hands moved as though he were trying to describe the terrors Emran suffered.

No words formed an appropriate response to the story. The silence demanded a response; anything to break the uneasy tension.

"A white man?" Ayan looked at his empty hands. "The white are strange."

"I do not understand that the official would allow a vacationer to harm a worker," Akbar said.

"The woman? Did she want to cause trouble?" Ayan sighed. "I have seen many foolish white women in Calcutta."

"Many of the white women on the ship are foolish. Their taste for an assault. She . . . they hide behind their fans and laugh."

"The supervisor was wrong."

"Emran knows he did nothing wrong, I hope." Akbar nodded.

"That much he knows. But before yesterday, Emran believed that the passengers were more innocent than the whites in uniform. It gave him hope. But now..."

A ripple went through Ayan's heart, breaking it in two. "Hope." He did not say any more. He did not tell Akbar that he lost hope. His father did not call him to the sea. Even if he lived when Ayan dreamed the dream, no Lascar lived long enough. The sea promised Kazi hope. The whip stole it.

He closed his eyes and allowed his mind to conjure up images. They wavered and grew strong. Kazi teased the girls as they went about their work. The warm afternoon sun lulled all but the most determined worker to sleep. Then Kazi laughed, his teeth stained red. Ayan jumped.

"Maybe Emran is better off without hope," Ayan said sadly. "Illusions are deadly to the minds of men."

"More of your mother's wisdom?" Akbar's shoulders slumped.

"No. A lesson I learned myself."

Ayan put the soup bowl on the floor. His stomach tightened. He hated the days when they never served bread. It settled the pains in his stomach. The soup provided enough nourishment to keep him alive and filled his stomach enough to remind him how hungry he was. The pain intensified and started to grip the stomach muscles.

He lay a long time deciding whether to sleep on his stomach or back. A full belly might have made it possible to sleep comfortably on his stomach. As it was, the muscles cramped beneath the weight of his body. Spasms in his back muscles prevented sleep. The solution lay in finding a comfortable position on his side. It offered several hours rest, until slumber relaxed his body and he slipped to his back.

Ayan woke from his sleep with a scream. Fire from the furnace scorched his back. He had fallen into the engine room fire. As the pain intensified, Ayan forced himself up. The pain subsided slowly once the flesh tore away from the dirt-encrusted fabric.

"What am I doing here?" The words came out in a sob. Ayan looked around, almost expecting to see in the darkness. He did not belong here, on this ship, among these men. This was not the work of a man. Allah created this existence for a hell-spawned beast. Tomorrow, another day of hell lay ahead. He suffered the torment of the fire and life as a Lascar. Who tormented men's souls? Ah, yes. The Cruel One.

He lay down and whispered, "Sleep." The command escaped his lips as oblivion overtook his body.

CHAPTER 9

"Pork today."

Ayan could not believe his ears. A large, scornful smile adorned Omar's distorted face as he looked across the table.

Ayan nodded and looked down before the man could notice his disdain. He did not like Omar, but many of the ship crew did. The man appeared gifted by Allah.

Omar had hair on his arms, despite the weeks of drudgery in the engine room. He also possessed a wife back home in Yemen.

Ayan hated to admit that envy tainted his mind, because Omar had experienced life with a woman. Ayan glanced up. How could a man with such cruel features manage to win a wife? Omar's nose also invaded half of his face. Ayan could not remember a time when his mouth ever closed. Now, he smiled about eating pork. How did a man as twisted and corrupt as Omar receive so many favours?

"Too expensive," Ayan mumbled. He did not want to discuss the matter any further.

"Bite your tongue!" Omar yelled, drawing attention from fellow Lascars. Ayan slouched low on the bench to hide a flush of embarrassment.

"I saw it when I passed the kitchen. Irish bankers cancelled their trip." He pointed at himself with a flat thumb. "The whites are showing compassion."

"Compassion?" Ayan hissed, unable to stop himself.

Ayan lifted himself out of the chair and leaned forward across the table, with his balled fists resting on the wood planks. The girth of his shoulders and arms blocked the rest of the room from seeing Omar's shocked face.

"Would Allah agree with you, my friend?"

"Allah," Omar smiled, glancing at the galley with a sparkle of amusement in his eye, "does not exist in European culture."

"Blasphemy!" said Ayan, shocked at Omar's bluntness.

Omar leaned back. "Have you seen Allah at sea?" He looked around. "Has anyone seen any sign of Allah since boarding this ship?" Ayan's anger grew.

"How dare you, man! Allah can hear you speak. He hears you think, too."

"Would he rather," asked Omar with a self-satisfied sneer, "see me dead? And leave a young widow?"

Fury provided Ayan with the strength to remain standing. He looked around at the room full of hollow eyes.

"This ship, The Bengal, wrecks your body." He punctuated each word. "It softens your wits."

Not one person responded. The room full of men stared blankly at him. A sudden realisation swept over him. These men died in mind and spirit a long time ago.

"I will not let them bruise my spirit!" vowed Ayan.

Omar spat on the floor. "You have no more choice than I do. They will take what they want. They will do what they want."

Ayan sat and shook his head. "It should not be this way."

"How will you, a Lascar, stop them?"

"How?" It seemed clear. "Leave the ship."

"Only a fool would think such nonsense!" Omar laughed at Ayan's statement.

"You let them destroy you," Ayan sighed, not wishing to be heard by either mate or ruler. "They treat you like swine and they feed you swine."

Omar leaned forward. "I'm willing to wager," he said, "that when the dark meat is laid on the table, no one will have regard for Allah."

Ayan slammed a fist onto the table top. "You curse! You curse yourself. You curse me. You curse our people!"

"I ..."

"You are no longer a man. I shall regard you as...."

"Ayan!"

Ayan whipped around and instinctively ducked to avoid the Cruel One's whip. Instead of facing Omar, Ayan's eyes locked with Akbar's. It took a moment to realise that Akbar's tone had nothing to do with Omar's blasphemy. His friend's tortured face revealed a dreadful tragedy.

"Emran!" cried Akbar. "The sea took him."

The other Lascars turned their attention to Akbar and Ayan.

"An accident?" Ayan asked.

"He jumped."

Ayan's knees buckled.

"He spoke to me last night." Abkar whispered.

"What happened?"

"He starved." Akbar's eyes told the truth, but his words told a different story.

"He was punished again?"

Akbar looked away. "By the same man. It happened several times since we last met."

Ayan shook with rage, but refused to allow it to overwhelm him. The table was full of men eating an oily, deathly grey meat. A plate cooled on the table before him. The smell turned his stomach. Omar grinned.

Ayan stabbed a piece of meat and ate it. Inside, he silently wept for Emran. The plate emptied. Ayan did not care for the rules of a religion that allowed a small boy be tortured to death; starved and frightened. There was no one to hear his cries for mercy.

Omar laughed sarcastically, "Allah forgives you. What is Allah to us? Do you think we will meet him? And, if we do, what then? Will he ask us to go below where he will not smell our stench?"

Akbar wept openly, crying his brother's name.

"If Allah cared," a Lascar farther down the table interrupted, "he would at least provide us with halal."

"Halal?" one of the supervisors laughed. "Shall I clean a stateroom for you too? What does Allah care for you? All of you traded your souls for berth on this ship. You do not belong to Allah. You are not Muslim or Hindu. You are Lascars and your soul belongs to the captain."

Ayan wondered what Emran said to Allah the moment they met.

CHAPTER 10

All the Lascars had ceased working. The ship had docked in Portugal the previous night, and for the first time in what seemed like weeks, the engines had been allowed to idle.

Lascars did not enjoy freedom, even when the ship was in port. They were rarely allowed on deck and there were definitely no opportunities to go ashore. But it did not matter anymore. Ayan's thought about Kazi more than ever. Kazi was Ayan's strength and as Ayan quickly learned, Emran had been Akbar's strength.

Both men grieved in their own way. Ayan worked harder, barely earning a harsh glare from The Fat Ones. Work was a blessing in disguise, Ayan thought, because it removed the focus from his grief. Without the constant lash to deal with, the muscles on his shoulders healed and strengthened. While the other men in the furnace room weakened, he grew more resilient. However, the grief had a more adverse effect on Akbar. It appeared as though his personality had been completely erased, leaving behind a hollow, emotionless shell.

Akbar's presence caused him discomfort. The memory of Emran was their only bond. It was not only Emran who had died that night. The men's fear of the supervisors died, too.

Ayan wondered how the minds of men worked. He strived to please them because he feared them, but their lust was insatiable. Then a day came when Ayan leaned on his shovel and stared defiantly at The Fat One's, patiently waiting for the beating to be over so he could resume his work. The paddle was raised and poised in the air. A worried look flashed across The Fat Ones' faces. They glanced at each other and backed away. That was the last time they tormented him. Not even the threats of The Cruel One could force them more than a few feet in Ayan's direction.

"There was a word Emran used before he died," Akbar

whispered. "I did not understand it at first; a white word." Ayan gestured for Akbar to continue.

"Slaves," he said, as if the word held a curse. Ayan shook his head, not comprehending.

"We are the slaves. Like bond slaves." Akbar looked over his shoulder. "They pay us in food. There is no money."

"We are slaves?"

"Worse. Animals. An animal works for food and freedom, nothing more. Eventually, one way or another, it finds both."

"I need the promised money."

Akbar leaned back. "I need my brother. We are paid with food very little food."

"They promised wages."

Akbar chuckled. "Dead men do not need coins," he said, using the supervisor's threat.

"That is why the beatings grow worse," Ayan sighed. "The more time we sail. The more beatings we suffer Why?"

Akbar shrugged. "They mean to kill us before we reach home."

Ayan recoiled at the statement. Surely that couldn't be true. Why would his father have beckoned him to such an existence?

Akbar continued. "I heard a word, Caribbean. Many slaves are free there. One for three. One broken Lascar is worth three slaves. Supervisors talk. They do not think we can learn their language. I have. I have listened."

"The world never changes," Ayan said sadly. "It seems that the strong survive, but only to suffer more humiliations."

The conversation made Ayan think back to when the mission teachers pushed him and Kazi into the streets. They survived. Many did not. Kazi and he often took on the unenviable task of carrying the corpses to the carts to "clean the streets". It was unpleasant, but sometimes it was the only alternative to starving. The difference here on the ship was that the supervisors did not send out the old to make room for the new, they just worked them till they died.

"Did Emran jump?" Ayan yelled.

Akbar didn't flinch.

"Did Emran jump?" Ayan yelled a second time.

Akbar lifted tear-filled eyes. "I do not know."

Ayan clenched his fist, but then realised that he did not feel anger, because it did not matter. His whole life amounted to little more than an exhausting cycle of arrivals and departures. He shuddered at the realisation.

"Tell me what you've been thinking, Akbar."

"The one you call The Cruel One . . . I watch him. He is ill. That is what makes him cruel. Some days he spends hours in the kitchen, near the stove. I've seen him many times. He bends over a pot on the stovetop. The Lascar cooks are afraid of him. I thought he was spitting in our soup."

Ayan bit his bottom lip in frustration, because his friend was keeping him in suspense for too long.

"Hurry, before we are overheard," urged Ayan.

Akbar paused for several long moments. "He is inhaling steam from the pot. It's merely boiled water."

"His lungs?"

"Yes. A lung infection; a breathing problem. The steam helps soften what is inside him."

With a rueful smile, Ayan replied, "It does not soften his temper."

Akbar grew more serious and hissed, "Which is why he deserves to go."

Ayan stared hard. Akbar's words echoed too loudly in the dark alley. He stepped into the opening and checked to see if anyone had overheard. He searched Akbar's eyes for a trace of humanity, something to indicate that his words were no more than an attempt to shock. Only darkness stared from the depths of Akbar's soul.

"I'm friendly with the men in the kitchen. I've yet to talk. I wanted to keep it between us. We can find others to help," encouraged Akbar.

"What are you saying, Akbar? Speak plain words." Ayan glanced over his shoulder.

"Do you want to run, Ayan?" taunted Akbar.

Ayan thought carefully before answering. The bruises on the bony areas of his body, the aches in his muscles and the welts on his skin all spoke to him. As did the tight muscles that were still healing from the lash. He threw away his plan; the childhood yearnings and the hopes for Kazi.

Akbar shifted his weight. "An answer?"

"Yes," replied Ayan resolutely.

Without wasting a moment, Akbar continued, "We push him into the boiling water. The man you call The Cruel One. I'll do it myself. Allah be with me."

"Allah is not at sea!" Omar's words echoed in Ayan's head as clearly as if the man stood in the alley behind them.

"One of the kitchen crew can do it. Or... someone in here. I know three other men who want out," suggested Ayan.

"Nobody of high rankings goes into our galley kitchen. They're afraid of catching a disease. Only this cretin appears. We shall wait 'til we dock in London."

"Then what?" asked Ayan.

"Then, we damage him. We cause a stir."

"It won't work," replied Ayan pessimistically.

"We do it before the meal is served," Akbar continued, ignoring Ayan's doubts. "The Lascars in the dining room will shout and argue. It's a noisy ship. The supervisors will need to bring order."

"And how do we escape?"

"If a man like him is injured there will be a lot of attention on him. The guards will be confused. We can just step off the ship."

"He will speak," said Ayan.

"The water will burn out his tongue," Akbar replied stony-faced.

"What of our spirits? Can we harm this man?"

"This man," Akbar, sucked in a breath, "is no more than a demon in human form. I will have no problem dealing with him if I stand to gain my freedom."

Ayan moved toward the door. "You are upset. You will feel differently in a few days."

Akbar closed the door, blocking Ayan's exit for a moment.

"Ayan, The Cruel One protected the white man while he brutalised Emran."

CHAPTER 11

The Bengal had now arrived in London. At last, the final destination. The dank smog of The Old Smoke hung low, souring the air on The Bengal's deck. A fitting setting for All Hallows Day.

The mist swirled. A dark image, draped in a black cloak, glided silently through the fog. Eyes, dark holes hooded by heavy brows, stared without seeing. The monster politely tipped his hat to a woman who was dressed as a kitten. She giggled, the movement making the white fur of her costume flow like lotus blossoms in a soft breeze. The man then leaned forward and whispered in the woman's ear.

Ayan suddenly felt that he was being watched. He shuddered and fled in the direction of the ship's belly. Two monsters blocked his way. Ayan stood back and let them pass. Ironic, how many of The Bengal's officers elected to wear a monstrous costume. It hardly seemed necessary for a monster to don the external wrappings to prove it.

He headed to the comfort of a familiar area. A Lascar passed, sporting a red nose. He passed another, scratching vigorously around an ornamental, fake moustache.

Supervisors moved through the lower decks. One met Ayan's eyes for a brief moment then moved on. They grabbed up a couple of sycophants to join the fools and passive types given the honour of leaving the ship. Ayan never expected to be allowed off the ship. Slave, the word rang as if he said it aloud. Enough strength remained to make Ayan too valuable to lose. The crew only lost the broken men.

Ayan looked over his shoulder and wondered how many of the privileged few would live to return to their duties tomorrow.

* * *

Several dozen Lascars gathered in The Bengal's lowermost

station to listen to one mate's tale of London. A crowd pressed Rakesh into a story. He smiled, enjoying being the centre of attention. "Rakesh the Loud", most Lascars called him. It came as no surprise that he had been chosen to leave the ship. Rakesh spoke English and charmed the whites with calculated compliments and expertly executed grovelling. Ayan took a seat and focused on the story.

"Perhaps the whites wish to be animals. I have never seen so many humans dressed as birds, snakes, and crocodiles. And what clothes these people can create, so fine it would cost me my entire home. A man could curry the Rajah's favour to offer such a costume as a gift, offered in abject humility."

"Which is not to say," grinned a man with whitish hair, "that you have a home beyond this craft."

"And whether your wife," said a young boy no older than thirteen, "is still your wife."

Rakesh smiled tightly, feigning forgiveness for the youthful jab. He let the silence settle and prepared to continue his performance. Rakesh raised a hand at his elder, as if toasting an imaginary glass.

"Indeed, the words you say have meaning. For who knows whether my home still stands. But the splendour. Imagine the silks worn by a woman. Not the thick coarse fabrics of the whites, but the fluid dresses of a courtesan draped over with features from birds of paradise. Imagine a fabric that glittered like one had plucked the stars from the sky and sewn them by hand, it would pale against the adornments worn a night ago." Rakesh continued.

"Most honourable men." Rakesh fell into his native storytelling manner. "It honours me to share the wonders I saw in London. One white gentleman had me laughing half the night."

Ayan leaned forward, captivated.

"We stood in a circle, in the public square, watching a man

juggle pins of fire. What a talent this man possessed! I now understand why Allah chose to reduce me to 'sweep floors', for no talent flows within my veins . . ."

"Not at storytelling. Tell us. Leave the flowery words for the whites," Ayan said.

"It is not becoming to speak low of yourself. The whites taught you that." A dirty Lascar spat on the floor.

A clean Lascar in white linen turned and frowned. "What do you know?"

"I know that Allah tests men. Men are measured by their deeds, not by the tasks they do."

An argument erupted. Ayan sighed. Few of the men understood what they argued about; they just quoted dogma, yelling to sound important. Allah tormented him. No other explanation made sense to Ayan.

Ayan did not argue, but held his own council. Allah placed him before the coal fire, merely a test to see how much hardship he would endure. He knew, just knew, that Allah prepared him for far better things.

The argument continued, some gleefully declaring themselves subordinates. They bragged that they understood. Allah created the caste system. Was this not to teach a man how to aspire to enlightenment?

Rakesh took a dramatic pose to regain control. "Brothers. Why argue over issues you do not understand? We are merely playing out our lives in a cosmic scheme that is far beyond our ability to understand. What do we know of the forces that bring a child to life, or take the life of an old man? Do we pretend to have wisdom beyond what we, as Lascars, were given by Allah?"

Ayan wondered about this. His respect for Rakesh waned. The man did harbour a warm heart, but what use is warmth when it was given to any who would take it? In a perfect world respect belonged to those who earned it, and never to those who demanded it. Ayan did not believe in a caste system.

"Please, endure but a little longer, and I will continue the tale." Rakesh feigned to weep, a storyteller's ploy to regain control of the audience. "When the juggler finished his wondrous act, quite a different spectacle developed. This spectacle did not play out for public view, as only my fellow travellers and I perceived the events that were a delight to my eye and a wonder to my mind. What happened before my eyes, the white people reached into their coats and pants' pockets and pulled out coins to place in the juggler's hat!"

A roar of laughter erupted. It echoed from the steel walls, causing many to cover their ears.

"They dropped coins on his head?" asked Little Lalit. A man elbowed the kindly teenager who was regarded more for his good looks than his mental agility.

Rakesh's eyes glittered, delighted for the misunderstanding. He replied with a merry shake of his head. "No, no, no, we could only hope!"

The Lascars laughed at the joke on their taskmasters.

"The juggler's hat lay upside down on the ground. I failed to notice it before, but apparently he placed it there before the show. It appeared before my eyes, and the eyes of those around me, that this man expected the gift. He carried the hat for the expressed purpose of gathering coins. And the way the white men offered up their money, made one wonder if they did not have bellies in which to put food. The coins left their hands with utmost casualness, as though the performance left their minds devoid of thought or common sense.

"And so as the crowd cleared itself away, I approached this most talented juggler. I intended to compliment him on what had been a truly astonishing spectacle. He seemed like an approachable gentleman. I accepted it as my honour to present him with some good praise."

Ayan admired the way that Rakesh's verbal dexterity held the audience captivated.

"Upon walking up to the juggler, I bowed..." Rakesh demonstrated just how, and said, "Where did you find such grace and talent? My goodness, I think I have never been so impressed in my life!"

A small crackle of laughter arose from Rakesh's audience, not so much out of amusement as in acknowledgement of the storyteller's fake composure as he pretended to grovel before the street performer.

"He graced me with a smile and expressed his sincerest feeling of flattery and said to me in his British accent: 'Oh, Lord only knows. I truly think I just pulled it out of my hat.'

"You could only imagine my amazement. I did not know the expression he was using: 'I pulled it out of my hat.' So in an instant, my mouth dropped open, and I looked down at the juggler's actual hat!"

Rakesh's attempt at a British accent incited a riotous burst of laughter, so loud and hearty Ayan wondered if the white partygoers on the top-deck heard. Lascars traded giddy smiles, patting each other's shoulders and aimed their thumbs at Rakesh with admiration.

Ayan rubbed an ear that nearly imploded from the laughter, both his own and those of his workmates.

"He looked at me. I looked at his hat. And I said in the most sincere astonishment and with utter seriousness, "Do you mean, if I had money, I could juggle too?"

The resulting laughter threatened to rupture The Bengal's hull. Ayan chuckled as he left the room and headed toward Akbar's bed. He was surprised to find him beneath the covers so soon after Rakesh's story.

"Have you been here long?" Ayan asked. "You missed a good performance."

"I heard my share from here," Akbar replied.

"Pretty amusing about the hat!"

Akbar let out a soft groan. "I never heard details, only a pack of hyenas."

The warmth of laughter ebbed slightly. For a moment Ayan thought of retreating to his own bed. Laughter and friendship were valuable commodities to a Lascar, more valuable than jewels. Ayan weighed the feeling of being a man again, against their nightly discussions to escape. After a moment, loyalty to Akbar prevailed. He patted his friend's shoulder and sat on the bed.

"He has a way of telling tales, that Rakesh. Have you ever spoken to him personally?"

"Allah forbids it. Certainly not. I'll not trade breath with a man who befriends the whites."

"He kids about them as much as the rest of us." Ayan shrugged and then let out a soft sigh.

"He is," frowned Akbar, "all things to all people. If he lived among dogs, he would learn to bark."

Ayan chuckled at his friend's morose mood. The kind of laughter that loathes itself for laughing.

"When is it time for us to carry out the plan?"

"I'll know the time when it emerges. My energy levels tend to wax and wane. When strength hits me again, we shall proceed."

Ayan felt dismayed by Akbar's selfishness. "Bitterness leads to death. I wonder. Is it freedom you seek, or revenge?"

Silence settled between the men. A voice startled Ayan.

"Of what do you whisper? It sounds devilishly grave."

It was the boy who joked about Rakesh's wife. Ayan failed to recall his name, but it was apparent that he and Akbar were acquainted.

"You use large words for such a small boy." Smiling, the boy extended a hand toward Ayan.

"What is your name?"

"Ayan? And what do you call yourself?"

"I call myself a brave and holy warrior," the boy replied, "but everybody else calls me Noor."

"What do you do aboard this floating coffin?"

"I assist the medics," Noor replied, "up near the captain's quarters. All day, I twist out blood from rags."

"You'd be less busy if someone threw all the whips overboard," Ayan said, winking at Noor and smiling ruefully. Even Akbar joined their laughter.

"Depends on who that someone was," Noor replied.

Ayan cocked a thumb at Noor and said, "I like this man. Shall we ask him to sit?"

Akbar studied Noor with great concentration, scanning his arms, legs, neck and chest, looking for signs of the warrior he had joked about.

"Yes," said Akbar, "we shall ask him to sit."

Noor plopped beside Ayan on the rim of the bed. The three of them talked until long after the other Lascars fell asleep. With each new Lascar that went to bed, the trio's whispering grew quieter and quieter…and quieter.

Ayan knew he should sleep, but resisted the warning that reverberated in the back of his mind. He thought back to Lady Achala's words. His path lay in the people he helped. Ayan wondered about the dark-eyed woman who would love him. Sleep dulled his mind. He did not worry too much about his future or fate.

He felt the warmth of being part of a trio again.

* * *

Ayan leaned against the wall of the shower room. He finished washing his face, feet and stomach. Now he let the trickle of water, leaking from the suspended pipe, wet the healing sores that laced the muscles on his back. He swished a toe through the muddy puddles on the floor. He often thought the foul water caused the rash on most Lascars' feet. The saltwater burned the sores, but the Lascars soon learned to tolerate the pain. The men who avoided the sting of saltwater on an open sore, died.

Ayan splashed the water on his face and drew in a delicious

breath of cold air. He turned to Akbar, whose intense shivering had little to do with the cold water. "Perhaps this is unwise, my friend. You seem ruled by jittery spirits."

Akbar quickly shook his head. "Tonight is the night. We cannot wait. There are five days until the steamer sails to the new world."

"We have five days to plan."

"No," Akbar's eyes snapped. He made fists, working out the pain in his hands. "No. The longer we wait, the more wary the watch will become."

Ayan nodded at the logic. Most of the escape attempts happened as The Bengal prepared to ship out, and men became desperate.

"If we wait, we will die. Or be sent to Jamaica as a slave. What good will you be to your brother then? Do you think there will ever be a return ship from Jamaica?"

Ayan closed his eyes.

"We were fools," Akbar growled. "I lost a brother because I was a fool."

"Do not say such things."

"Ayan, you are a fool." Akbar grabbed Ayan's shoulder and spun him around. "When you signed up... do you remember that day?"

Ayan nodded.

"Where were the Lascars from the inbound trip? Did you see them fighting for a new berth? None returned."

"My father returned, several times."

"Maybe, but your father didn't sign on a slave ship." Akbar pointed his finger with authority.

Ayan held his tongue. He could think of no retort.

"It wouldn't be hard," Akbar continued, his face softening into a smile. "I have been thinking. We can be out of the ship within the hour."

Ayan laughed.

"Seriously," Akbar insisted. "Only people on the ship are Lascars and a few guards. It is a matter of getting on deck and then we jump."

Ayan followed as Akbar's hand did a swan dive toward the muddy sludge that covered the floor. Akbar picked up one of the large buckets which held their excrement.

"Are you coming?" he asked over his shoulder as he disappeared into the dark corridor.

Ayan froze. If they succeeded then Ayan would forfeit the money he earned, the money Kazi needed to survive. If he stayed, then he would never see his brother again. His breath came in deep gasps. He reached down, but his hand wouldn't pick up the bucket. He couldn't abandon his brother. He stared at his filthy, blood-soaked legs. He stared into the dark corridor. His heart failed him. His courage failed him. Ayan sat down and put his head in his hands. A sob escaped him before he could control his emotions. He prayed to Allah.

"You will not have a second chance."

Ayan jumped at Akbar's voice. He took the pails from Akbar's hand and blindly followed him out the door.

"What about the others."

"Do you want to risk Kazi's life by waiting?"

"We arranged to all go."

"Then wait. You wait," Akbar stopped and looked directly into Ayan's eyes. "You wait until it is too late. Then you look at them and remind yourself that you forsake your brother for them."

"I am not..."

"If you do not get off this ship ... yes, you abandon your brother for them." He stuck his thumb toward the belly of the ship where the others slept.

Akbar went up the stairs. Ayan followed.

They moved through the labyrinth of the ship for several minutes, climbing continually higher. Ayan tried not to think about what waited on the ship's deck.

Akbar reached the deck first. Ayan followed for several yards. The men shared a hopeful glance as they rounded the back of the ship.

"You!"

Ayan paused. Akbar continued, deaf to the order.

"I'll shoot."

Akbar slowed to a stop.

"You! What are you about at this time of the night?"

"Emptying pails." Akbar lifted his slightly.

The guard sniffed and moved forward. Ayan gasped as the butt of a musket crashed into the back of Akbar's head. The man fell in a dead heap. Both guards laughed.

"Well, Lascar. Empty your waste." The guard put a foot on Akbar's back and pulled a revolver. "Do not return in time and we kill this one."

Akbar's eyes rolled slightly. Ayan wondered if his friend was already dead. His stiff legs took him forward, closer and closer to the edge of the deck. He lifted the pail and dumped it. The sound of water lapping against the edge of the ship. The cold, black water rolling in low waves. All beckoned to him. It would be so easy to slip over the side and disappear into the water. He didn't dare to turn his head.

He paused for only a moment then returned to Akbar. The guard rested a foot on Akbar's back and flicked ash on him as he smoked. Ayan picked up the other pail and emptied its contents. He hurried back to Akbar's still prone body and helped his friend up, turned his back on the guard and carried Akbar down below.

The Lascars grew restless. Two days passed. Akbar grew restless. Ayan prayed for the storm to stop. Both men talked about ways to escape. They agreed that it would be futile to try another direct plan. They needed a diversion. Ayan did not sleep anymore. He lay awake, or sat in the dark waiting.

CHAPTER 12

Loud shouts and screams broke the silence. Two men had tried to escape. The guards beat them to death and left them in the hall as a warning to the others. The confusion and anger didn't touch Ayan as he continued to stare at the floor and continued to plan.

Late in the night he stood and walked toward the deck. He didn't stop until he reached the upper level. He didn't think. He didn't stop. He just walked. He didn't stop until he was face to face with the barrel of a pistol burrowing into his chest.

"You going somewhere?"

Ayan stood. His breath was slow and even. The gun cocked and dug deeper into his chest. Ayan didn't move. He was tired of fear. He was tired of obedience. Dreading Kazi's face exhausted him. He wanted it to be over.

His head lowered until he looked into the guard's eyes. He stared deep into the man's eyes. He saw a foolish man. He suddenly realised that the guards were stupid. They were nothing to be feared. He wondered why he had ever feared them.

He turned on his heels and returned to the sleeping bunks. He smiled. He smiled for the first time in months. He needed to find Akbar and tell him that he had a plan that would work.

The ship stopped rocking. The men looked at each other. The hull of the ship was cold now that the steam engines were barely burning. The storm chilled the steel hull, draining the last warmth.

The group of men huddled together below decks, carefully hatching a plan. Tonight the ship would fill with the English crew. Akbar pushed the issue at every chance. Why did they need the English crew, unless there would be no Lascars to stoke the fires on the return trip.

Tomorrow morning passengers would board the ship. The idle English crew would be given whips and the task of guarding the

Lascars. Ayan guessed that there were two hours before lunch. Two hours to get everything right. Two hours for everything to go wrong.

The plan was simple. Ayan would follow Akbar into the kitchen and assault The Cruel One when he stood by the stoves. The thought of attacking an ill man left a coppery taste in his mouth. Even The Cruel One deserved mercy, but to afford it spelled death for Akbar, Ayan and as a result, Kazi. He played through the assault in his mind, working every movement, every step and every mistake. No matter how many times his mind played over the impending attack, Akbar failed to function efficiently. A minor mistake, a hesitation and The Cruel One turned. A question niggled at the back of his head, "Would he stop?" Months of pain and abuse destroyed his soul. Akbar did not doubt he could attack The Cruel One, but he refused to say whether he would stop before The Cruel One's blood stained his hands and his enemy's eyes pleaded for mercy.

Ayan's duty was to overturn some shelves of kitchenware, make plenty of noise and intensify the inevitable confusion. The plan had expanded. Noor and two other Lascars, Avid and Farook, had been brought in on the plan to escape The Bengal.

Ayan felt a pang of guilt that he cared nothing for Noor or the other Lascars. Their participation, lives, or possible deaths were nothing more to him than a tool to facilitate his own escape.

The smell of food wafting through the corridor turned Ayan's stomach. The time was almost upon them. So much could go wrong. Last night, the storm tossed the ship and kept the whites on shore. That should have been the time to make their escape.

He turned to his friend, trying to focus his thoughts and silence the voices.

"Friend," Ayan nodded.

"Freedom," Avid replied, and disappeared down the hall. "Fire," he whispered in English and grinned.

Ayan did not doubt that Avid would successfully use the

cigarette to set fire to the dry firewood outside the Captain's quarters.

Ayan went over the plan with meticulous detail. He pictured himself moving through every stage of the plan. His mind played the scenes in his mind. Avid upstairs causing chaos. Ayan and Akbar far below in the kitchen, attacking The Cruel One. The whites and the other Lascars would panic. Few Lascars understood English, compounding the problem. Ayan shut his eyes and imagined himself elbowing his way upstairs as throngs of Lascars and whites ran to help. He would reach the deck where Farook and Noor would be throwing dozens of sacks of wheat into the water and drawing the whites and their guns to the back of the deck. The five would then slip over the railing, strong arms taking them to shore in a few quick strokes.

The noise in the dining room drew Ayan out of his daydream. Voices rose in anger as everyone fought for hard bread and thin soup. He sat at a table with a clear view of the kitchen and forced the food down. He felt too nervous to eat, but knew it could be his last for some considerable time. Akbar sat across the table, looking as nervous as Ayan felt, with sweat streaking his forehead.

A rasp sliced through the noise. A choking cough. Ayan held his breath, afraid that The Cruel One would sense their plan as he passed. Ayan felt, rather than saw his enemy pass behind him. The Cruel One gurgled as he pushed his way toward the kitchen. Ayan closed his eyes, envisioning the pot of steam.

"Can we do this my brother?" Ayan whispered.

Akbar's wide eyes dropped to his bowl.

"Yes, but not too abruptly. Give him a few minutes."

The tenseness drained from Ayan's body, replaced by a heightened awareness. His eyes closed. Instinct identified everyone in the room by the sound of their breathing and their scent. The aroma of onion. The scent of fear. The tremor in a man's voice who was about to die of fatigue and abuse. A man breathed heavy, the sound strained by the pain of a recent beating.

Ayan didn't want to eat anymore. Each moment took too long. They must wait. The guards must finish their meal and head to the deck to smoke cigarettes. Once all the guards were upstairs, Avid would start the fire. There must be time for the fire to grow before he sounded the alarm. If the fire was put out too fast, if the guards didn't run downstairs to fetch Lascars to help put out the fire, if Avid were caught…Ayan gulped down his fear. Too many things could go wrong. He slowed his thoughts.

Akbar would shout that the Lascars were needed to put out the fire. Not too loud. Not loud enough for The Cruel One to hear from the kitchen. Ayan would wait until the Lascars left the dining area. He would then move into the kitchen.

A calmness settled. The sounds faded. Time slowed. His eyes met Akbar's in silent affirmation. It was time.

Only the image of Kazi, firmly held in Ayan's mind, remained real. There was no other choice. Escape would unite the brothers. The rice shop could provide all they need. Ayan saw himself walk across the field. Kazi's excited greeting echoing through the evening silence.

"Help!" Avid's voice pierced the dining room chatter. "Fire!"

"Fool," spat Ayan. He leapt to his feet. A fierce snarl rumbled through his chest.

"Too soon," whimpered Akbar.

Ayan spun, reaching the kitchen in two strides. The plan evaporated.

"I'm supposed to move first," Akbar screeched.

Ayan paused only for a second to wonder why Avid didn't wait until the guards went top side to smoke. It was too late to improvise; he must proceed with his part nonetheless.

Ayan dodged sweating chefs, moving deeper and deeper into the forbidden domain. The cry of fire moved through the kitchen. Cooks blocked Ayan's way as he tried to find his prey.

The confusion in the kitchen turned to panic.

"You!" A guard pointed at Ayan. "What is happening?" He moved forward when Ayan didn't respond immediately. The guard threw one cook to the floor.

Ayan looked deeper into the kitchen. Then at the guard who had almost reached him. If The Cruel One saw him fighting with a guard, he would become wary. He must strike quickly, and without warning.

The guard's eyes widened as he stopped only a few inches away. Ayan looked down, shocked. His hand remained on the hilt of a butcher's knife. Warm blood oozed down the blade and stained his skin. The guard looked at his blood stained uniform in disbelief. A sound gurgled in his throat as the lifeless body fell to the floor.

Ayan stood motionless and let all his fears drain away. He was now the hunter. Ayan gripped the dripping knife tighter and turned back to find The Cruel One.

A horrendous form stood in the kitchen alley, blocking his way, red-faced, moist with steam and mucous. The Cruel One's eyes burned. The death he just witnessed excited him. A sneer twisted the upper lip.

Ayan hesitated a moment.

"Slave," he chuckled.

"Animal!" Ayan screamed and threw his body forward, his focus on the blue eyes that glittered behind the blotched red skin and filthy hair. He rose into the air, dropping with his full weight.

Ayan brought the knife forward, but The Cruel One grabbed his wrist. Ayan fought to twist the knife into the man's fat belly, but The Cruel One drove his elbow into Ayan's nose, snapping his head back. Black spots formed in front of his eyes and he dropped the knife. Ayan drew from the strength he'd built after months feeding the furnace. He drove into his foe and in one swift movement he half picked up the heavy man and threw him to the floor.

Ayan's fist landed on The Cruel One's cheek bone, splitting it. Blood splattered across Ayan's face. A roar of rage erupted from the man, who surged up, only to meet another blow. Ayan pounded and pounded. His full weight behind each punch. Revenge for every lash, every kick, and every taunt. Finally, The Cruel One lay still. He was alive, but badly injured. Ayan reached for the boiling pot and stood over The Cruel One, pausing for a second to allow him to take in what was about to happen.

"Mother!" he screamed. "Mother . . ."

Ayan slowly upturned the pot, aiming carefully for his face. The putrid soul was now blind.

"Ayan?"

Ayan spun and crashed into a pile of pots sending them to the floor. They clattered underfoot as he struggled backward.

"Ayan!" screamed Akbar. "We must go now!"

Ayan fingered the hot pot for a moment. He turned and quickly, deftly, forced the hot metal against The Cruel One's mouth. The man's scream tore flesh from his lips. Ayan turned to Akbar.

"He cannot talk now."

Lascar chefs still struggled to leave the kitchen. One man tried to climb over his friend. A well-dressed Lascar, from the upper deck, stood frozen. A yellow wet spot stained his pants.

"Run!" Akbar hissed and turned.

Ayan realised that he'd only been in the kitchen a few moments. It felt like ten lifetimes. Suddenly, the room grew unkind. The walls narrowed, menacing. The memory of the dream. The darkness, the water, the pain. It all flooded back. Ayan needed to escape the lower halls of The Bengal.

"If we are not overboard before the whites find their guns, we are dead."

Ayan looked at the door just in time to see his friend disappear into the darkness through the open door. Ayan turned back on the Lascar who wet his pants. He wondered if he should stop the man from squealing. He hesitated. The man had not moved. Ayan tossed the empty pot toward the man.

"Do not move!"

They made their way through the kitchen and dining room into a main passageway. Ayan stepped back to avoid a collision with The Fat One. Ayan dropped his gaze, avoiding The Fat One's eyes.

"We must help the Captain," Ayan screamed, dimly amused by his own theatrics.

The Fat One hesitated and then headed toward the engine room.

"We must help the Captain," Ayan yelled into the darkness once again before running after Akbar.

The men ran towards the stairs leading to the upper deck.

"Fire." The call echoed back and forth down the passageway.

"Have we waited too long?"

"Talking will not help us, move."

"Which way?" Akbar and Ayan were tangled in a group of men rushing for the upper decks.

The basement cleared as they reached the top levels. They raced faster, gasping for breath as they scrambled up the last steps and into the blue-grey evening light. It quickly turned into a journey of terror when they reached the Captain's deck. Men raced with buckets of water, black shadows dodging flickering flames. The fire's roar drowned out the men's shouts.

"Here, take this."

Ayan took the bucket shoved in his hand. A white woman ran frantically along the deck, a small black boy carrying her bag. She struck any unlucky Lascars who blocked her way. Behind her, women screamed in terror. White men fought to remove their wealth from the ship. Whips sang in futile brutality. The Lascars cringed back from the flame. Clouds of smoke cloaked the deck in a choking blanket.

"Good," Akbar yelled over the noise. He motioned over the

edge.

Ayan leaned back against the rail and looked over his shoulder. Numerous white sacks floated in the water, just as had been planned.

A white man looked over the edge, a rifle in his hand, the flames dancing on the gun barrel. The white man shot Ayan a dark glance and ran into a billow of smoke.

"Did they make it?"

Ayan shook his head. "Only Allah knows."

"We need to move now."

"Wait." Ayan grabbed Akbar's arm.

Akbar turned. Far away, the cries of horses and the clanging of a bell grew closer. Shouts from the shore made demands in English.

A shot rang out. Akbar almost jumped from his skin. Ayan steadied his friend.

"Wait."

Another shot rang out. Lascars, their nerves taut, bolted, screaming in fear. Even Lascars carrying out orders ran headlong into the fire, or over the rail, in blind panic.

A dark figure ran from the cloud of smoke. Ayan stood still as the white man raced past with two others. The primal hunting instinct drove the men to chase what was running. They raced past Ayan and Akbar barely noticing the two men standing by the rail. A shot split the air, pierced by a scream, as the men found suitable prey.

"Now!" Ayan grabbed Akbar's shoulder and fell backward, dragging his friend with him.

Their bodies hit the water hard. The cold stole the air from their lungs and cramped their legs as the darkness swallowed them.

Ayan's lungs burned. His body twisted, desperately searching for the surface. His body went limp, the cold stealing the strength from his muscles. He floated, waiting to die. His eyes fixed on the only beauty, a red spot floating on the water. His mind screamed at him.

The red spot.

Something about the red spot.

He tried to think.

A hard blow struck his shoulder. He gasped in a mouthful of water as his body dragged to the surface. Ayan screamed, filling his lungs with air. His arms and limbs surged to life, flailing against the water. Ayan heaved for a moment. The blackness cleared. His eyes focused.

"Ayan," Akbar cried. "Allah be with you."

"You saved me," Ayan choked.

"Do not talk."

"Thank you my friend."

"Ayan, we must swim. Stay below the surface. The white ones are still shooting anything that moves."

Ayan nodded.

"There are boats in the water. Hurry."

"Do not lose your way under the water."

Both men took a deep breath and sank below the surface. Ayan swam until his muscles refused to move. He surfaced a few feet from the dock.

"Here!" a shout echoed across the bay. "There is one here."

Ayan looked up. A man stood on the deck. The red flames of The Bengal washed over the dock making it as bright as day. Water splashed beside Ayan's face as a bullet landed less than a foot away. Both men dived back beneath the murky water.

Ayan emerged for an instant, took a breath of the cold London air and then submerged again. They had come so far, to fail now would be unbearable. Finally, they found themselves well under the deck, covered by the darkness. Ayan looked out into the night, where The Bengal lit up the dock like the morning sun. The hollow echo of boots running on the dock disrupted the silence. Ayan hugged the wall, as far under the dock as possible.

"We did it Akbar," he whispered.

"We shall see, Ayan, we are not clear just yet."

"Hey, you two. When do we get out of this cold water?" said a voice.

Avid trod water nearby. "You were early."

Ayan smiled. "You were late."

The men laughed between chattering teeth.

"I do not know," Avid said between chattering teeth.

Suddenly, the sharp crack from a gun filled Ayan's ears.

Ayan stared where Avid had been. A flower of blood bloomed across the water's surface.

CHAPTER 13

Ayan climbed onto the shore, soaked and hungry, with barely enough energy to crawl. The men turned to the harbour and watched The Bengal. It now looked as if the entire ship was on fire. Ayan watched as the orange flames lit up the black sky. He could feel ice in the air in the cold November night. Several boats floated around the ship. A few of the boats pulled bags of grain. Ayan didn't care whether they stole the grain or helped The Bengal. He was free.

Screams and shouts still carried across the water, punctuated with the crack of rifles. In the distance, horses screamed and thundered through the woods. A few Lascars cried out loudly as the beasts ran them down and recaptured them. Ayan realised that others took advantage of the chaos and tried to escape.

Together, Ayan and Akbar crawled through the woods and collapsed in a clearing, shivering in the bitter cold night air. Another Lascar skulked through the undergrowth, snapping twigs and breaking branches. Farook crawled on the ground next to Ayan and collapsed in a heap. The men remained tense. Twigs cracked. Ayan crouched, ready to pounce. A small man walked through the woods clumsily. His breathing heaved with each step. Farook slipped behind a tree.

"It is not a white man," Ayan whispered. He did not see the person who stumbled through the trees, but his ears alerted him. Light footfall meant a small man approached, or a boy. The uneven breathing came from pain, not over exertion. The person weaved his way through the woods in uneven and broken steps. Back from the direction of the harbour, white men carrying weapons could be seen slipping onshore.

Ayan tensed. "Noor." The word slipped out before he remembered to avoid alerting the whites who hunted the escaped Lascars.

"Over here," Farook called softly. "This way, boy."

The boy stumbled into view. A hand hung limp at his side. Noor stumbled to Akbar and crumpled onto the ground. He lay still for several moments before Farook reached over and shook him.

"He is hot as fire." Farook brushed the boy's cheek. "Where is Avid? He should be here by now."

A lump choked Ayan. He opened his mouth several times. The words did not come out without igniting the images of blood pumping as the body thrashed in the water. Nothing erased those few moments. Ayan wondered if anything would ever wash away the horror of watching a body explode in the black water.

Time passed.

Farook paced. "I will go find him."

"No." Ayan reached out and caught Farook by the hand.

A frown darkened Farook's eyes. "I must find my cousin."

Ayan opened his mouth, and shut it.

"Ayan . . . what do you know?"

Ayan's eyes burned. The truth choked him. The memory blinded him.

"Ayan?"

Ayan shook his head sadly. His mouth opened, but no words escaped.

"Is Avid hurt?"

Ayan shook his head, and coughed out a single word, "Dead."

Farook stood abruptly. "No." He clasped his head. Farook shook his head repeatedly. "No. It cannot be," he wailed. "It must not be." His body started to rock as he babbled. "I vowed to his father. I vowed that I would protect him on my life." Farook's eyes bulged. Fists started to flail at an invisible enemy. "I vowed I would not return home without Avid at my side. I vowed. I vowed."

"I saw it." Ayan grabbed his hand to restrain him.

Farook tore his hand away and stalked into the darkness. "I

vowed." The words echoed from the darkness.

"What happened to Avid?" Noor whispered.

"We must be quiet. They are still hunting us."

Noor wheezed. The sound turned Ayan's blood cold, a vaguely familiar tenor to the sound, an unmistakable rasp. Eventually, exhaustion overrode adrenaline and the men dozed off.

Ayan dozed only lightly; Noor's wheezing disturbing his sleep and making him think of Kazi. The morning chill woke him. The sun hung low. Ayan shivered. The morning was peaceful. No more sounds of the ship's engine. They could see London in the distance.

Noor lay silent beside Akbar. Farook lay beside him.

Ayan lay with his back to the others and watched the blackened silhouette of The Bengal out on the bay. Smoke billowed from the stacks and darkened the sky directly above.

"Noor does not move," Farook whispered.

"Have his nerves ceased to function properly?" Akbar asked. "My mother's sister suffered from nerves that did not function properly."

"Most likely the infections from the white men's lashings took too much strength from him."

"Let him sleep," Akbar whispered. "He needs time to heal."Ayan sighed.

"Ayan?"

"What!"

"Ayan?" Akbar asked curiously. "Are you angry?"

Ayan sighed.

"What do we do?"

"I do not know," Ayan sneered. "You are the one who makes plans."

"We are off The Bengal," Akbar whined. "The plan worked."

"It did not work," Farook growled. "Not for all of us."

"It will grow colder here."

The cold water numbed Ayan's feet so long ago he was not

sure he possessed the ability to walk.

"We will remain until Noor is better."

No one challenged Akbar's plan. Nothing could force the men to move, not even a white hunter. Ayan laughed, thinking that they were now four free men, yet they could not move to save their lives. However, if The Cruel One appeared, they would be able to move. Not only that; they would probably board the ship and work a day's labour before collapsing. No. Ayan's mind rebelled. "No," Ayan whispered.

"Never again." The voice whispered in the back of his mind, soft as a dove's coo and strong as a storm at sea. The words bore deep into his soul. Never again would he allow himself to lay in humble acceptance of another's anger or brutality.

The Cruel One's face danced before him, the red skin peeling under the boiling water. A new sense awoke inside him. It stirred in his mind, silent as a tiger, strong as a bull elephant. It promised to remain dormant, asleep, until needed and then it would strike. Attack anything that tried to hurt him.

He wondered if the last few months had turned him into an animal, or a man. Either way, only Allah offered the power to help, the promise of hope.

They remained in the woods until the bitter wind forced them to move. Ayan rose.

"No," Farook objected.

"I will not die," Ayan vowed.

"He must return for Kazi," Akbar stated as if explaining Ayan's vow to Farook. But, he did not move.

Ayan rose and started to walk away. He heard Akbar stiffly climb to his feet. Farook paused, then jumped to his feet and ran to catch up.

"Ayan?" Akbar turned to look back.

"Do not look back," Ayan ordered.

The three men walked away, shoulder to shoulder.

Behind them, Noor lay in the spot where he collapsed the

night before.

* * *

"Fud, please, fud," Ayan begged. The man swung his cane forward, creating a mute barrier between the woman he escorted and Ayan. The woman blustered nervously and grabbed the man's arm. Ayan did not understand the words, but he understood the reassuring tone. Ayan did not understand why these people feared a beggar.

Akbar rolled his eyes. "The oo sound, not the u sound."

Ayan snarled and turned away.

"No one learns their harsh tongue easily. It took my brother and I . . ."

Both men grew sober at the mention of their brothers.

"Food, please, food." Ayan tried again with a reassuring smile.

Ayan begged for several hours to no avail. The whites responded to their pleas with outright hostility, or blatant arrogance.

"Warm water. Sweet fruit. Working hard in the morning under a bright sun. A warm sun."

"Akbar, do not." Ayan did not want to hear Akbar cry for his home country. The autumn wind bit their skin and chilled their lungs. Akbar fell silent.

A woman glanced at them, pity in her eyes. Ayan did not move. He learned long before that pity from an English woman did not mean mercy. He wondered if the bitter wind hardened the white people's hearts.

"Maybe we can try begging for money again."

"To what purpose?"

Farook crept around the corner and slid down beside Ayan and Akbar. Ayan turned to greet him and then changed his mind. Farook's disposition remained bitter. His anger burned hot. Akbar and Ayan sat silently, waiting for him to speak first.

"I lost a brother," Akbar started softly.

"Did you take a white man's life for it?" The words dripped

with anger.

"Allah does not want revenge. Not for a brother." He turned to Farook. "Not for a first cousin."

"No?" Farook leaned back and grinned. "Allah may not want revenge. It is something I want. There are many different ways to kill a white person. A rifle, to silence their words like they silenced my cousin is a good way to find revenge."

"It will not dull the pain"

"Who are you to speak to me? You killed a white to save your own life. What difference is it to kill to save your life, or to seek vengeance."

Ayan and Akbar traded sober glances.

"I did not kill," Akbar sulked.

Farook stuck his thumb out, pointing to an invisible horizon

"You do not think all those deaths were the result of your plan?"

"Cheap," said Farook, and spat. "Not one person gave me a single penny."

"Not even the kind-hearted ones will share their food."

"No colour in their flesh and no blood in their hearts."

"You keep looking at them with such cold eyes, Farook," said Akbar, "I guarantee the blood flows nowhere near their hearts."

The veins tightened in Farook's neck. "What am I supposed to be? Their slave? Again? Do these people never see that I am a man? Perhaps I should throw my shirt off and bend over for a whipping?"

"Yes," Akbar grimaced. "They have no reservation about sharing the edge of a whip."

"Hush," Ayan interjected, flicking his eyes from Farook to Akbar and then back again.

"There is no use fighting amongst ourselves. If we don't work together, we'll end up like Noor."

The mention of the boy's name had the desired effect. Both men sank into silence.

"There is nothing we can do for our lost," Ayan sighed. "We do not even know if we can keep our own souls and bodies connected. We have no power to help others."

"We have the power to help ourselves," Farook interrupted. He waited until Ayan and Akbar realised he had something worth listening too. "I found a shelter."

"Shelter? How much."

Farook shook his head. "Not a room. A shelter, between two buildings, in the city. It is small. Between an alleyway. The floor is gravel and concrete. There is something overhead. It will keep the rain off. It looks like a shelter made by other beggars."

"Are they still there?"

"I do not know," Farook shook his head. "There is no smell of rotting food."

"It is better than sitting here."

"It is protected from the wind. We have a better chance of staying warm."

"What if they come back?" Akbar asked.

Ayan rose. "Farook, show us the way."

They crossed several alleys and lanes before arriving between the buildings. Some men had created a cave between two walls. Boards had been wedged between the walls creating a roof that would not hold heat in, but would hold the rain and sleet out.

"We can be comfortable here." Akbar went deep into the back and curled up against the wall. He spun excitedly. "It is warm. The wall is warm!"

"Warm?" Farook knelt beside Akbar and placed a palm on the wall. "It is."

"There must be a kitchen or fireplace on the other side." Ayan sat with his back to the wall and sighed.

"Now," Farook sighed, "for Halal to eat."

"Be thankful for what you have," Ayan sighed, "but I too would like rice, or a good bowl of curry."

"We should only eat Halal," Akbar quoted.

"Our faith and Allah are not in England."

"We ate pork to survive on The B-B-B." Akbar hung his head.

"Those are words," Ayan rebuked him. "We are not on the sea anymore."

"We may not be, but we still must eat defiled food," Akbar sighed.

"I would do almost anything for a good bowl of rice."

"My mother made wonderful curry. It took her months to mix and age the spices. Many people bought her curry mix."

"A bowl of curry and rice."

All three looked at each other then broke out laughing. What nonsense. They didn't even have garbage to root through for food. The chance of seeing an elephant or snake charmer on the London's streets was greater than the chance of them finding a bowl of curry.

* * *

"Where is he?" Farook growled, his fists clasping into balls. "It has grown dark since he left."

"He'll be back," said Ayan, watching the small wooden panel they added to serve as their door. "Akbar is a loyal friend."

Ayan doubted his own words.

"It has been more than an hour." Farook threw his hands up

"We needed to trust someone. Akbar is too small to defend the shelter against the others. We all made the decision together."

"You did not need help defending the home. Who is to protect Akbar?"

Ayan chuckled. "And who would expect a thin, rag covered man like Akbar to have any coin to steal."

"They will see the food bags." Farook slapped his hands together.

Ayan shook his head. "Akbar is hungry. He will not let anyone take his food."

"I should have gone."

"This is tiresome. Akbar knows how to barter. You do not. Let it rest. If Akbar has robbed us, there is no way to find him. Our money is gone. Becoming angry will not fill your belly."

Farook paced along one of the walls. Ayan could not help remembering how eagerly Akbar volunteered to fetch the food. Supposing the man had a selfish heart. What then? When would Ayan and Farook eat next? The starkness of this question was maddening. For the sake of preserving his sanity, Ayan forced himself to believe that Akbar would return. He sat by the warm wall and watched the door and waited. And watched the door.

"The pig!" shouted Farook as the minutes wore on. "I can imagine him now: putting fresh bread into his mouth. His guts swollen."

"Do not speak of bread to me," said Ayan, with the slickness of the drool on his tongue.

"Do not speak of anything," Ayan said. "Akbar does not know the local language. He travels with obstacles. Nor does he know how this society works. Patience. He will learn what he needs to know for food so he is not robbed by the farm merchant."

Ayan sensed he might be addressing himself.

Farook spit against the wall as footsteps echoed from outside the shelter. Ayan and Farook looked at each other, fear and relief vying for control. Ayan assessed the texture of the footsteps. Did it sound like . . .?

"Akbar!" Both men screamed the name at once.

Farook laughed, for the first time since his cousin Avid's death. Ayan and Farook crowded Akbar as he squeezed through the door. Farook grabbed for the cotton sack. Ayan laughed. Perhaps Farook had a hint of telepathy. The bag smelled of bread.

Akbar grinned and pulled out a fat, rounded bun, the corners of its surface flaking with a bit of poorly baked flour. Akbar broke the bun into even thirds. They gulped the food down, their hunger removing the desire for water, or manners.

Farook verbalised their private thoughts: "That's all?"

"The coins," Akbar breathed, moving his tongue about his

mouth to relish the taste, "Were not worth much."

Farook exploded. "You snake. You ate our food!" He threw himself at Akbar.

Ayan took the full force of the attack. Akbar crouched in the corner and whimpered. Shaking his head. "Allah is my watcher. I did no such thing."

"He's a good friend," pleaded Ayan. "This man would not do that."

Farook turned on Ayan. His face a flashback to a nightmare, the Fat Ones face danced before Ayan's face. Farook could be mistaken for a devil. "How do you know?" he screamed. "You just wish for peace. Peace and quiet, yes? No fighting? Life is a fight and you are a child. A child without a home. We must behave as clawed creatures in the jungle if we are to gain anything."

"You ramble, Farook," Ayan said evenly. "We just ate food. There will be more. Akbar did not steal from us."

Farook darted toward the door. He tore it open. "Starve, if that is your choice. It is not mine."

"I never ate the food. I never ate the food."

"You never ate the food. I believe this."

"I never ate the food," the whimper continued.

"I know you are good." Ayan patted Akbar.

"You are a good man. And you will help us return home." Akbar said with a tear in his eye. "Home?"

"Yes." Ayan leaned back. "You will once again walk your village. A respected man who has travelled the world. Men will pay to hear of your adventures. You will be asked to entertain rich men. You will tell them about defeating the white men. You will tell them about tricking the whites and escaping The Bengal."

"...and you my friend Ayan will return to Kazi with enough money for a doctor. The rice shop will flourish. People will travel long distances to see the wonderful treasures you brought from the farthest corners of the world. They will eat rice and drink tea.

Your cousins will marry into good families and wear colourful silks. They will laugh and raise fat babies. You will wear fine clothing and be respected. You will visit and tell me stories of the Punjabi and Rajahs. You will share stories of princes and foreign treasures."

"You will keep a room for me." Ayan said with a smile.

"And you for me."

The darkness settled between the buildings. Distant voices drifted down from the windows. A woman laughed. A child screamed.

"Are you tired?" asked Akbar, indicating that it was time to sleep.

Guilt tainted Ayan's response: "Hungry… just hungry."

* * *

"What are you doing?"

"Marking the days."

Ayan looked at the wall.

"I learned it from the older ones. The ones from the upper deck who were not . . . killed or sold as slaves." Akbar traced the lines. "Each day you draw one on the wall. When each finger has a mark, start another line. There are a certain number of marks between ports. The ones who work on the deck can tell when they will arrive in port when there are certain numbers of lines on the wall."

"Why do they do this?"

"The whites become happier when they are near a port. They bestow more favours. It is worth the effort to grovel and curry favour at such times. A Lascar may be offered a half-eaten plate to carry back to the kitchen. Or, they may be asked to clean a room with a full plate of scraps left in a cabin."

"How will this help us?"

Akbar paused. "I do not know. We did survive for three hands. That is one half of a month. That is the time it takes for a seed to break out of the ground and grow a thumb."

Loud shouts from outside froze the men.

"You men in there. Come along, there. That is a good fellow."

"Who is it," Ayan covered Akbar.

"They are London constables. They are the authority. We must go with them."

"I will not return to a ship as a slave," Ayan hissed.

"Come along, gentlemen. You cannot stay in there."

Akbar slid around Ayan and opened the door. He grovelled before the police officer. A rosy cheeked man stared in at Ayan.

"Hello there, gents." He touched his cap. "You cannot stay here. It's a bit draughty, wouldn't you say? We've a nice place with a warm meal to warm your bellies."

Ayan's heart fell to his stomach. Akbar translated for Ayan. The London constable spoke proudly of their city. London, being a modern city, offered limited housing for people like them. Akbar explained that Ayan must not fight the officers or he would be put in a cell.

They strode down the streets into a dingy, smoke-stained section of town. They rounded a large building and entered a small green door. The constables seemed well-liked by the people who worked at the house. Arabs moved in and out in a steady procession. The constables nodded and left them at the door. The place reminded Akbar of the mission orphanage, except here, there did not seem to be any rules.

Ayan entered a small, crowded yet decent structure. They were shown to a tiny room with no beds, chairs, or tables. They slept on the floor. The men in the surrounding rooms peeked out. Ayan assumed by the languages spoken and their dress, that they were Sikh, Chinese, and Malayan. Akbar spoke with authority, as if he lived in the house for some time. Some of the other men were gamblers and wayfarers, but most were beggars.

A timid woman at the end of the hall peeked out. Ayan looked down and smiled at her. She had eyes like the women at home, shy and friendly and always seeming to be laughing at some delightful joke. But, fear shaded this woman's eyes. Ayan smiled at her and was disappointed when she darted back in her room.

Ayan entered the room and closed the door.

"With two of us begging, we can afford to stay here. It is warm." Akbar could hardly contain his excitement at their good fortune.

Ayan withheld his own opinion. He had seen too many good things offered by the whites that were, in fact, tricks that forced them into slavery, or worse.

Ayan woke early in the morning. He wished for a basin of water and laughed at his foolishness. Akbar leapt up happily, eager to start the new day.

Ayan stretched and entered the hall. The dark-eyed woman opened her door. A man made a rude comment in Bengali. Ayan opened his mouth to rebuke the man, when the woman uttered a violent curse that almost burned his ears. Akbar laughed and wished the woman a good morning. Her eyes narrowed.

"What is your name?" Ayan asked.

"My name is no affair of yours, slave."

Ayan squared his shoulders. "I am no slave."

"You were," she laughed. "No man in this place has muscles like you unless he was a slave. You are Sylheti Bengali, or Hindu?" Ayan noticed that she relaxed slightly, but still kept her distance.

"Sylheti." Ayan smiled.

"I am Italian."

"You speak our language." Akbar grinned.

"I speak your language, and mine. I speak Hindi and English."

"Then you can tell me your name."

She grinned. "My name is Louisa. Some call me Lascar Louise."

"You can learn languages?"

"Yes." Louisa smiled.

"Can you teach?"

"I am teaching Ayan to speak English." Akbar laughed.

"Akbar is just learning himself. We have only been here for half a month."

"Almost a month," Akbar corrected, "and we are beggars."

"I am also a beggar." Louisa smiled. "Come with me and I will show you some good places to ask for a coin."

Ayan followed her outside, listening intently.

"It is easy. Watch. Shillings," she said, jingling a handful of coins. "You never have them all in your hand. Only enough to make a noise, but still make it look like you will not eat."

"Shy-lens," replied Ayan.

Louisa smiled and shook her head. "Shih, shih, shih," she emphasised the first syllable.

Ayan got the hang of it, and said, "Shih, shih, shih."

"Lings," she chirped.

"Lings," he parroted.

"Shillings," she said, raising her hands.

"Shy-lens," Ayan declared. Louisa collapsed into laughter.

"You have some work to do," she told Ayan in his native tongue, patting him on the arm.

Ayan warmed to the touch. He had entertained many women when he sold rice, but all belonged to another man. To touch them would break a sacred taboo. Faiza and Mirvat were different. Faiza grew up so innocent and sweet that he never imagined any man touching her without the utmost respect and reverence. Mirvat, he smiled, would laugh at a man who touched her.

Ayan did not own enough to have a wife. But, the idea of a woman as a friend warmed something deep in his stomach. Mirvat sometimes smiled at him in a way that made him feel shy, but her laughter always made him feel foolish.

Louisa's voice and manner made Ayan feel strangely shy, something he never felt when talking to a man. He spent as much time as he could with Louisa over the next days. They quickly developed a bond, unlike any he had enjoyed with a woman before. Akbar was not offended at all. He too had made a group of friends, and they would disappear for long stretches of time, returning with coins, but never talking about where they went.

Louisa and Ayan made a good team. People were willing to give Louisa money. She believed that Ayan's size prevented people from pitying him. He did not know if this was true, but agreed if it meant spending the day with her. Louisa strayed farther from the lodge with Ayan at her side.

"You are my good luck," she teased.

Ayan smiled. It suited him to stand aside and glower at men who treated Louise roughly. Even the white sailors and dark-clad rich men who hid in black carriages, withdrew from Louisa when Ayan stepped forward. Louisa blossomed in her new found freedom. Her laughter and jokes attracted attention. Ayan remembered the story about the street performer. Louisa did the same. Instead of begging, she entertained.

Ayan loved the days when she swung her skirt and sang songs in Italian. She stood outside theatres some days and sang sweet songs from operas. Ayan never understood what an Opera was, but the gentlemen in long black coats and white scarves threw coins if their silk draped wives enjoyed what they heard.

A woman clapped after one of Louisa's songs and begged for an Aria. The man spoke Louisa's Italian fluently.

She stepped back and stood tall. Her eyes moistened as she sang a song so beautiful that Ayan's chest tightened. When she finished the man bowed low and tossed her a coin. Louisa squealed and ran across to Ayan.

"A crown. He gave me a crown." Louisa danced around and sang. "A crown. He gave me a crown. A gentleman gave me a gold crown."

"A crown?"

"Much money," Louisa laughed. "Much money."

The smile on Ayan's face did not reach his heart. He looked at the gentleman. A gold and silken woman fluttered on his arm. Her eyes adored the man. Her voice worshiped him. Other men turned in envy at the woman floating beside the gentleman. Ayan knew wealth. He knew about respect and noblemen. But, for the first time in his life, he felt the bitter disappointment of not being a man which could draw a woman's laughter and delight in the same way this man enthralled his escort and excited Louisa.

Something about the way Louisa's hair shone in the sunlight reminded him of the woman he thought of as mother. He now knew she had been a prostitute, but that never changed the way his heart remembered her. She made Ayan want to be special and earn her approval. Louisa's smile possessed him. It worried Ayan that she held the power to make his heart swell. He wanted to earn Louisa's approval.

The crowd moved into the theatre. Ayan watched Louisa laugh for a few more minutes and then touched her arm. She looked up, surprised. Ayan looked down into her eyes. His breath sped up. "Teach me English."

"Milk," Louisa said, pointing at the bottle in a passing child's hand.

"Milk," Ayan repeated. That was an easy one.

"Bird," Louisa said, pointing up at the sky.

"Burr," Ayan said back, knowing from her smile that said it wrong. Ayan's teeth ground together. He set his jaw. "Bird."

"Drum," Louisa said, aiming a finger at the instrument being carried by another street performer leaving the area of theatre.

Ayan did not reply. He smiled at Louisa.

"What?" Her head tilted sending a cascade of dark hair tumbling off her shoulder. "Tell me. You have a secret."

"I have a fabulous idea," he said in Bengali.

CHAPTER 14

The drum roll echoed off the walls of nearby buildings. Ayan stood tall, beating a tattoo from the skin. He smiled. No one looked down at him. The cold glitter never left the white's eyes. The change, though subtle, was noticeable. The whites did not look through Ayan now, as if he were an untouchable. They looked at him.

Louisa wandered farther down the street leaving him alone. He played, letting the hands hit the drum in rapid succession. A few of his friends stopped begging and danced, picking up the pace as he let the hands fly in an ecstatic frenzy. He broke into a religious song. The Bengali words fascinated the whites and added more energy to the dancer's convulsive jubilations.

Ayan paused, shaking out his wrists. A thunderous applause brought a blush to his cheeks. The basket held a few coins, good for a morning's work, but it would be better soon.

"More," several of his friends called.

"I must rest," Ayan said in a breathless voice. "My arms are ready to fall off." Ayan felt bad for disappointing them, but they must leave if he hoped to make real money that afternoon. He looked up and down the street for any sign of Akbar or Louisa. He sat, feigning fatigue to dissuade the last friend hanging around.

"You will play again?" a young boy asked.

Ayan sighed. Begging turned a man hard. "Maybe later," he promised the boy. He tossed the boy enough coins to fill his belly. A white grin split the grimy face as he tore off down the street toward a sweet meat vendor. Ayan whispered a quiet blessing to Allah for permitting him to climb from slave to beggar and from beggar to businessman again.

Horses clattered down the street, their heads pulled high, forcing their eyes to flair and their feet to prance high. After the streets filled with fine carriages, the cabbies appeared, their worn nags plodding heavily. The cabbies' lives were hard. Ayan could leave the street when his basket filled. He could step in out of the cold. Many times he stood under the shelter of a theatre and played for the crowds as they left, while cabbies remained in the wind and rain awaiting their fares leisure.

The layers of English society were as complex as that of Calcutta. The layers of the wealthy and the layers of poor intertwined into a tapestry of life that Ayan found intriguing.

"You are asleep?" said Louisa.

"No, just waiting," Ayan smiled up at Louisa.

"You are a gentleman now? Sitting away the afternoon?"

"I am waiting for you and Akbar," Ayan replied.

"You speak about me when I am not here?" A voice teased from behind them.

"We do not," Louisa objected to Akbar who crept up behind her. "Ayan here has decided that he is a wealthy gentleman sitting in the club all afternoon."

"I do not." Ayan stood. "I was waiting for you to arrive."

"You did not do well." Akbar kicked the basket with his toe.

"I did well enough to share with the boy."

"Dickie?" Louisa smiled. "You are too good to that boy. He only follows you to fill his belly."

"You should not give away so much of our money."

"A few pence will not hurt." Louisa made a face at Akbar. "Ayan is good. We will earn the coppers back. No street hacker attacks coins like Ayan's drumming."

"Your dancing attracts a larger audience than my drumming." Ayan toyed with frayed leather holding the worn drum together.

"We are exotic entertainers." Akbar bowed low.

Louisa spun lightly, her hands flipping her skirt and flashing her lower legs as she spun.

"Exotic performers who entertain noblemen and world travellers."

Akbar took Louisa's hand and they spun happily. Ayan took up the beat and sang loud enough to rise above the street noise. He smiled. She never looked more like Faiza. Her shy eyes hid deeper pains than Faiza ever knew, but her soul shone through. Life would not defeat her. Ayan learned from Louisa that Faiza may be quiet and gentle, but those did not equal weakness in a woman as it would in a man.

In fact, Louisa taught him that a quiet gentle woman possessed more strength than the bawdy women, who met the beggars when they returned at the end of the day and tried to coax them to trade coins for companionship. Those women preferred to share their favours with several men and then drink themselves into a stupor. Their odour and behaviour disgusted Ayan.

"We are a novelty," Louisa chirped merrily. Ayan snapped out of his meditation.

Louisa put her hands on her hips and mocked Ayan's sober mood, "We are like the gypsies who travel in Italy."

"And people pay to watch a novelty." Akbar laughed. "We will give them something worth stopping to watch."

Ayan focused on the drum's steady rhythm, matching the drone of the religious songs with the cadence. The street throbbed and ebbed like waves on the shore. People moving in all directions, each one moving in a straight line, but never colliding. Shoulder to shoulder, dancing their dance, void of rhythm, existing in a dance that long ago lost the meaning of life.

The trio worked hardest when couples and families strolled down the street. Their laughter and excitement added to the performance. The crowd faded, soon to be replaced by hordes of bank tellers and clerks. Louisa, Akbar and Ayan relaxed while they filled the streets and made way for their throngs to pass. They rarely tipped street performers, or even noticed that they existed.

Ayan looked up after a long while. Akbar undulated in some mock Hindi dance while a man stood patiently, prompting a lesson about foreign cultures to two young boys who stood in awe. Ayan laughed. The thought that an arrogant Englishman would believe the nonsense they did to earn coin actually represented their cultures.

A familiar movement caught his eyes. Enemies. Three jugglers moved close enough to attract the young boy's attention. One juggler tossed a knife high into the air and back flipped before catching it. The juggler flicked a hand gesture at Ayan, and then flipped backward again. The youngest boy squealed.

"Darkie," the juggler's friend laughed. He stuck his tongue out; the jester protected by the brute.

Ayan played louder to encourage Louisa and Akbar to continue dancing. The father led the boys away.

Four teen boys took their play. Their voice mocking Ayan's song, jeering them. The jugglers openly taunted now. Their jibes followed by pebbles dug from the gutter.

"Sootbag." Akbar stopped dancing at that insult. Louisa crept behind Ayan's shoulder and pressed close.

"What are they saying," Akbar whispered. His face turned bright red. "What are they saying? Woman."

"Akbar!" Ayan snapped. His arm closed around Louisa, pulling her farther away from the four youths. One spat on the ground at his feet. A light shower of spittle draped his arm.

Ayan's eyes narrowed. "Ignore them," Kazi's voice echoed in his memory. He stopped moving. His senses alert. His body relaxed into a crouch that was not perceivable, especially the four fools who stood in front of him. He sensed the jugglers moving back, their street sense warning them that the game ran amiss.

Ayan understood enough of their words to realise they found him dirty and felt insulted by his presence. The feeling was mutual. A constable strolled up the street, his baton flailing loosely on its leather strap. The boys sauntered away laughing. Louisa whimpered, her tears wetting the back of his shoulder.

"Trouble here men?" The constable eyed Ayan suspiciously.

"No trouble," Louisa leaned around Ayan's shoulders. "No trouble."

"Want no trouble, sir." Akbar's head bobbed in the manner he learned as a deck slave. The constable levelled a stern eye on Ayan.

"And you young man?"

A muscle twitched in Ayan's jaw.

"It would be a shame to see you slapped in chains and your young missus and family left without anyone to protect them."

The constable tapped his helmet with the edge of the baton. Louisa withdrew at the gesture. The constable turned his gaze to Ayan. "It would be a shame now, to leave such a fine lass on her own."

The thought of Louisa alone cleared the fog from Ayan's mind. He relaxed and nodded slightly to the constable.

"Right now, let's move along." Akbar picked up the basket. They walked soberly as Akbar counted the money. Louisa hung off Ayan's arm.

"We have enough for a sweet after our meal," Louisa said.

"I do not feel like a sweet today," Ayan replied.

"It is not every day we have enough left over for sweets," Louisa pouted.

"Many of our friends never taste sweets."

Louisa threaded her fingers through Ayan's. "It is a hard life here."

"It is a hard life anywhere," Ayan countered.

"Not like here. Our skin is dark." Louisa held her hand out to inspect it. "Look," she pointed to a filthy scullery maid. "She is no better than I. Yet, she is permitted to work inside, away from the wind. Away from the snow."

"Snow?"

"You will see soon." Louisa pressed closer and spoke, more to herself than to him. "I hate the snow. It is wet like rain, but colder than the sea. Buildings grow cold. Not the type of coldness after a storm. This cold is hard. It bites with teeth like a mastiff. It holds like hunger in the belly. Then, when it has taken all it can, it melts into water, soaking the body. It brings fever and delirium. Many die. In the spring the lodge will have many rooms empty. Snow," she shuddered, "I loathe it. It is the only thing that can steal the life from a strong, healthy man."

"Loathe?" Louisa laughed. "Yes, loathe. It means to despise with all your heart and soul."

"Loathe," Ayan repeated. His mind playing over the thought of water that bit hard and hurt like hunger.

"I can understand the word loathe," she sighed. "I understand the word in three languages. That scullery maid cannot, and never will. Though, it matters not here. In this country I am dark skinned."

"It will get better."

"You do not understand," Louisa cried. "She can work in the warmth. If I were fair, I would work in the warmth. My days would start in a bakery, kneading dough. All day my hands would fly, making bread and sweet meats."

Ayan fingered Louisa's soft hand, unsure if the thought of calluses pleased him. "Against my skin, yours is very fair."

"Not fair enough. Not fair enough to earn a position working in a bakery."

"You want to make bread?" Ayan queried, certain he did not understand what Louisa really meant. "You sing well."

Louisa laughed. "In Paris, or Italy, I might sing on a stage. These very people who look through me as if I am invisible would applaud me and noblemen would beg for the favour of visiting the back parlour to see the dancing girls and divas."

Ayan smiled. "Is that where you learned to sing?"

"In an opera house. My mother danced the ballet until she became older. Then she sang in the chorus. I sat still as a statue every night. My mother said, "Learn the words dear and you will never go hungry. Learn the words and you will never need to beg."

"You did learn the words." Ayan smiled remembering her performance.

"Yes," the word hissed. "I learned the words, and came to England, but my skin was dark. They do not let dark women sing or dance. Even famous divas must powder their face heavily."

"That is why you want to bake bread?"

"No," Louise laughed out loud. "No, silly. I do not want to be a baker."

"But, you said . . ."

"I said I could not work in a bakery." Her eyes beseeched him. "I do not want to work in a bakery. I just want to be warm when the winter winds blow."

* * *

"Where is my drum? Where is my drum?" Ayan cried, in both English and Bengali. He paced the lodge, banging doors. Most men shrugged and slid away, the truth hid behind poker faces.

"Where is my drum?" Ayan yelled.

"Where did you last see it?" Akbar trailed Ayan around the building.

"In our room; where else? I put it beneath my clothes before my bath." Ayan snapped. The old wood panel splintered under the force of another blow.

"It did not walk away," Akbar said, sulking from Ayan's rebuke. "We'll find it."

A dull thud stopped Ayan in his tracks. The blood ran cold chilling his heart. A muted smack emitted from down the hall. A few steps farther, he stopped and listened. The clamour grew loudest behind a chipped door. Nikolai.

He pushed the door until it rested against the wall. The Russian, Nikolai, smiled with unclouded cruelty. "Sounds good, no?" he looked up from his spot on the floor, his back resting against the wall.

"You need practice," Ayan hissed. "You must purchase your

own."

Nikolai's smile deepened, deepening the wrinkles in his face into rivers of blackness. "I would," he shrugged muscular shoulders, "but this one, I like. I like, very much."

Ayan pounced like a cat. Before Nikolai could react to protect himself, Ayan was on top of him. Anger fuelled Ayan's assault. He grabbed Nikolai around the throat, thrusting forwards smacking his head against the cold hard wall.

Akbar screamed. The giant Russian winced at the blow and dropped to the floor. Ayan stepped over him and took the drum from his hands. The anger faded. The Russian stood up slowly, visibly shaking. Ayan's shoulders spanned farther than Nikolai's, but the Russian outweighed him by a stone. Ayan braced for a retaliation blow.

"You leave me alone," said Nikolai, struggling to prevent his voice from wavering. Ayan leaned forward. The Russian's face blanched. Ayan stared at a ghost. Nikolai shook with more fear than The Cruel One, when Ayan had stood over him with a boiling pot. Ayan laughed. Nikolai had much bark, but zero bite.

The Russian breathed heavily. Ayan turned his back and walked from the room. The hall cleared as he walked. Men backed away and lowered their eyes. Ayan walked into the street to clear his head.

Rain pounded the cobblestone. Wind drove sheets of rain against Ayan. He walked streets far beyond his normal territory. The tall dirty buildings gave way to tall walls and gates that protected gardens and family homes.

A lamp lighter doffed his cap and climbed the ladder to light the street lamp. His piercing whistle echoed long after they passed in the night.

The dawn's chill drove into the bone, making a man wish for the comfort of home. Street hawkers wheeled their wagons into the markets. Ayan moved closer, drawn by the warmth of their fires. A fierce-eyed street hawker nodded slightly.

Ayan returned the gesture and moved toward the fire. The men laughed and chattered. Rag-draped women huddled in the street sorting vegetables, flowers, or bread. Children crept close, stealing the scraps of beans, or a fallen tomato. Eventually, streets lightened and working men headed to their jobs. It was time to return to the lodge to rejoin Akbar and Louisa. He hurried the next hour, drawn by the promise of her smile. Louisa's ability to restore his good mood drew him like a moth to a flame.

A crowd stood outside the lodge. He moved through them, certain Akbar and Louisa had already left, but hoping to find someone who could direct him to the corner they worked today.

"Louisa?" Ayan grabbed a man's arm, not caring who he asked. The man shook his head and pulled away. Ayan looked around. The crowd moved away clearing a path. "Louisa?" Another man shook his head.

A surge of desperation flooded the senses blinding the eyes, deafening the ears. He started to run down the hall. "Louisa!" he screamed.

"Do not cause a disturbance," the lodge owner yelled up the stairwell.

Ayan ran to the stairs and looked down. The man stood below looking up. "I need to find Louisa."

"She is gone."

"Where?"

"Gone."

"Where do I find her?" Ayan said in a desperate voice.

"Are you deaf? She is gone." His hands gestured wildly. "Gone . . ." The man sighed. "To Spain. She travelled to Spain. You know, the country."

Ayan took the stairs two at a time and hurried to check all the rooms. A couple of minutes later Ayan reappeared looking visibly shaken.

"When?" Ayan croaked, unable to believe it could be true.

"Last night," replied the lodge owner

"You are wrong! She would not leave like this," shouted Ayan. "There must be some mistake."

"I am sorry, Ayan, but it is true. Louisa came and thanked me for looking out for her when she first arrived here. It is too late, my friend, you will never catch the ship. It left berth before dawn."

Ayan staggered outside and collapsed on a bench. It was cold and miserable, mirroring his mood. The rain had turned to wet snow. How fitting that this harsh weather appeared when Louisa left him. Ayan looked strangely at the white slush. It lay a moment, pristine against the miasma of life, then mixed with the street filth and disappeared. He rose and went looking for Akbar.

The city had turned grey under the onslaught of this new cold snap. Darkness settled early driving Ayan back to the shelter. He repeated the search for a few days.

"My money," the lodge owner cried every time he saw Ayan.

Ayan started ducking in later and leaving earlier, to avoid the man. The drum lost its magic. No one wanted to stand in the snow and listen to music. The whites bundled between heavy furs and long cloaks as they hurried by. Women hid their heads behind heavy veils, faceless phantoms that travelled the street. Men lifted the collars of their great-coats and lowered their hats. Cabbies and coachmen coughed roughly as they sat high above the horses, their breath turning to smoke like creatures of the night.

Ayan continued his search, until finally, he turned a corner, and literally bumped into his old friend.

"Where have you been, Akbar? I have been searching for you. I thought you may be hurt somewhere."

Akbar turned around and looked at Ayan. He looked dazed.

"I have been to a far, far place," Akbar replied. "I was talking with Emran," Akbar said dizzily, his eyes stared as if frozen in their sockets. "He rarely said much, but now he talks. Some days his voice never stops."

Ayan's heart cried.

"Emran asks where his mother is. He is looking for her. I tell him to travel where the water is warm, but he cannot understand."

"It is enough that he remained with you, brother." Akbar fell silent on hearing Ayan's kindly words.

"Peace," Ayan whispered. "Let yourself be at peace."

"I cannot," Akbar cried. "They will not let me."

Ayan looked down the empty alley.

"Every night they come and wake me," Akbar said.

"No one comes in our room,"

Ayan reached over and held his friend's hand. The skin burned under his touch. Ayan let go, helpless. "No one enters our room."

"They do. They all do. All the men I killed."

Ayan frowned. "You killed no one. If The Cruel One died, the fault was mine."

Akbar shook his head, "I killed him. I let an evil whisper in my ear. I ate my anger and made it possible to bear the pain. It trapped me."

"You speak foolishness," Ayan replied.

Akbar looked at Ayan like they met for the first time.

"Foolish? The foolishness that resulted in many men's death. I did not understand Farook's words until much later, until they came to me in the darkness, asking why I killed them."

"Peace," Ayan sighed. "Be at peace. They do not blame you for their death. Each man made his own choice."

"I convinced Farook and Avid to take part in the plan. Avid did not want to play his part. Farook and I pushed him until his courage failed. Now, Avid is dead."

Ayan moved away, and took a place on a corner. He tried desperately to conjure up enough heart and soul to coax music from the drum, and a few coins from the passing crowd. Akbar needed to eat. The drum thudded lifelessly under his hand.

People passed without noticing him. Ayan started singing a religious song. The words wrung the pain from his heart. The eyes may not weep, but his heart wept bitter tears. A few coins tinkled as they hit the cobblestone.

Ayan took the coins and entered a pub just over the road. The landlord eyed him suspiciously.

"Please, a bowl of warm, thick soup, and I will leave."

The man leaned on the counter and stared hard for a moment. "You will take it with you?"

"Yes," Ayan tried to smile. "It is for a sick friend."

The landlord chuckled. "That won't save you a few coppers, friend. Let me see your coin."

The man looked at the coins and shook his head. Still, he filled a broken mug to the rim with hot stew. He tossed in a thick slice of bread.

"Thank you," Ayan nodded.

"Come again," the landlord called, and then paused. "But not when there are patrons inside, do you hear?"

He returned to the corner. "Akbar? Where are you?" Ayan followed footprints through the sticky clumps of snow. "Akbar?" He walked between the buildings, and checked the small holes were a man might hide.

Ayan spied Akbar sitting in the back of an alleyway. The dusk settled early under low storm clouds. The storm broke in the distance, letting a brilliant shade of pink highlight the city's filth. Instinctively, Ayan slowed as he approached his friend. "Akbar, I have soup for you." He leaned close.

Akbar's body was warm, but hung limp when Ayan tried to rouse him. Ayan held his friend tight to his body, trying to warm him. He put a hand over Akbar's face. He felt no breath but the palm dampened.

"Akbar. Wake up. You must wake up." Ayan shook Akbar roughly.

Akbar's eyes fluttered once and shut. Ayan leaned close. "I

bear witness that there is no God but Allah." Ayan leaned closer and repeated the words. "Repeat them."

"I bear ..."

It took several moments for Akbar to force out the last words. The men's eyes met. Akbar's whole countenance changed. The angry bitter Akbar faded. Ayan saw the forgiveness of Allah wash over his friend. Akbar settled into a sleep full of peace, something he never once enjoyed while alive.

Ayan clutched his friend tight to his chest, rocking back and forth in the snow. He heard the sound of sobbing in the distance. The sobbing grew louder until he realised he cried openly.

"I bear witness that there is no God but Allah." He waited, begging Allah to take his soul. Life held no promise for him. The cold settled into his bones. Ayan's teeth stopped chattering. He sat numb.

"Kazi," he cried. He looked up. Kazi sat beside him, looking particularly pleased with himself. "Kazi?" Ayan tried to move but lost feeling in his limbs. Kazi did not move. He did not talk. He just looked sadly at Ayan. "Brother? How did you come here?"

Kazi sat in his pious pose that he used at the pool to inspire people into parting with their coins.

"I have missed you so much, brother. I tried to make the money for the doctor."

Kazi shook his head and smiled.

"How can you be here, Kazi?" Ayan struggled to clear his head. "Am I dead?" Akbar lay, a dead weight in his arms. Ayan saw the street but could feel nothing, not the cold, not Akbar's weight. Only Kazi moved and looked around as he did when a boy.

"Are we both dead? Did you die?" Ayan's heart broke. "I am sorry Kazi. I tried to save you. Please forgive me."

Kazi turned his head and smiled.

Ayan struggled to rise. If he were truly dead then he should be able to meet him again in the afterlife. Ayan cried. "Have I let you down? Will we never be together because I let you down? Please forgive me Kazi. Please forgive me."

Kazi spoke for the first time. Ayan smiled, believing his brother said the funeral prayer for him. They would be together at last. Free from hunger and cold.

"When an affliction befalls the believers, they say, "We belong to Allah, and to Him we are returning."

Ayan listened to the voices; they combined and confused his mind. He tried to separate them, desperate to hear Kazi's prayer.

"Those who reverenced their Lord will be led to Paradise in throngs," Kazi's voice faded. He looked over and closed Akbar's eyes.

"This one's alive," a coarse cockney accent broke through Ayan's stupor.

"No!" Ayan tried desperately to grab Kazi. "No. Don't leave me Kazi. Don't leave me."

Rough hands pulled Ayan away from Kazi. "This is a big un." The voice made it impossible to hear Kazi's prayer.

If only he could hear the funeral prayer, then he could remain with his friends. He screamed as the men's hands closed over his arms and dragged him across the street. Ayan's eyes cleared. He looked around. Akbar's body lay on the wagon beside him. Louisa spoke truth. Snow did bite like a vicious dog. It caused a pain that held tight, like hunger. Ayan woke as the men dragged him down the familiar halls of the hostel.

"Don't leave 'im 'ere to die."

"Not my affair." The cockney voice laughed. "Yours now."

Ayan lay, waiting for death. He woke from time to time. He cried for Kazi. Once a man in a red turban stood in the doorway looking at him, Ayan screamed in horror. Kazi must have died. Why else would he have seen him, and heard the funeral prayer? Akbar had died. Louisa had left. Ayan learned that there is one thing to be feared more than all others – being alone in the world.

CHAPTER 15

"What are you doing?" the constable shouted roughly.

Ayan looked up. His body remained in a kneeling position on a mat. He looked at the constable. Arm muscles tightened as he waited. He looked at the drum on the ground beside him. As the streets of London filled with immigrants, it became harder and harder to find a quiet place to pray. Winter had passed and spring had arrived. The city constables became more irritated and abusive with each passing month. He decided it best to leave the constable in ignorance of the prayers and focus on his drum playing. The English understood money far more than they understood spirituality. The police officer stepped forward.

"Drums." Fear gripped Ayan's chest. He understood the question, but did not understand enough English to explain.

This officer moved like a dragon. His club swung lightly against his leg. The eye muscles flinched. With predator grace, the constable moved forward.

"Drums?" the word slurred over a thick accent. His voice rose. "Did you light that fire?"

This question was so shocking as to nearly stop Ayan's heart. Some four blocks away, off in the distance, a residential establishment was pouring out blackish smoke. Ayan had been half-aware of the fire over the past several minutes, but his thoughts were devoted to his prayer. What form of unreason had provoked this officer to ask such a startling question?

"Do you hear, darkie? Did - you - light - that - fire?"

Ayan understood the threat behind the condescending tone. A cloud covered the sun. A spring chill cut through his clothing. Ayan looked around. Nothing appeared to be out of place. Whites passed, ignoring the drama unfolding around them. Two young men chatting close by caught sight of the constable. They looked suspiciously at Ayan and moved away a few feet. The constable kicked the basket. The basket jingled, but the few coins did not spill over.

The constable pointed toward the fire burning in the distance, with the tip of the thin black club.

"Darkie. I asked you a question. Did you light that fire?"

The words rang between the buildings, attracting attention. Women raised their hands to their breasts, startled. They moved closer to the men, or pulled young children into their skirts. The two men stepped away briskly. The circle around Ayan and the constable widened.

Ayan opened his mouth to deny any knowledge. His hand stung. Ayan looked down at his empty hands. The constable's club had struck him hard, just below the wrist.

The drum hit the ground and bounced. The constable's foot flicked out and kicked it hard. The fragile wood snapped and the jumble of tangled strings. The skin came to rest against a pile of mud-soaked garbage.

Ayan stood helpless. His hands were yanked behind his back. Cold steel shackles were snugly fastened around his wrist. He stood, mute, the mangled wood only a few inches beyond his reach. Thick hands yanked him to his feet. The shackles bit deep into the soft flesh of his wrists. It didn't matter. Ayan's hope shattered with the drum. There was no reason left to fight.

* * *

Ayan stared at the ceiling. The stench of unwashed bodies and foul breath mixed with the odour of stale urine on the floor. It took all his willpower to focus on the ceiling instead of the smell.

The dank cell was filled with dark bodies, but no faces. No one tried to make out the man to his left or right. The poor light from a single window filled the room for less than an hour a day. The darkness agitated the hardened men. Anger and frustration boiled below the surface and only the threat of a beating from the constables waiting beyond the door kept the room from erupting.

Ayan learned in the past months not to aggravate these men.

They cared about nothing and had less to live for. He turned slightly and tried to sleep. Images floated through his head as he escaped into the world he remembered. His mind drifted to the fields and house he left behind. The rice fields lay beneath a blanket of water. Spring rains washed the dark odours from the forests. The paths to the rice field smelled fresh and clean at this time of year. Kazi looked at him, no lump on his lip. He laughed. "Don't worry, brother."

Ayan walked up the path towards their little house, eager to embrace his brother.

"You will be fine, my little Ayan. Allah does carry you upon a gentle wind." Kazi smiled wide and held his arms out.

Kazi laughed and danced a few steps. Ayan's tension eased, replaced by a smile. How nice it felt to flex the muscles in his cheeks. How rare a smile. Ayan never understood the wealth he possessed. He appreciated the good brother who made smiling so easy.

"This one doesn't belong here." Kazi's tone altered, curious and cautious.

The distance between Kazi's face and voice became startling. Ayan looked hard. The voice did not belong to Kazi. "Is another spirit speaking through your body?" Kazi looked up and smiled

. "Goodbye, brother."

Ayan struggled to focus his gaze, unsure if he was still dreaming. The vile stench made him suspect that he was indeed, awake. The man before him wore a black suit and the letter "t" hung around his neck. The man's skin was white, yet his face gentle. "He doesn't belong here," the man repeated. "He's a musician."

Ayan looked up. The way the man said, "he's a musician," caught Ayan's attention. The tone held respect. He remembered. It all flooded back. He knew these men. The clothing was different. The manner and movements didn't change.

Louisa used the term "missionaries." They read from the same book of myths that the mission teachers of the orphanage did. The cobwebs of sleep left Ayan's mind. He looked into the man's eyes.

"Let's go, my son. We'll get you a job."

CHAPTER 16

Ayan fell. The little boy stood over him, laughing. Ayan looked at his hands. When did he grow old? He did not understand the term, a decade, but his employer stated that Ayan had been with them for a decade. Ayan never learned to track time like the white people did. He recognised the seasons, but the past and passage of time, seemed an obscure aspect of life.

Ayan hugged the boy's legs.

"My daddy," Allie laughed in a chirping English accent, "says for you to come see him."

A hot blaze swept Ayan's body. Old Mr Jennings was about to pass from this world. His sickness had progressed - gradually and then not so gradually - over the past three or four years.

Time passed so fast. At one time life promised to stretch eternally for Ayan, now, the friends he knew reached middle age and grew old. They faded and died. He looked at the child and smiled. The fate that drew him away from Kazi came full circle. His heart still ached for home, but he learned that home travelled in his heart. No one replaced the dear friends he lost. Each person brought something special to his life. Each person left a gift. Even those he once believed that he hated had played a vital part in the journey he called life.

"Lead on little one."

Ayan felt honoured to be summoned to speak to the man. He held genuine respect for his employer. The missionary saved his life twice, a decade before by freeing him from jail. He saved his life again by introducing him to Mr Jennings. He gave Ayan a place to work, but acknowledged Ayan's intelligence and never treated him like a servant.

Lionel Jennings sold soap and shampoo, some of the finest in all of Europe. Ayan secretly maintained that he was the perfect employee for such a man. Ayan valued cleanliness and grooming above all. He also offered assistance and advice on products used to clean difficult odours and stains. Most of Ayan's knowledge came from living in the belly of The Bengal, in the lodge, on the street and in jail. Ayan amazed himself how a smart man like Mr Jennings never knew of herbs and chemicals that were common aboard ships and in London's lowest hovels.

"Do not run too far ahead," he called to the eager child. The boy waved over his shoulder and bolted around a hedge.

Ayan hoped Mr Jennings illness did not affect his mood. He could be condescending at times - especially when asking Ayan to hurry with his morning meal - but, the man was blessed with a warm heart.

A lump formed in his throat. He dreaded his employer's inevitable departure. One day, the man walked through the door wearing a red cap. A flood of memories and emotions flooded Ayan, much as he felt now. They weakened his knees and caused a throbbing pain in his head. Ayan knew his father was not alive and did not call him to the sea. But, the image of his employer wearing the red hat touched something deep inside that never faded in the years they were together.

Ayan could clearly remember the first time he met Mr Jennings.

The missionary knocked on the door and smiled over his shoulder. Ayan stood back, wary. He understood about employment, but had never worked inside a white person's home. House servants wore uniforms and behaved modestly. They went about their master's business. The constables ignored them and the boys in the street did not harass them. Ladies did not withdraw in horror and place their hands on their children.

The Jennings' servant, an Eastern Indian Ayah named Ishra, opened the door. Her thick accent colouring the English words.

"What do we have here?" Mr Jennings said startled to see two men waiting to ascend the grand front porch.

Mr Jennings stood tall, almost eye to eye with Ayan.

Ayan's first impression was that the man glowed from within. He had a kindly face that appeared to want to break into a smile, and the warmest, friendliest eyes Ayan had ever seen on a white man.

Mr Jennings held out his hand. Ayan withdrew, worried that he was being deceived into breaching protocol. A slip could land a Bengali back in jail. He looked at the white skin, wondering if it felt different from his. Would the white leak into his hand?

"Do not be rude, man," the missionary admonished.

Ayan nodded and bowed. He stepped forward and took Mr Jennings' hand. The vigorous shake brought a roar of laughter from Mr Jennings. The grip tightened and the gentleman's other hand folded over Ayan's hand for a moment before they broke away.

Mr Jennings touched Ayan's arms. "My Lord! What are you hiding in there, blocks of concrete?"

Ayan did not comprehend what the man was saying. He knew what "hiding" and "concrete" meant but his arms were meat and flesh. He stood still, accustomed to letting whites examine him. He did not twist and pry Ayan's muscles like the supervisors on The Bengal had. In prison they poked and prodded, selecting men to work within the jail.

"Welcome." Mr Jennings slapped Ayan's shoulder hard and turned to the missionary. They lead the way into the home, chatting like old friends, while Ayan followed at a respectable distance.

A grand staircase wound up the wall. Huge doors, made of etched glass and polished wood shone beneath the overhead lights. Dark wood lined the wide halls, framing beautifully detailed furniture. Ayan did not finish taking in all the wonders before the Ayah hustled him into a room. She remained in the hall and closed the doors.

There were as many children as there were pieces of furniture. Lace-ruffled girls in tight curls played with paper dolls, while boys wearing copper-toed shoes clamoured for the men's attention. Ayan thought that surely not all the children could belong to Mr Jennings. Two house servants sat sedately in a corner, as quiet and still as statues. Occasionally they would gesture towards a child, a stern look of disapproval enough to tame any over-boisterous behaviour. Ayan recognised them as nannies by their uniforms. The house had enough energy and volume to compete with a robust schoolyard.

He felt like he had entered another dimension. He cast his mind back to the girl dancing beyond the latticed stone wall at the brothel. Her sad eyes staring vacantly as the men watched and gorged on sweet fruits. Often he had caught a glimpse inside windows. Usually, servants bustled around rooms as ladies busied themselves with needlework. Now, this room woke something deep within him. A glass mirror on the wall continually drew his attention. The gilt frame glittered.

Ayan looked at his reflection for the first time. Deep, thoughtful eyes stared back. His impressive stature filled the mirror. He did not see the cowering, submissive form he expected. Akbar mastered the stance the English expected of a Bengali. Even Kazi knew when to grovel. Nothing about Ayan's image reflected back a subservient attitude or broken spirit.

Mr Jennings placed a hand on his shoulder and led him room to room. He pointed out certain pieces of furniture and said words like "baroque" and "marble" that Ayan didn't understand. Ayan tried to pay attention, but his eyes kept seeing things that distracted him. Ayan stopped dead in the entrance of one room. Stars hung above a long table polished as shiny as the mirror in the first room. Mr Jennings laughed heartily and explained that the stars were glass, polished crystal glass. A long cloth ran down the middle of the table, white as newly fallen snow, and smooth as silk.

A tall statue of a young female, holding a jug on her shoulder, stood at the end of the room. Her body partially unclothed, the statue stood a mute guard. Mr Jennings spoke proudly of a trip to Rome. He touched the statue lovingly, explaining the efforts expended to acquiring such a treasure.

The servants' stairs were barely wider than a woman's body. Ayan turned sideways as he made his way up the dark stairwell. The upper rooms were for sleeping only. Each one had a coal fireplace in it with a polished brass grate to protect the rugs. Thick drapes covered the window wells, protecting the room from the winter's wind, while letting in the summer's warmth and light.

Oil lamps sat on polished tables, their chimneys shining brightly above bowls of golden oil. Red felt and salt floated in the oil, preventing them from exploding. Ayan knew this from his days on the ship. A young, upstairs maid blushed as they barged in on her. She hid the duster behind her back and bowed. Mr Jennings greeted her jovially and reached for a book. Ayan opened the book and looked at the printed words. He turned a couple pages. One page had a picture. Mr Jennings explained how they made a lithograph. Amazed, Ayan touched the picture. He did not understand the words used to describe the lithograph, but he understood the concept of printing. Women in his village often carved woods and vegetables and then used them for printing designs on their silks. Some of them rivalled the ornate decorations on the gilded page.

Mr Jennings led the way back to the main floor using the main staircase. It was wide enough to accommodate the passage of two or three elephants and although the one between the second and third floors was not quite as large, it was still sizeable enough for a tall man to sleep on. He wondered what crowds entered the house to demand such a wide staircase, but did not ask. He wished to be off the polished stairs and back on the rugs.

With each new step, he sank deeper into luscious reverie. Would this be - could this be - his actual new home?

The tour led into the back kitchen where a plump woman was

introduced as the cook. She put her hands on hips and bragged about her pots. She pointed to a cupboard and told Ayan never to open it. Ayan looked at Mr Jennings. The old man winked and leaned back. The cook opened a paper cone. Ayan looked hard at the dark cone. The cook said that if anyone stole any of the sugar there would be a punishment for the offender. Mr Jennings finally laughed at her and ushered Ayan out of the kitchen.

"Maddy owns the kitchen. It is her kingdom. She protects the sugar as if it were gold," Mr Jennings laughed.

"I will not touch sugar," Ayan promised. "I will not touch sugar." Ayan was not sure why anyone would want to touch the dark substance, but the snap in Maddy's black eyes warned him that she made no idle threats.

"What do you do for money?" Mr Jennings asked.

"I play drum."

"A musician. Very nice. I am afraid I have no use for a musician."

"I worked on steamship, The Bengal." Ayan's voice caught on the name of the ship that nearly destroyed his life. Mr Jennings looked strangely at him but did not comment.

"I owned a shop. I grew rice. We sold rice." A voice deep in his mind warned him to stop with the mention of rice. Mr Jennings appeared to be the type of man who would frown on the production of betel nut.

"A merchant," Mr Jennings' voice rang with admiration. "I believe we will get along well, my man."

Ayan never realised that he had been a merchant. He spent so much time wishing to be a respected member of the village that he failed to see what he had.

"I grew good rice. My brother and I."

"A brother?" Mr Jennings smiled. "I have a brother. Haven't seen him in long time, but we very close."

Ayan held his hands high, palms together. "My brother, Kazi and I, this close . . . until I leave. My brother is ill. He has cancer.

I write to him but he does not reply. I came here to work, save money and send it to Kazi. He needs money to see a doctor."

"Pity," Mr Jennings sighed. "It is a pity what desperation forces a man to do. I'm sorry to hear that."

They were climbing another set of servants' stairs at the very rear of the house. The air chilled as they climbed. The walls were bare of windows. Wall scones held unlit candles.

The winding hall ended in a door. Mr Jennings opened the door and stood back against the wall, giving Ayan room in the narrow space to enter. A gentle light flowed from within. The discoloured, plaster walls were bereft of the shining gorgeous oak that lined the wider halls in the family areas of the home. With a wave of his hand, he motioned toward the door.

"And this, my friend, is your room."

Ayan wasn't sure which thrilled him more, the word "friend" or "room." For a moment, he was torn between approaching Mr Jennings for another handshake and approaching the doorway to see what waited behind it. He paused. The first choice would prove awkward. He opted for the second.

A simple, solid oak bedstead stood against the wall. The rope had released over the years, leaving a sag in the middle of the bed, but the thick straw mattress looked extremely comfortable. His fingers touched the oak. He briefly feared that he would ruin it.

"I do not want to be responsible for an expensive bed." Ayan frowned. The words sounded rude.

Mr Jennings burst into laughter. "Do not worry. This is an old bed. I am sure that you cannot do it any harm."

Ayan looked down. The bedroom touched his heart. Years of pent-up emotion surged to the surface. A thick, hot, red line of embarrassment moved up his neck and coloured his ears. He could not stop tears from flowing down his cheeks.

Mr Jennings cleared his throat. "I believe we will get along just fine, my man." He stepped to Ayan's side, comforting him and frightening him in equal measure. He withdrew and squared his shoulders. "Well, we must present ourselves with respectable decorum when we descend."

"Thank you," Ayan said.

"Gone are your days of poverty."

Ayan nodded. Gone were the days of glorified closets and overlarge roommates. Ayan looked back into the room. His room. The space was sparsely yet tastefully decorated. On the floor was a colourful and rounded rug. The edge had frayed and been sewn several times, but the colours still held some of their brilliance. Translucent curtains of fine cotton covered the windows. The room's rear wall contained a towering bookshelf, carved from strong reddish wood, upon which stood enough tomes for Ayan to learn the English language three times over!

"Books."

"Yes," Mr Jennings nodded. "You remember?"

"Can I . . . can I touch them?" Ayan asked.

"Touch them? Why would you want to touch them, my man?"

"There are stories in them."

"Yes, and information. History." Mr Jennings moved into the room, his enthusiasm ignited. "Here, this one tells of life in England one thousand years ago. Think of it. The wisdom of the ages locked on a white page. We live in amazing times."

Ayan picked up a book. He recognised a symbol on the spine. He opened it. Deep blue and gold pictures danced before his eyes.

"Bengali?" Ayan asked.

"Bengali, yes. You can read?"

"No." Ayan shook his head. "Home." He pointed to a picture of an elephant carrying an Eastern Indian Rajah. Ayan turned the pages, some symbols he recognised. "Allah." He pointed to the page. He flipped a couple more. The mountains loomed in the distance. His hands carefully caressed the images. Dark-eyed women in saris walked down a path. His eyes welled. "Home," he whispered.

Mr Jennings put his hand on Ayan's shoulder. "You must

learn to read."

Ayan looked up. He stared wide eyed at his employer. "Read?"

"Yes. I will make sure you learn how to read. When it will not interfere with your duties, of course."

Ayan wanted to do several things at once. He wanted to stretch on the bed, start learning to read the books, embrace Mr Jennings - and clean his entire mansion that very instant. He placed the book carefully back on the bookshelf.

With great concentration, he addressed his employer, "You would . . . want me to . . . clean?"

Mr Jennings stared at Ayan for a long moment. Ayan dropped his head, self-conscious. Was his English too poor? Were his tears visible? He did not mean to make his employer ill at ease. Thoughts zipped through Ayan's mind, seeking to unravel the mysteries upon the old man's face.

"No...you do not start your duties today. Rest. I'm sure it was exhausting, riding over here in that carriage. Puts me straight to sleep almost every time. Get some sleep. We'll give you your assignments tomorrow or the next day."

"Sleep?" asked Ayan, looked out the window. The light shone bright and warm outside, high above the city.

Mr Jennings roared with laughter. "Yes, Ayan, sleep. Hopefully you haven't forgotten what that is."

"Yes, sir. No, sir."

A gentle knock disturbed them.

"A lunch for your manservant, sir."

Ayan stepped back. A young girl put a tray on the table. "Cook thought he would be tired after the journey from the city."

"Biscuits and stew. A fine first meal." Mr Jennings lifted a white cloth. "Fresh buns and fruit spread. It seems that you've impressed the cook."

Ayan surveyed the tea tray. The subtle aroma of dark tea filled the room piquing his hunger. The stew held thick chunks of white meat and multi-coloured vegetables. Ayan's heart sank.

Pork.

"Chicken stew, left over from yesterday's pot pie. It was a delight."

Ayan's relief shuddered through his entire body. He did not want to appear rude and turn down his first meal. "Will I serve you first, sir?"

"I have my tea downstairs, but thank you," replied Mr Jennings.

"Do I wait for the others?" Ayan asked.

"Others?" Mr Jennings' eyebrows shot up.

"To share the meal."

"This is all for you, my man? It is good tea, granted. Do not despair. We will feed you a larger meal for supper."

Ayan's eyes flew open. More? More food than this?

Mr Jennings shook his head a bit and then laughed his way down the winding corridor. Ayan sat down. He slowly sipped the stew letting the good taste cross his tongue as long as possible. A thick layer of butter had already melted into the biscuits. He held the fruit pot in his hand and dipped the biscuits in the sweet mixture of preserved fruits. He sipped the tea while sitting on the bed. Ayan stretched the meal as long as he could before he lay down. Gentlemen slept the afternoon away. Merchants slept the afternoon away. Ayan never slept the day away in his life.

CHAPTER 17

Ayan excused himself to Alfred's delight. He stood outside Mr Jennings' door until he had gained his composure. He stood tall, straightening his jacket before entering the room.

"Come closer, Albert," Mr Jennings said, waving a bony hand in his direction.

Ayan responded to his English name without reaction. This was the first time the old man had referred to him as Albert when they were in private.

Alfred followed Ayan's tracks across the room to the enormous bed. Ayan long enjoyed the fact that his boss had given him an English name that so closely mirrored that of his favourite son. But, by no verbal agreement, the name was only used in the presence of company. Ayan stepped self-consciously across the room. It was rare for Ayan to be in Mr Jennings' bed chambers when he wasn't cleaning.

"You fill my heart with emotion," Ayan said, not attempting to conceal his sadness.

"And you fill mine with gratitude," said the old man.

Little Alfred looked from one man to the other, and broke into tears. He fled soundless from the bed chamber.

"There is," said Mr Jennings, "more bad news than that of my death. My wife and children will live with my sister. You and Ishra will not follow. There is no place for you in their estates. I could not secure employment for either of you."

Ayan swallowed. He assumed that his business skills had improved enough so that his employer would let him manage the business. He knew that such was not the case, in most cases, but he studied English, learned to manage a business. He watched. He learned.

Mr Jennings coughed painfully. "I will leave money for the period after you leave. It will be enough for you to live on for a few months. Maybe you can invest it. I often thought that it was a pity you were not born white. I am sure the making of a great business manager is in you. If only . . . I am sorry. I did not plan it this way. . ."

Ayan didn't know what to say. He wanted to protest that he could manage a business, but he understood. No white man would accept a darkie as a boss. Ayan took his employer's hand in his.

"I also have a letter of reference. I've instructed my solicitor to assist you in any way. If you need help obtaining another position, you are to approach him immediately." Mr Jennings lay back in the deeply cleft pillow. He held out a hand. "Over there, on the table. The letter is there. Fetch it. I want to know that it is safe on your person before I . . ."

"Sir." Ayan crossed the room blindly. Two white letters lay on the table, one addressed to Albert.

"I wish I had the money to keep the house open. I am sorry. Abigail will come out soon. She must be presented properly. I cannot risk her making a bad match. She must marry well to protect the entire family."

"Yes, sir."

"Everything hinges on her marriage. The boys will attend school in York. There is enough money to carry them through Oxford, but beyond that, they must make their own way in the world. It all hangs on Abigail's ability to make a good match. Poor Abigail, such a burden for one so young."

"Sir, I could watch them . . ."

Mr Jennings eyes flickered. "They are going to the country. I am sorry. The tolerance for foreign servants is very negligible. I fear that you would hinder, not help, Abigail's opportunities."

Ayan bit his tongue until blood filled his mouth with a coppery acidic taste.

"My child," emotion strangled Mr Jennings.

Ayan stood by his bed, the way he stood behind the desk all

those years, patiently waiting his master's leisure. The room stilled. Tears flowed down Mr Jennings' chalky cheeks.

"I wish you a good life, Albert."

"You have," said Ayan, leaning close to his employer's ear, "made it so fine, so very good, sir."

The two men waited.

Feminine wails broke the absolute silence, ruining the ambiance. Both men wished to pass the afternoon like they had passed so many others. A clergy broke their solitude briefly. The undertaker introduced himself quickly before taking up his post in the hall. Ayan stood to be introduced to Mr Jennings' solicitor. He watched the man's eyes as Mr Jennings instructed the solicitor to help Ayan find employment. The solicitor addressed Mr Jennings politely, promising to carry out his last wishes. But Ayan knew that no aid would come from that venue. The solicitor ignored him as he left the room.

Ayan closed the thick drapes against the night air and returned to his post. They waited, the older man taking his very last breaths, the younger feeling older than he had when he woke that morning.

CHAPTER 18

Ayan stopped his work and watched the festival. Queen Victoria's Golden Jubilee, hosted by England's Royal Family, filled the streets of London. Never before had he seen so many people gathered in one place for the sole purpose of celebrating. The brilliant colours of the decorations were so magnificent as to stay with him while he slept.

Very few dark-skinned people ventured into the streets during the festival. They had little reason to celebrate. Ayan, had grown to trust many people of light skin, and moreover, his work as a street cleaner, offered the opportunity to walk among the festival goers, sweeping up their litter, with relative obscurity.

"Hey darkie!" yelled a voice from nowhere.

Ayan turned to see who taunted him. A heavy blow snapped his neck back, blinding him. Sharp pains spread from his already swelling eye. A wobbly moment passed before Ayan realised he'd been hit in the face with a rock.

"Pick up the trash, darkie!" the Englishman yelled.

Ayan looked around the crowd. Several faces bore sympathetic glances, but that would change if he tried to fight back. He eyed the offender through blood-soaked lids and swallowed his anger. With the mob already excited from the festival, any retaliation on his part would only end badly for him.

He wiped the blood and resumed work. He picked up his broom and continued sweeping. The crowd faded into the street. Within two steps no evidence remained of the confrontation. Ayan leaned on the broom for support and pushed hard.

A bolt of black lightning hit the back of Ayan's skull. He staggered and fell to his knees. With bleary eyes, Ayan scanned the ground. A brick! He grit his teeth. He could snap his broom in two and stab this devil.

"Enough! Shame!" A cultured feminine voice rose above the

crowd. "Be gone before I fetch a constable!"

Ayan searched the crowd for his champion.

Phoebe Hillary was Mr Jennings' niece, daughter of the woman with whom the Jennings children now lived. Her cool eyes and commanding stance alerted all to the presence of a Lady. Instantly, several gentlemen came to her aid, eyeing Ayan and the whites with critical concern.

"Can I be of assistance?" A middle-aged man said.

"Viscount." Phoebe lowered her lashes and blushed. "I apologise. I meant no disrespect."

The Viscount offered her a gloved hand. "None taken. I was merely passing and noticed your servant being molested."

Ayan understood the title Viscount meant a man of utmost importance. He lowered his head, and bowed, willing to accept humiliation over causing Phoebe any shame because of his actions.

"Would you like me to address this situation for you?"

Without needing a reply, a constable materialised from nowhere and dispersed the crowd. Phoebe blushed and curtsied prettily. The Viscount bowed low, took her gloved hand and brushed his lips across the fingers. "A pleasure, my dear."

The nobleman tapped his hat and strolled off, amused by the encounter. The constable followed. The moment the nobleman disappeared into the crowd, Phoebe spun, rage and disgust bending her brows. She stepped in front of Ayan and addressed his tormentor: "How dare you ragamuffins harass a hard-working man. Be off with you!"

Ayan almost laughed at the transformation in Phoebe. A perfect Lady in the presence of the Viscount and a stalwart champion of her own when standing alone. The man put his hands in the air, as if being arrested and vanished into the crowd.

"Are you okay, Albert?" Phoebe said to Ayan.

Ayan bowed with respect. "Yes, Lady Phoebe." Ayan was more than okay. Phoebe's appearance was almost worth the brutality he endured at the hands of the fool. "I think so," he replied, touching the throbbing back of his skull. "Some humans have concrete in their veins."

"That doesn't mean they have to throw it," said Phoebe.

Ayan smiled at her quick wit, so like Mrs Jennings.

"Have you been eating well? You're thinner than you were last I saw you."

"Some people," he told Phoebe, "care more for spending money on festivals than giving it to beggars."

"Have you been begging?" Phoebe asked aghast. Her eyes narrowed, their depths showing her deep concerned.

"At times," he answered. "I have held various jobs, cleaning, sweeping and working on the docks. Somehow, each day manages to give way to the next."

"You try to speak in a happy tone," said Phoebe, "but I hear the tones of sadness."

Ayan never liked to think of himself as sad, but he wondered if Phoebe was onto something. "How do you mean?"

"Sad people think in terms of days," she answered. "Happy people think in terms of years."

"Here." She fished out a large quantity of coins.

Ayan closed her hand. "No, I cannot take it."

"Pooh." She glared at him. "Of course you can. It isn't much, the cost of a hat. I do not need another hat as much as you need a meal." Her glove slipped over his fingers and gently pried them open. She turned his hand over, palm up and deposited the coins in the palm. "We will talk no more of this."

"Thank you."

"Have you sought help from the estate's solicitor?"

"Once. I went to the office, but they made me sit in the foyer until the office closed. I returned the next day but was told not to return."

"We shall see about that." Phoebe gave her head a pert tilt. "You take care of yourself. And, eat more."

Ayan agreed and watched her pass into the crowd.

* * *

Ayan gave serious consideration to the truth of Phoebe's words, for though he was happy, he always thought in terms of today, neither days nor years. All that existed was the moment, shining in a way that seemed nothing short of holy.

He stood on the corner waiting for Phoebe.

Phoebe appeared with the bluster of a March wind. Ayan followed at a respectable three paces behind as they strolled the streets. Phoebe often chastised him for his foolish class rules, expressing her annoyance at turning her head around to engage in pleasant conversation. In reality, she rarely turned. Instead, she merrily chattered about topics learned in books. The most recent museum exhibit, the foolishness of French fashion, or a horrific courtship between her friends, that was doomed to disaster before the hapless couple weaned their first child.

Frequent letters arrived from home, admonishing Phoebe for refusing an invitation, or slighting a Lord. However, Ayan's presence was not only tolerated, but encouraged. The presence of a guardian, or servant, put Phoebe's bohemian spirit in a more respectable light and reflected on her "studious" parents who had the foresight to protect the young woman's reputation for the time she would come to her senses and enter into an appropriate marriage arrangement.

This afforded Ayan the freedom to enter her apartment, although he never took advantage of the situation, fearing her father's retribution if a gossip chose to put a slanderous twist to their relationship. If that happened, they would both lose their freedom, Ayan to prison, Phoebe to the confines of her father's estate and perhaps, the prospect of marriage that she heartily detested.

"Why should I marry or work for a wage? If I did either of those things, all the art lessons you paid for would be in vain!"

Ayan found camaraderie with the young woman. She too was

shunned, not because of her skin, but because of her refusal to marry. Ayan loved to chase away young noblemen who thought Phoebe possessed the charms and discrete manners to make a highly acceptable mistress. His black eyes and massive shoulders sent the boldest of Phoebe's consorts scurrying.

Ayan grabbed one man and shook him vigorously. A constable ran to the man's aid, but at Phoebe's well-versed, and mock, faint, the constable backed away and addressed the young man. Ayan stood stunned. He expected to be dragged to prison. Instead, he had new respect as the servant of a young Lady.

"I do not think I will return home for the Christmas season."

"That may be folly," Ayan boldly suggested.

"It most assuredly is a folly, but no more than spending the month of December being paraded past provincial boys and old merchants as if I were a prize mare. You are a man. Do not mock me. You will never know the burdens a woman must bear. To think, at my age, I should be endowed with at least four children and do nothing more with my life than await my husband's pleasure."

Ayan laughed at the thought of Phoebe awaiting anyone's pleasure. "Your brother claims you were spoiled," Ayan taunted her.

"You scoundrel." Phoebe levelled her best glare at him. "Will you never stop tormenting me?"

Ayan smiled in response. He loved igniting her temper. Her cheeks flushed prettily and her tongue's edge sharpened.

Phoebe's mood dampened. "My father has pressed the issue more determinedly lately. I believe he sees my future in widow Jennings' situation. I am sure she is a more taxing burden on my parent's social life than on their financial situation. But with young Al receiving such high accolades from his school masters, and the youngest coming out next year, I am sure they feel the pressure."

Ayan didn't know what to think, so as his custom, he held his tongue. But, Phoebe's father suffered very little. The demands they placed on Mrs Jennings to serve the role of widower were exploited to the fullest. He did not know what to think. The poorhouse was a dreadful place, full of ladies who fell on hard times. It was London's shame, and its greatest open secret. Mrs Jennings' fate, without the charity of Phoebe's father, and a proper title of her own, would be to slave away the rest of her life as a seamstress in the poor house.

Phoebe often admonished her peers in polite society about the cruel fate of women who had neither social status nor wealth to offer future prospects. Few listened. Most chuckled indulgently, chiding the weakness of her woman's mind for believing such foolishness. Ayan never chided her. He had been to the poor house. He saw how the women lived.

"You should consider your father's wishes," Ayan whispered. He did not want to hurt Phoebe, but he could not endure the thought of her forgotten, sewing sheets, as the years stole her youth.

"My father is not concerned with my wishes. Do you believe he suffers?" Phoebe brushed a hair from her face. "He could live a life of leisure until he died and still pass on a king's ransom to his heirs."

"He is caring for the Jennings." Ayan felt uncomfortable. "He did not need to do that."

"True."

"He does have the legal right to force you to marry."

Phoebe sighed. "Ayan, your wisdom is sharp as a sword, and precisely what I need at the moment."

Ayan set up her stool and easel. Phoebe sat and focused on the canvas.

"I know what I'll do! I'll marry you. Then Mommy and Daddy will be proud!"

Ayan choked on his shock. "Lady Phoebe. It is not Lady-like conduct." Louisa called such behaviour flirting. Though he would be hard-pressed to explain the word's meaning if somebody asked him.

"Your father would be angry."

"Which is precisely why I'd do it!"

He watched her paint the blue-green river, beyond the rose hedge. He pointed at the canvas.

"You do have talent."

Phoebe smiled. "Thank you, sir."

Ayan stood behind Phoebe, hands folded behind him, eyes alert.

"One day I'll look like that, all frail and wrinkled."

Ayan followed the direction she looked in. An old woman ambled across the lawns, tossing bread crumbs to the swans.

He knew Phoebe was cuing him to say something. Startled, he opened his mouth and let the words come out: "No you will not--oh, yes, you will. I'm sure of it!"

Phoebe's eyes flared. Ayan grimaced. Her mouth dropped with mock astonishment. She flattened her drawing hand on the table, letting her pencil roll away.

"Albert Miah," she gasped, pronouncing Ayan's English first name and proper last name, "do you tease me, again?"

Ayan played a dangerous game. He attempted to reveal his affection for this woman, in a harmless way. Apparently, this flirting business required a level of finesse that he did not possess. He shook his head sharply. What was he doing?

"I did not mean any harm. I am a foolish old man."

Phoebe's eyes laughed at him. "You are a complex man." She returned to her painting.

A line of sweat lined his lip. Fear's grip refused to let go. One word from Phoebe that he had made an advance, no matter how innocent. Ayan refused to think of the consequences, except to remind himself that the penalty for a darkie who even touched a white woman was death.

* * *

Ayan followed Phoebe on trips that often took them far beyond their own section of the city. Families and couples filled the avenue, enjoying a Sunday stroll. Phoebe met several friends and acquaintances, stopping to share gossip, learn who attended what parties, and who committed which indiscretions.

Ayan's attention was drawn to a shop window across the cobblestone. The merchant displayed an assortment of gleaming horns and polished drums. Ayan took a few steps without realising he left his post.

"Phoebe," a foolish, heavily endowed girl cried. "Your servant is leaving his post."

Phoebe looked casually over her shoulder. "I fear that I forgot the time. Please, accept my excuses and tell your mother that I will call upon her next day I am paying visits."

"Well!" the girl huffed and flit away in a flurry of silk and lace.

Phoebe chuckled and waved Ayan forward.

"I used to play an instrument," he said, remembering his brief stint as a musician.

"In your village?" Phoebe asked.

Ayan tapped the glass and replied, "Not too far away from this square. But a long time ago, still."

"Would you like me to buy something for you?" Phoebe offered, her warm tone touching something inside of Ayan's heart.

Ayan looked into her eyes. "Your father awards me a small allowance to work for you. I ... I do not understand."

"A gift. There is no reason why you cannot accept a gift. The season is almost upon us. My father gives each of his servants a gift on Christmas morning. There is no shame in accepting one from me."

"I do not want to diminish your allowance," said Ayan.

"I buy gifts for all my friends. I have enough money to buy gifts for people I care for."

"You care for me?" asked Ayan.

With a smile, Phoebe nodded.

"Then the only gift I want from you," he said, "is for you to continue caring."

In the space between them, their dangling hands tapped gently against each other. Ayan's spirit filled with warmth.

CHAPTER 19

Mr Bradford Hillary was beside himself. He stormed across the drawing room, waving a newspaper in Phoebe's face.

"It's all over the press!" he screamed, his volume shaking the walls. "This arrangement is an insult to your culture. I will be assaulted when I enter my gentleman's club. Your mother is stricken."

Yvette Hillary, Phoebe's mother, stood beside the globe in the corner. She looked healthy and robust. An unopened bottle of smelling salts and a perfumed lace cloth offered the only evidence that she was stricken.

She never looked at Ayan, instead, looking at her daughter as she spoke. "You can address yourself by a Christian name, Albert, but a word will never make you clean."

"The French. That is who to blame." He spun on his daughter. "It is those bohemians you associate with. Filling your head with nonsense. I should have married you off years ago."

"Father-"

"Do not use that word with me." His rage silenced Phoebe.

Phoebe sat on the sofa. Her hands hung limp in her lap.

"I've two summonses from The Earl of Suffolk, and The Duke" He spun. "And you! Thirty years ago, I would have never even been in the same room as an Indian, let alone suffered to tolerate one inside the walls of my own home. I can have your head for this."

"Father, things are changing."

"Changing? Changing! You expect me to believe that this ... this ... travesty. A heathen tempting my daughter? And you! How am I to find a man to take you off my hands now?" He threw his hands up. "The only thing that could be worse would be if you had become pregnant!"

"Bradford." Mrs Hillary blanched visibly. Her husband's anger gave her a real reason to faint. "I..."

"Don't you talk to me!" His eyes bulged. He shook his finger at Mrs Hillary violently for several moments before finding his voice. "You indulged her as a child. Art lessons. Schooling. How blind I've been. I should never have listened to you. Schooling for a girl. Look what has become of her. My soft treatment of you. I stayed my temper. I indulged you. And look what it has reduced me too. I have lost several business associates. I will be forced to sit in The House of Lords and endure the humiliation of knowing that my daughter not only committed a public indiscretion but with a ... with ... with a ..."

Tears welled in Mrs Hillary's eyes.

"Sir. Times are changing," the family barrister interrupted. "In a few weeks this scandal will be forgotten. This is not the abomination it would have been a decade ago. It is still possible for your daughter to live a respectable life. I may be able to find her a position as a governess. It is folly to fill a woman's head with knowledge. They are too frail to handle the pressure, but it may prove valuable…"

"Shut up!" Mr Hillary roared. "You imbecile. I am not worried about my daughter's ability to earn a living. She can live in the cottage in York for the rest of her life for all I care. How are we to save the company?"

"In the Americas," the barrister tried again.

"In the Americas, he," Mr Hillary pointed at Ayan, "would already be dead."

"The wheels of progress turn, even in the Americas," Phoebe murmured.

"The wheels of progress turn? Not for my daughter. Not in my house." His fist slammed into the desk. "They do not turn so much that you share your life with an alien."

"Sir," said Ayan.

"Alien!" he screamed.

One of the guards drove a fist into Ayan's stomach. He

buckled, but remained on his feet.

"How dare you address me?" He fell backward into a chair, exhausted by his rant. "How dare you address me? A servant does not speak unless spoken to."

Ayan's passion drove back all reason, overpowering his common sense.

"I will speak to you not as servant, or subordinate," he yelled back. "I speak to you as a man! Your daughter and I love each other…"

"Silence this man's dirt-ridden tongue!" the old man shouted.

Blows reigned until Ayan's legs weakened. Phoebe screamed. A heavy silence filled the room when the beating stopped. Ayan coughed, gasping for breath. He pulled himself up again and faced Mr Bradford. "We shall love each other. Yes?"

Phoebe lifted her eyes, confused. Her eyes were far away. Ayan rephrased his question, "Am I correct, Phoebe?"

Phoebe's senses returned suddenly. She looked at him with two moist eyes. "You never need to ask," she said.

Mrs Hillary rested a palm on the globe and spun it around gently. Mr Hillary's eyes bore holes in Ayan.

Mrs Hillary walked to her husband's side. "I once had three daughters," she whispered. "Now I have two."

"It is not enough," Mr Hillary growled.

"Isn't it? Where will they go? They cannot live in society without them both facing prison. They cannot move to the colonies without him facing death. Africa? I do not think the Boers will give them a warm welcome. Will he return to Bengal with his bride? All the Indies and beyond are a part of the Empire. The ways of England are the ways of the world. They will live to rue that."

Her chin lifted. "Let them live with their curse. Let them suffer their shame."

Despite his immense distaste for this woman, Ayan thought of his own parents, how they might react if they knew. A fluttering of guilt halted his heartbeat. Phoebe's hand slipped inside his. Love swept all else from his heart.

Phoebe held her head high and smiled at Ayan.

"I am not sure," the barrister uttered.

"Shut your useless mouth." Mr Hillary shot the insult at the barrister.

The pair walked out of the drawing room with their fingers intertwined. No one watched them leave the room.

The next few days blurred. He did not remember the trip back to Phoebe's apartment. A simple letter met them demanding they vacate the rooms immediately. They only attempted a stroll once. Ayan ushered Phoebe back to their apartment, away from the rude gestures and angry comments, away from the curious stares. Phoebe's friends turned their heads discreetly and crossed the cobblestone at their approach.

Their attitude stunned Ayan. "Fools."

"No," Phoebe's broken spirit laced the words. "They are only doing what they have been taught from childhood."

"They treat you like you are…dark-skinned."

Phoebe sighed. "I am worse. I fled their ranks. I deserted their society and that is an unforgivable sin."

Ayan tore another notice of eviction from the door and opened it. Locked in their room he soon despaired of ever finding a solution. Phoebe's crying persisted for days. Ayan ran out of comforting words. He empathised with her loss of family, but failed to understand why she now grieved over the very institution she railed against for so many months. He started to take long walks in the night. It comforted him like it had in the winter when Akbar died. He tried to find a clergyman who would marry them.

The first clergyman drove him from the premises and closed the door. The second spat in his face.

On the fourth day, Ayan decided to address Allah on the matter. Though he preferred to use prayer as a means of reverence, this time he used it as a means of request. He hoped Allah would be patient and not deem him greedy. He crossed through a sunny park, wishing he had the peace of mind to enjoy its tranquil beauty. He strolled and inhaled the woodsy air and began half-thinking and half-whispering his plea: "Allah, I beg your patience and I ask for your intervention in this world. Should you not grant me such intervention; I ask that you grant me strength in its place. I am not wise to the ways of women. I ask, very simply, that you grant Phoebe peace. Please settle her mind so that she may be equipped to absorb the recent changes in her life. I beg for this with great humility and without expectation of..."

Ayan felt the force of strange eyes upon him. He stopped and turned to see an elderly lady upon a bench with a sack full of seeds in her lap. Pigeons gathered near the lady's shoes. Her glare was familiar to Ayan; it was the glare of a disapproving white person. He stuffed his hands in his pants pockets and began moving again.

"If you want to please her," said the elderly lady, "then you must talk."

Ayan stopped walking and turned toward the lady. "But all we have done," he replied, "is talk. It's continued for days."

"I didn't say you should talk. That's her job. You're to listen."

"But how will that lead to solutions?"

The old lady sighed as though she'd been having such discussions all her life. "We're different creatures from you, you know. We don't want your solutions."

"We have problems you would not understand." Ayan spoke respectful of her age, but annoyed at her advice.

Her gravelly chuckle grated his nerves. "All men think they face the same problems."

"I am dark."

"I can see that."

"She is . . . light."

The woman's brows lifted. "Well, I am sure the gentry took that one with a grain of salt."

Ayan shook his head, not understanding the sarcasm.

"I seem to recall several stories in the bible where colours mixed. Did not King Solomon have one thousand wives from the four corners of the earth? I am sure they were not all the colour of an Israeli."

"I do not know the stories in the book of myths."

The woman chuckled again.

"I also seem to remember an English Queen who married a Spaniard King. I do hear that they are quite dark-skinned. Ask your lady what she thinks of that."

"But the law…"

"The law has left you alive. A blessing that you must give thanks for daily. I've lived a long time. I've learned many things. One of them is that people are more interested in their own petty vices than they are in the greater good. Time heals all wounds. You will see."

Ayan watched the birds feasting at her feet. "You are a beggar woman." Her quick glance made him lower his head in shame. "I apologise."

"And you speak with excellent clarity and a finely cultured voice, for a dark man."

Ayan nodded in respect. "I only meant that I do not think you understand our plight."

"Ah," the old woman chuckled. "You prove my point. Caught up in your own vanity. You stand there believing the entire world is against you and yet, you do not see past my skin." Her head tilted slightly. "I once worked in Eastern India, Bengal to be exact."

"I am from Bengal," Ayan started.

"I thought so. I was a lady, but when I grew old enough to come out, my father had little money or social status to afford me many opportunities. I did not cry. Instead I pledged myself to the church. I spent many years as a missionary. I worked in orphanages and poor houses. How many years," she sighed. "How many years I worked among the poor without ever seeing them. I only saw dark-skinned heathens who needed to be taught the truth. My truth. I never knew love until one day when a young girl touched my heart."

The old woman's attention returned to her birds. Ayan waited several moments for the story to continue. The woman fed her birds as if she had never spoken to him. Ayan turned to leave. He remembered the mission teachers, their harsh ways and their rules. He never thought of them as ever growing old. This woman represented everything that he learned to hate and somehow, as he thought of her spending her last days feeding birds in a park, there was nothing left to fear. Like the shadow of a tiger outside a home would drive fear into a man's heart, until they lit a candle and saw an old cat placidly strolling through the night. The fear and hatred he'd carried in his heart for so many years melted away as if it were never there.

"Let her talk," a gravelly voice called, just before he was out of earshot.

As Ayan hurried home. His steps hastened. Allah blessed him far beyond what he asked for. He found strength and peace over the fears that haunted him for so many years and he sent a blessing to ease Phoebe's suffering.

* * *

Tears streaked down Phoebe's face. As if he were an actor who had been given direction, Ayan engaged her.

"I want you to tell me all that is inside you. Make me understand what you're suffering. I wish to experience this as husband and wife."

"But," Phoebe said, "we are not married."

"We are not? Who says? What is a marriage? Does a piece of paper hold the power to make us married when our love does not?" He caught himself. The woman instructed him to listen.

As it turned out, those were the last words Ayan spoke for over two hours. He listened as she spoke about her childhood. Days. Events. Routines. Each tale detailing parents who were both loving and yet so controlling and concerned about appearances that they snuffed her spirit. She forgot her pain and related glorious holidays when her family ventured into the country to enjoy wonderful picnics. Many took place on weekdays. Mr Hillary's abundant wealth often became the focus of a story. He paraded his beautiful daughters and boldly bragged of the culture and refinement they enjoyed. He chose to give Phoebe an education, bragging about his forward thinking and how women in the Americas were being educated. Anything good enough for girls in America was good enough for his daughters. Then, he would dismiss the French scholars and western-travelled governesses and happily insist that his children not attend lessons, while he directed their carriage to landscapes of beatific loveliness.

Tears welled again, spilling softly onto her cheek.

"Father entertained several business associates. He never saw colour or race when it came to business. He often invited a diamond merchant who brought diamonds from Brazil. Once the diamond merchant spilled a bag of diamonds onto the table and let his daughter, Betsy and I play with them. They shone like stars on the black velvet cloth." Her fingers traced circles in the air.

Phoebe curled under Ayan's arm. Her head perfectly fit the hollow of his chest. She twisted slightly and pulled up her knees so she was completely cocooned under his arm. Ayan's fingers stroked her calf absently as she talked. His warmth relaxed her into a dreamlike state. They lay tangled amid a blanket of her hair, his soft breath on the nape of her neck, her eyelashes brushing his arm with butterfly sweeps.

"Now, men like Betsy's father are the true gentry. American farmers own estates larger than the city of London, and men like my father are unable to adjust. The fact that their former servants are now wealthier than they are, sticks in their craw. And, because they are beyond the reach of the English crown, in the Americas, or Africa, they have no power to, as my father stays, restore order."

Ayan stroked Phoebe's hair. He kissed the top of her head lightly. He wondered how her head could be so full of book knowledge, but her innocence bordered on naive when it came to matters of the world.

"One day, we thought it would be fun to trade dresses, but Father didn't want Betsy to wear my dress. Betsy's mother was a Jew. It was the first time I learned about his hatred for those who were "bringing down the British Empire." His words were, exactly "stinking like a crafty rodent." Betsy overheard what father said. We played quietly the rest of the afternoon. She never came over again and I never received another invitation to play. I never understood. Betsy had a yellow, diamond baby ring. She let me wear it. Her papa gave it to her because the stone and his girl, were both rare and both valuable."

Phoebe laughed hoarsely. "Father was angry. Betsy's father stopped bringing him diamonds. I think that is when his hatred for anyone who was not British turned to hate. Until then, he concerned himself more with commerce than politics."

Ayan listened fascinated that he could loathe the parents yet love Phoebe. Even more remarkable was the fact that as he learned of Mr Hillary's nobler deeds, he found himself feeling sympathy for the man. Could it be that souls possessed both good and evil? And if so, could the good defeat the evil, or vice versa? Ayan stared at the wall, mystified.

He knew that Phoebe's parents would not accept their union, but the venom her father spewed startled him. Phoebe, his daughter, he treated her like she was "stinking like a crafty rodent". He knew that Phoebe's title did not offer her any accord in the society she both detested and needed desperately. Her world of intolerance and arrogance left little room for a man to bend the rules, and none for a woman. In truth, her father still owned her and had the legal right to do as he willed.

"It sounded so simple when she said it . . ."

"Who?" Ayan said after several moments.

"Josephine Butler. I attended a Social Reform meeting of hers in London. She regaled against the new divorce act that permitted a man to seek a divorce and denied a woman. Her arguments against the institution of marriage for women who preferred to engage in a career, or to purse a business venture, made sense. I understood what she spoke of. My mother owned a diamond encrusted broach, passed down for several generations. It did not belong to her after marriage and indeed, my father sold it to finance his fledgling company. She still weeps."

"Josephine Butler. This woman does not believe in marriage?" Ayan frowned.

"No," Phoebe shook her head slightly. "She believes that a couple may marry if they make an agreement in public. She does not believe the church should control marriage. In fact, in Scotland, a man and woman only need to pledge to each other in front of witnesses and they are married."

Ayan nodded. "It is the same in Eastern India where the Colonial government established Qadi, a Muslim judge who records the Nikah."

"Nikah?" Ayan sat on the side of the bed and scratched his chin. The word almost defied definition. "A marriage in Islam is an act of worship. Yet, more. It is the giving of a gift, a solemn contract of mutual respect."

"Like in England," Phoebe laughed. "Women are married as a contract to maintain and protect wealth and status quo between the families."

Ayan shook his head and smiled. "No. For one thing, in my religion, the woman receives the dowry. Not her family. It is to protect her against her husband's death, or a divorce."

Phoebe jumped up and kneeled beside Ayan, her hands

resting on his thigh. “How lovely. Your religion allows a woman to divorce? In England, a man may divorce his wife, but never the other way around.”

Ayan leaned back, relaxing for one of Phoebe’s long stories.

“I had a friend in school. Her father divorced her mother. We were told never to talk about it. But one night she told me that her mother had been sent to a poor house. Can you believe it? She said that many of the women in the poor house are titled, but they are not heiresses and have no power. Their husbands just tossed them away .... what are you laughing at?”

Ayan ran his hand through Phoebe’s hair and pulled her close enough to kiss. “I did not laugh at you, dear one. I merely appreciated your passion.”

Phoebe eyed him suspiciously and then snuggled under his arm. “Is there a ceremony?”

Ayan tried to remember. At the moment, he only thought of how soft her hair felt. “A woman is expected to consent and there is a simple wedding.”

“No big church? No dress? No feast?” Phoebe almost pouted.

“A simple ceremony in the assembly.” He stopped short of telling her that he knew of no assembly, or Imam to perform the nikah, is the ceremony. It is more worship of Allah than a party. In Eastern India, your father would ask your consent to the marriage and the amount of the dowry. I would express ‘qubul’ and accept responsibility.”

Phoebe looked up and laughed. “Is there a ceremony for this?”

Ayan flushed. He did not want to admit how little he knew of his own religion. The life of a beggar and Lascar did not offer the opportunity to study the Quran. He could read very little Arabic and could only recite the prayers by rote, but he did understand a few of the passages. He thought a few minutes before carefully constructing a truthful answer. “I do not remember any incident of a formal ceremony. Nor do I remember any writings about the matter. Though there may be teachings on this but I have not heard of them."

Phoebe smiled and took his hand. "I solemnly agree and consent to be your wife."

"I have no dowry to pay," Ayan teased.

Phoebe took both his hands in hers and smiled. "Your dowry is worth far more than jewels or gold. You offer me freedom, love, safety, security and your heart. What more could I want for a dowry?" Tears rimmed her eyes.

Ayan kissed her tear-stained cheeks.

Phoebe brushed a light kiss across Ayan's cheek. He pulled her close, unsure why she was so happy, but delighted.

"Now," she said, "We only need to find another apartment to live in."

"I have found some prospective rooms."

"Oh, where?" Phoebe smiled up at him.

"Whitechurch."

"Whitechurch will be a lovely place to live," she said, her voice void of conviction. "When will we be married?"

"Tomorrow morning," Ayan promised.

"Then we must move the next morning."

"Another notice on the door?" Ayan tightened his grip.

"An officer of the court. We must vacate these rooms by noon, day after tomorrow."

"Then we go to our new room."

"Yes." Phoebe twisted a lock of hair.

"You are disappointed with your situation?"

Phoebe sat pensively for a moment then spoke slowly. "If I want to marry for love then I must not expect to remain in a social class which considers marriage a business transaction. I love you. I am just torn. My father has been good to me."

Ayan cleared his throat: "I will never ask you to stop loving your parents but I cannot ask you not to love me."

Ayan sighed heavily. Silence filled the room.

"My brother.... Kazi, I miss him dearly. I will never stop loving him."

"You've never mentioned him before!" Phoebe said looking concerned.

"It hurts to talk about him. He is ill.....cancer. He doesn't write. He has probably gone. I will love him for the rest of my days. He lives in my heart." Ayan looked down at the floor.

"You must not think of the worst. Perhaps he is waiting for you," Phoebe said.

"Yes, he is probably waiting for me in his grave. If I am truthful, I never expected to see him again when I left home."

The room fell silent. Phoebe sat on Ayan's lap. The chair that carried them squeaked against the hardwood floor. She looked deep into his eyes, and said, "Thankfully, I intend to love you for the rest of my days."

* * *

The morning frost glistened on the hedge roses. The couple walked hand-in-hand through the streets of London. They rose long before dawn, but the sun hung high in the sky before they reached the Fleet Street Market. The crowds of couples hoping to marry had dwindled. Only one of the freelance clergy remained, lounging on the wide, stone steps of a theatre.

Phoebe slowed, suddenly shy.

"Wait here."

Ayan crossed the market to a poor flower seller. He carefully counted out two pence and accepted one flower.

"What do you have?" Phoebe tilted her head and smiled.

"I have two gifts for you." Ayan stood tall and smiled down at his bride. He produced his left hand and held it, palm up. "Clover."

"Four leafed clover." Phoebe laughed lightly. "Be mine! Of course I will be yours... forever."

Ayan brushed his lips across her forehead and then stood up. He produced his right hand "Chrysanthemum."

Phoebe raised her brow in feigned impertinence. "Red my

love. The colour is very important."

"I know," Ayan whispered. "Red for, 'I love you'."

Phoebe held her flowers while Ayan discussed their marriage with the clergyman.

The man looked around Ayan's shoulder and whistled. "I hope her father knows of this, my man, or you'll face your day in court."

"My business is none of your affair," Ayan asserted as he placed a coin in the man's hand.

Ayan handed the piece of paper stating that nothing hindered their freedom to marry. The clergyman stuffed the paper in his pouch. "Write your name here." He handed the page to Phoebe who wrote her Christian name, using her maiden name for the last time. He handed the paper to Ayan who wrote his name.

"Albert?" The clergyman's eyebrows rose in amusement.

"Albert Miah," Phoebe stated. Her crisp cultured tones caused the clergyman to pause uncertainly. He scrawled something on a piece of paper and handed it to Ayan. "Do you have a ring?"

"A ring," Phoebe looked up at Ayan in horror.

"Do not worry, sweet one." Ayan pulled a narrow band, woven from strands of copper wire he found behind a newly renovated building. He placed it on Phoebe's finger.

"That is all?" Ayan looked at the clergyman.

The man looked uncomfortable. "I guess I could say the marriage words. T' won't make a difference. Your married, and legally to boot."

Ayan bent down and kissed Phoebe. She steadied herself on his arms.

"You are now safe from my father," Phoebe sighed.

"Friend?"

Ayan stepped protectively between his new bride and a dark-skinned man who had approached. He wore the marked face of an Arab. He held his hands up and lowered his head respectably. He stood bowed for a moment before rising.

"I notice friend that you marry today, yet such a strange way to marry for one such as yourself. Would Allah truly be pleased at the way you take a bride? I would feign to call you friend, as a worshiper of Allah and the last prophet. However, at this blasphemy, I wonder if my eyes deceived me and my senses fail."

Ayan's brow furrowed. Phoebe frowned, and held his arm.

"Ah, I see that you are mere children in the light of Allah. An unfortunate soul as yourself brought here by the cruelty of a white master and abandoned. Tell me if it is not so? And your bride? A gentle heart that is by all means worthy of Allah for chastity and sobriety light its soul. Would you not wish to please Allah? For it is most fortunate that I may be of humble assistance."

"We have no money," Phoebe said.

"Most assuredly, gentle dove, for what woman from a noble family would marry here, in this cesspool, if she had the opportunity to marry before in the assembly and proclaim that "God is one." He lifted his arms dramatically and looked to the sky in prayer. "Who only asks for complete surrender to Islam, according to his Prophet Muhammad, Peace be upon him."

"I am Christian." Uncertainty tainted Phoebe's voice as she clung to Ayan's arm.

Ayan looked down into his troubled wife's eyes. He did not want to cause her grief, not on her wedding day. He wanted to bring her joy, but his heart also warned him that the Arab was right. He did dismiss the teachings of the Prophet in his lust for a bride, and his love for Phoebe.

"Am I to change my religion?" Phoebe directed the question to Ayan.

"That, sweet dove," the Arab said before Ayan moved, "is only right. For doth not your religion demand submission from a wife in all things? Is it not possible that it is the light of Allah which drew your heart to love this man? Maybe, oh favoured one, Allah saw your sadness and unsatisfied heart and sent this man to guide you to enlightenment."

Ayan eyed the Arab sternly and put his arm around Phoebe, preparing to walk away.

"Please, friend, come this way."

"I have no money," said Ayan.

"I require no money, friend. I was passing this morning and Allah said to me, my son is lost and looking for the way. I paused, for my day is full of my own concerns." He bowed dramatically, "But who am I to question the divine request of Allah? I said to Allah. This man does not know me and may beat me as a thief or worse. Allah in his divine wisdom chastised me as a foolish child, for does not he always desire his best for those who live for Him?"

"You are most eloquent." Phoebe smiled and bowed her head slightly. "We are honoured at your concern."

"Phoebe." Ayan took her by the shoulders. "I do not require you to convert."

"I know. That is why it is my wish. I want to please you."

Ayan stood and nodded. The Arab took this to mean agreement, and turned without a word and hustled away. He led the couple deep into Whitechurch, weaving through the cobble and stone, avoiding the alleys full of trash. He stopped outside of an abandoned store. Boards covered the windows and there were holes in the wall, through which shone thin streams of light.

"Is it not time to pray?" The Arab smiled and opened the door. He stepped aside and let Ayan and Phoebe enter first. Phoebe stopped short at the sight. Men on carpets kneeled over the entire floor space. They prayed, many in Arabic. Beggars and merchants knelt side by side, each one devoutly intent on their own prayer.

"You will wish to complete your own prayers first."

Ayan did not know what to do. He looked at Phoebe. "I must pray alone."

"Of course." She laughed and whispered, "I noticed that no

other women are here."

Ayan gave her a sheepish grin and moved between the other men. He found an empty mat and stood. He touched his head to the floor and proceeded to pray. The words came awkwardly at first. He did not feel self-conscious when praying on the docks, or along a park fence, but among these men who prayed devoutly in a sanctuary, he felt the lack in his own spiritual walk.

He spoke softly in Bengali. He noticed the Arab speak quietly to another Arab man, who was wearing a headdress at the front of the room. Ayan's heart leapt. Did an Imam make this sanctuary home? The man did not look like a holy man, but he did seem to have authority.

Men ended their prayers and mingled in groups talking excitedly. Ayan noticed several glance his way and nod with approval. Ayan rose and waited to be approached. The man in charge approached and nodded. Ayan liked his pleasant manner and laughing eyes.

"You wish to marry?"

"Yes, Imam, I do." Ayan bowed low.

"No, my son. I am not Imam. It would be too much of a blessing. I am merely a government appointed Qadi. Allah does not require the establishment of priesthood like the English, so we worship unhindered in our own place until the day Allah sees fit to allow us a Mosque for worship."

Ayan bowed low.

"Has there been an agreement?"

"Yes." Ayan smiled.

The Qadi looked Ayan over.

Ayan shuffled his feet uncomfortably. "The marriage gift to the bride will be deferred until a later date."

The Qadi looked over Ayan's shoulder. Everyone turned as if noticing Phoebe for the first time. "The bride agrees?"

"Yes."

"She has wakeel?"

Ayan shook his head no. "She has not converted."

The Qadi looked at his friend. "Most assuredly not. I do trust that you do not dishonour us? Her parents are aware of this situation?"

The Qadi did not wait for Ayan's reply. He waved Phoebe forward. She moved gracefully as if she approached royalty. Her face glowed as she approached the men. Relief swept through Ayan as she appeared to be enjoying the experience. She took his hand. A sincere smile reflected in her eyes. The Qadi smiled and nodded in approval.

"You have no guardian, but I see that you are no child. Would it please you if I stood as your guardian in this matter?"

Phoebe looked at the Qadi and then up at Ayan. He nodded in approval. The Arab handed a contract to the Qadi who turned to Phoebe. "This Nikah is a contract of marriage. We will register it with the court so your marriage will be recognised legally."

Phoebe nodded and smiled up at the Qadi. "There is none worthy of worship except Allah and Muhammad is His servant and messenger," he declared. "I invite the bride and the groom, and the guests in the assembly to a life of piety, mutual love, kindness, and social responsibility."

'By Allah! Among all of you I am the most God-fearing, and among you all, I am the super most to save myself from the wrath of Allah, yet my state is that I observe prayer and sleep too. I observe fast and suspend observing them; I marry a woman also. He who turns away from my Sunnah has no relation with me."

The Qadi bowed his head and prayed for the bride and groom, their families and the Muslim community. Then he prayed for the extended community.

Ayan and Phoebe signed the marriage certificate, and Ayan asked the Arab to witness. The man bounded forward his eyes glowing at the honour. The Qadi signed, and folded the paper.

Ayan shook hands and accepted congratulations. The crowd pushed on them as they moved through the door. Phoebe took a deep breath at the door.

"A friend?" the Arab man said.

"I will look for you at prayer times. When work permits, of course."

"I will be here."

Phoebe smiled as they walked toward their new home. "I believe I will be happy here," she sighed.

Ayan smiled. For the first time in his life he felt like he was home.

CHAPTER 20

Ayan turned down an unfamiliar street, as he led his bride to their new home. The city became dull as he approached the Whitechurch district. Gangs of men filled the street, moving swiftly from large brick factories toward the pubs. Ayan's arm protectively encircled his bride's waist. Phoebe became nervous as the streets narrowed. Spontaneous laughter erupted from several buildings as the night's merriment got under way.

Phoebe only stopped once when a grand carriage halted in front of a pub. A finely dressed gentleman stepped out of the carriage and waved the driver on. Two prostitutes instantly molested him, cooing over his favour. He tipped his hat in mock respect and led them both into a pub. Laughter flooded the streets as the door opened and closed.

A cabbie drove a white nag to the same building and a group of young, genteel businessmen stepped out. One turned and looked directly at Phoebe, before following his mates into the building.

"What?" Phoebe's voice was unsteady as her knees. Her hand grasped Ayan's arm for support.

"Something is wrong?" Ayan asked concerned.

"I... I..." Phoebe's face flushed. "I know that gentleman. He is married to . . . He is a friend of my sister's husband. I know his sister."

Ayan lowered his head, wishing he did not need to expose Phoebe to the darker side of London. "Hurry," he whispered, desperate to remove his bride from the debauchery that would flood the streets when enough liquor had been consumed.

Ayan turned down a street that became a warren of alleys that turned in on themselves. They weaved through buildings until finally they walked up two flights of stairs and across a flat roof.

Phoebe looked over her shoulder. Dark buildings loomed in

all directions.

"Most of the riot remains on the street. It is quiet up here."

"I have not been to this part of the city before."

Ayan did not know what to say. He turned the key and pushed open the door. Phoebe followed him into the cold dark room. Ayan lit a candle and watched as Phoebe surveyed the new rooms. He arranged the furniture in the same pattern it had been in Phoebe's old apartments, and wondered how she would adjust to the fact that they must share a bed chamber.

Phoebe picked up a wrap and put it around her shoulders. Her eyes fixed on the broken plaster on the walls and the black water marks staining the ceiling.

"There is much work around here. There are new factories and many opportunities for men, all men."

"My father said these are great times," Phoebe tried to smile. "The newspapers call it the industrial revolution."

"I will get a job, a real job. I will work in one of the factories. I will work hard. We can move somewhere better."

"Oh," Phoebe's eyes flew open. "I am sorry, Ayan. I did not mean to disparage you."

"Look at me," Ayan whispered softly, and reached for his bride. "Look only at me."

Phoebe stared into his eyes for a moment. The tension drained from her soft features.

* * *

"Another one." Phoebe cried in horror as she flew into her husband's arms.

Ayan braced himself as his bride flew into his arms. Every muscle in his body ached. The moment Phoebe fell into his arms she burst into tears.

"I cannot endure this. You are gone from sunrise to sunset. I cannot endure this."

"Hush, sweet one. What is wrong?"

"Oh, Ayan, it was so horrible." She turned toward the east wall and pointed. "In that building over there. I didn't want to hear but those awful charwomen stood on the roof and gossiped all day."

"Are you okay? Did anything happen to you?"

"No," Phoebe cried frustrated. "Another woman is dead."

Ayan relaxed, relieved that no one came for him, or molested her in his absence.

"They say the walls were covered with blood."

"Do not think about it."

Phoebe stepped back, aghast. "Do not think about it. That was the second one to die within two streets. The constables do not know if there is one murderer or two. I am here, all day, alone. How can I not think about it?"

"The women dying are women of ill repute. The man does not appear to be killing anyone else."

"What about the woman who was stabbed thirty times?"

Ayan looked at the small stove. His heart fell. His wife spent all day weeping and fretting. Once again she forgot to make a meal for him. His stomach pinched tightly. Ayan sighed and kissed Phoebe's head.

Ayan put another scoop of coals into the stove. "Do not think on such things. The world can be a cruel place, full of evil people."

"I cannot leave the house. I am imprisoned here, day by day."

Ayan sighed. "You may leave. I do not stop you."

"I cannot go out," Phoebe wailed. "Not with a madman murdering women."

"He does not murder women in the daytime. You are safe," Ayan reminded her. He put a stew on the stove and sat on the couch.

"Oh," Phoebe's voice softened. "I am sorry. I should have made a supper."

Phoebe dropped into his lap and pouted. "I had too much on my mind. I cannot think about anything but murdered women."

Ayan patted her hair. It had lost its lustre, but still felt like silk between his fingers. "I do not think about anything but you. You strengthen me. I could not endure the torment of standing in the same place all day, lifting crates onto wagons." Phoebe cuddled into Ayan's arms.

"You are the love of my life."

"I love you too," Phoebe whispered.

They sat still as the aroma of stew filled the room.

"Things will become better soon."

"They need to be, Ayan."

"I will work hard; we will be able to move somewhere a little better, in a nicer area."

"With more room," said Phoebe excitedly. "And a window that looks over a park, or some trees."

"I think you we will have to wait and see what we can afford," smiled Ayan. He was pleased to see a spark in Phoebe's eyes. It had been some time since it had been there and Ayan worried that it had been extinguished forever.

"I don't earn as much as…."

"And a cot for the baby!" interrupted Phoebe.

Everything changed in the weeks that followed. Ayan would finish his long shift at the factory and then rush to the docks to help load up carts with the goods emptied from the merchant ships that berthed earlier in the day. It was back-breaking work, especially after a full day at the factory, but Ayan wanted to get Phoebe out of their tiny lodging and into a half-decent apartment, before the baby arrived.

It still felt like a dream. Could this really be happening? Ayan Miah had a beautiful English wife? And was soon to be a father? How life had turned around in such a short time. The hardship and hard work were a small price to pay for love, freedom, and family. Ayan harboured a desire that once they had moved to a better apartment and the baby arrived, then perhaps Phoebe could reconcile with her family. Once they realised how hard

Ayan worked, how much they loved each other and what a great father he was, then surely they could start to accept him.

* * *

Ayan rushed home. Phoebe hated him working such long hours. He was glad the last woman murdered was several streets away. Maybe it would comfort Phoebe knowing the murderer did not walk the same streets she did. The yellow glow of the streetlights cast eerie shadows. The sun had set four hours ago. The pub landlords had taken the last of their patrons into the gutters two hours ago. The prostitutes had sent their clients home one hour ago. And Phoebe spent most of the night alone with her fears.

Smoke and soot stained his clothing, and a dirty rag covered a large burn across his shoulders. A physician gave him a powder to ease the pain. It dulled the agony, but the raw skin flared under his shirt. He rushed through the abandoned streets. A fire wagon rolled by, the exhausted firemen hanging from the side. The white-speckled horses pranced anxiously. Their noses flared at Ayan as they trotted past. Their hoofs rang off the cobblestone long after they vanished down the dark street.

Ayan hurried down a back alley, hoping to follow the labyrinth of alleys on a shortcut to his house. He turned a corner, slamming into a tall man, Aaron Kosminski. Ayan held his eyes for a moment. He held his breath, everyone did around Aaron. The man rarely bathed. His matted hair hung in long dreadlocks. Dirt caked around his ears and crusted on the edge of his clothing.

"Let me pass," Ayan stood firm.

Aaron's eyes narrowed. A chuckle rumbled in his chest.

"You and I have no quarrel. Why should we quarrel? We are the same? We are not like them, vile creatures. Are we? You are not a vile creature."

"Let me pass," Ayan tensed, sensing something was not right. Aaron kept his left side close to Ayan, hiding the right hand.

Ayan tilted his head to see. Aaron immediately jumped back. Ayan froze. He had seen that look before. Aaron's eyes burned, evil. The Cruel One had the same gleam in them the day he almost beat Ayan to death.

Ayan stared into dead eyes. They stared back as if from a corpse. A chill ran up Ayan's spine.

"You want to see?" Aaron lifted his right hand. A bloodstained knife lay in the palm. "We are not vile creatures." He spun around and loped down the street.

Fear froze Ayan to the spot. His mind reeled. He forced himself to walk to the corner. The street lay vacant. Ayan peered back to where he had been and saw that the mist had already swallowed Kosminski.

Phoebe! Ayan's feet slapped against the damp cobblestone. His heart pounded loudly in his chest as he took the stairs two at a time, up to the wide landing where they lived. As Ayan approached the front door, his heart dropped. The door was ajar.

"Phoebe! Phoebe! Where are you?" Ayan called out loud.

Ayan dashed inside but Phoebe was nowhere to be seen. Ayan's gaze was drawn to the table, where there lay a pristine white envelope. Ayan walked slowly across to look closer, knowing its contents would not be pleasing to him. Before going near the letter, Ayan poured some water into a bowl, and carefully washed his hands and face.

He picked up the envelope carefully, fingering the thick, expensive paper. The writing on the front was exquisitely neat and bore a single word, "Albert".

Ayan moved the chair from under the table, and slowly sat down. He held the envelope in both hands, afraid to break the seal, afraid to read the words that would break his heart. He lay the envelope down and stood back up. Several minutes passes as Ayan circled the room, unsure what to do. He put some water on the stove, more out of habit, than necessity. The water boiled, and Ayan made some tea. He sat down at the table once again.

The envelope had an ethereal quality, almost glowing in pulses, daring him to pick it up again. Ayan sipped at his tea, almost like he had made some pact with himself that he must open the letter when the cup had been drained. This act was drawn out for as long as possible, but eventually Ayan stared at black leaves in an empty cup.

"Ok," Ayan said to himself. "Let's see what news greets me after a hard day at work."

He carefully broke the Hillary Family Seal and pulled a single folded sheet from inside. He unfolded the paper and read the contents.

Albert,

Phoebe has returned to her family. We have known for some time of her predicament. We sent a servant to see her several weeks ago, and they reported back to us on the terrible conditions that you have allowed our beloved daughter to live in.

We have been following the newspaper reports concerning the awful murders that are happening right on your doorstep. You may not be concerned with Phoebe's welfare, but we are.

We sent three of our most trusted servants to retrieve Phoebe and to leave you this note. She may not be entirely convinced that she is doing the right thing, but I am sure that she will soon see the error of her ways.

Mr Bradford Hillary.

Ayan read the note again. Why hadn't Phoebe told him that her family had been in contact? He would never have forbidden her from seeing them; in fact he had hoped for some kind of reconciliation. Ayan read the last sentence over and over again. 'She may not be entirely convinced…' So Phoebe was pressured into leaving him? She was upset, and they caught her in a weak moment, vulnerable and lonely. She would soon realise what she had done. Phoebe would come home to him, he was certain.

A knock at the door shook Ayan from his thoughts.

"Phoebe? Phoebe? You are back?"

He ran to open the front door only to find two police officers staring back at him.

"Are you Albert Miah?" one of the officers asked.

"Yes, I am. What is the matter, Officer?"

"I am arresting you for theft and blackmail. I think we've met before, darkie!" The policeman grabbed Ayan's arms and forced them behind his back.

"What do you mean? There must be some mistake. I haven't done anything wrong, sir!"

"You are coming with us. Please remain silent."

"No, this can't be!" Ayan was led away by the two officers. His yelling echoed through the halls of the flats.

CHAPTER 21

"Ayan Miah!" screamed the young prison guard as he walked from cell to cell. "Ayan Miah!"

Ayan could not believe his ears. The fact that the guard was screaming his birth name rather than his English name was a very good sign, indeed. Only Phoebe called him by his birth name. Perhaps, at long last, she had sent him a letter! Ayan leapt from his mattress and nearly ran face-first into the steel bars.

"It is I, sir. It is I," he yelled.

The guard's boots clapped against the concrete floor. He stomped over to Ayan's cell, a sneer implanted on his doggish face. "You sure you can read letters, son?"

"Oh, yes, sir," Ayan said, waves of fear rolling over his body.

The guard shook his head a bit. "I don't know about that. Can you read my badge? Tell me what it says."

With that, the guard placed his hand over his badge, blocking it entirely.

"Certainly," said Ayan, an invisible frown twisting on the face of his soul, "it must contain your esteemed ranking."

The guard seemed to like this. His sneer disappeared and he smiled ever so slightly. He dropped the letter on the floor outside Ayan's cell and stomped away. Ayan descended, reached through the bars, and grabbed it.

"Curses!"

In his hands was a letter Ayan had sent to Phoebe weeks before. The post office had abused it with stamps - RETURN TO SENDER, UNDELIVERABLE -Ayan tore the envelope open and read his own words:

Dear Phoebe,

I may not be the wisest soul on Earth, but I've long believed

my instincts to be sound. And deep inside myself, those instincts tell me that you DO NOT believe your father.
I swear on the name of my faith that I stole no jewellery, money, or other valuables from your mother and father. Though I freely admit to not feeling warmth toward them, I would never violate them - or any person - in such a way.

Believe me when I tell you that your father set me up. Does he not set people up at the banks he runs? Have you not told me stories of his questionable dealings? In the brief span of our marriage, when I faced unceasing poverty and strife, did I ever once seize so much as a salt granule that didn't belong to me?

We loved each other, I believed. We loved each other, Phoebe. I am a man who had no love in his life, but when you came, you lifted me to new heights. Can you remember how it felt, my Phoebe? We were poor, but did we not have joy? If there was no love, would we have been blessed with a child?

I ask you, now, to look not with your mind, but within your heart. Which of the men in your world is more deserving of trust?

Love always,
Ayan/Albert

Feeling entirely pathetic, Ayan did what the guard had seemed intent upon doing: he tore the letter to shreds and then dropped the pieces into the toilet. Anger and frustration took over Ayan, and he collapsed onto his filthy mattress and wept unashamedly.

CHAPTER 22

Ayan stood at the cell window. Visitors filed through the narrow door and each one told a different story. He watched a rag-wrapped woman shuffle across the courtyard, a basket in her arms. The basket held a token for the guards and food for a family member.

The fair women, both wives and daughters, walked a gauntlet on the way to their loved ones. Few women possessed strong enough constitutions to return more than once. Those who did rarely returned after the first few visits.

Husbands visited their wives, but loyalty waned as time passed. They moved across the courtyard, shoulders down. Eyes locked on the ground before their feet. Ayan became expert at predicting their last visit. Something changed in the way they looked at the guards. When the husbands left the first few times, their eyes burned with anger. Eyes locked with the guards in defiant rebuke. As weeks passed guilt replaced the anger. Visits shortened. Shoulders slumped.

Ayan scratched another mark on the wall. He drew boxes. Each box held seven scratched lines. Each row held 50 boxes. He put a mark to indicate different special days. At one thousand days he sat back and stared at the wall all day, trying to determine whether one thousand days was worth grieving over, or whether it was a short time. One thousand days, including three summers. A child was still a baby after three summers.

He stroked his bushy beard gently, and returned to his study of the people crossing the visitor's courtyard. He no longer saw the figures clearly as they crossed the yard.

A gentlewoman entered the gate and crossed the yard. His breath quickened. He stared hard, trying to see clearly. The woman's movements touched his soul. The gentle way she tilted her head, the alert movements as she surveyed every inch of the yard. Her shape and movements were surprisingly familiar. She moved with divine grace, but as ethereal as she was, the guards refused to grant her permission to enter.

Heat burned Ayan's neck and cheeks. His fists clenched the bars, turning his knuckles white. His fist slammed against the wall. Ayan rubbed at his eyes, hard, with the backs of his hands, desperate to see clearly.

"Phoebe!" he shouted. "Phoebe!"

The woman scanned the cell windows, and stared straight at Ayan. This did not mean anything. Perhaps she was reacting to being yelled at by a criminal. Perhaps she never reacted to the name. Nonetheless, Ayan screamed again: "I love you, Phoebe! I love…"

His voice died. Ayan coughed and coughed, choking on his own emotions.

Ayan's eyes strained until pain shot through their sockets. He stared at the empty spot where the woman stood. The wind whipped into the cell. The yard darkened before the chill drove him from the window. He sat on the bed, a storm of emotions flowing through his veins. He looked at the marks on the wall. They meant something now. They represented the time it took to weaken his eyes so he could no longer see across the yard. Each mark represented a day that he lived with the memory of Phoebe's touch. The rows measured the time he lived without waking to the scent of Phoebe's hair. Four rows and four years. To Ayan, they represented his whole life.

He wished he could remember his dreams like the other inmates. Dreams kept men sane. He only remembered small pieces of his past: Lady Achala and her predictions, which all came true. He helped others and that lead him to Phoebe who loved him when every dream died and all hope was lost.

He remembered Kazi helping him build their farm. He remembered the day he met the thieves at the bean seller's shop. These memories comforted him. They did not dull the pain, but they did make the time pass easier.

Now, with his life half spent, he knew how to measure time. Four years represented the separation that divided Phoebe and him. It took four years for a man to forget, with certainty, what his wife looked like.

CHAPTER 23

Ayan walked through the open gates. His life half over, years wasted in prison, a ship's bowels and the streets.

"Albert Miah."

Ayan turned to the young guard, who nodded slightly. "Do not return."

Ayan returned the nod and stepped into freedom. Once again he stood on the street. A homeless man with nothing to show for a lifetime of work. Ayan didn't look at his empty hands. Instead, he looked at his opportunity.

He walked through the streets with his head held high. Unlike the first time he made this journey, this time he knew the city.

Ayan walked the streets for days, restless. The place felt different. Dirt caked to the walls of buildings and refuse filled the alleys destroying the haven he shared with Phoebe. Nothing seemed the same. Old brothels were abandoned and taken over by immigrant families, most of them were Jews from Europe and Eastern Indians. The onion and pork hawkers disappeared. Spice merchants took their place. And, for the first time, he found a store that sold real halal meat.

Ayan entered the store and looked around. He did not see any forbidden meat.

"I can help you?" the store clerk asked politely.

"This is halal?" Ayan asked.

"This is indeed halal. All blessed. None forbidden."

"You know this? "The man laughed. "You are new to the area? The Imam will tell you himself that my store sells only halal. I have never defiled the place by allowing forbidden meat through the doors."

Ayan looked around.

"You have come to make a purchase, maybe?"

Ayan's stomach growled. He stepped back. "No."

The man smiled. "Of course. It is only right that you sample the wares before you decide whether to patronise my humble establishment." The man ran to the counter and pulled a thick slab of cooked meat from under the counter. "You enjoy lamb?"

Ayan nodded before he could stop himself.

The merchant laughed and cut two thick slabs from the joint. He wrapped the meet in brown paper and forced Ayan to take the package. "It is not a gift," he said with a knowing smile. "I give you two slices of halal today and tomorrow when you find work, you come to my shop and buy your halal. It is a wise move on my part."

Ayan smiled, understanding the logic behind the merchant's generosity. "I will indeed return to your shop, many times."

He rushed down the street, looking for a safe place to unwrap and eat his meal. He entered an abandoned building and found a clean corner.

"Welcome," a voice came from the darkness.

Ayan covered his meat.

"Do not fear me. I am no thief. My name is Joleeka, a humble Hindu from Calcutta. I notice from your face that you are not born in England."

"Bengali," Ayan said. His eyes adjusted to the dim light. A thin man sat less than six feet from his corner. The man looked at the meat package, but never begged. "You would like some?"

"I have money, today," the man said. "I see that your hunger pinches harder than mine."

Ayan looked at the meat. It did not feel right to eat in front of this man.

"I must leave soon for mass."

"Mass?" Ayan asked.

"Yes, I attend night mass. I cause less offence then."

Ayan felt he should say something friendly, but nothing came to mind.

"You may come to church with me tonight."

"I am Muslim," Ayan explained. He broke a chunk of meat off and handed it to the older man. Joleeka paused only a moment before pouncing on the meat in a birdlike manner.

"How do you come to be Christian?"

"My story is long and sad." Joleeka chewed the meat carefully. "I came to England the respected man-servant to a Scottish Army Officer. My days were industrious and pleasant, until my master died."

"My master also died." Ayan offered Joleeka more meat.

"If not for my Christianity, I would not survive."

"Allah gives me strength."

"That may be," Joleeka muttered between mouthfuls, "but does your religion help you survive?"

"I do not understand." Ayan wiped his mouth and leaned back, comfortable for the first time in days.

"The English favour their Prophet Jesus above all. It is easier to live as a Christian. Not only does their charity increase for those who follow their religion, but their favour increases."

Ayan remembered Mr Jennings' anger when he caught Ayan praying. The thought of converting for the sake of a meal never crossed Ayan's mind until now. "Allah is The One In your religion, is this capitalised? Yes, it is ok to have it like this? God. The only true religion is to serve and worship him."

"Christians, Hindus, Muslims, is there any difference between each?" Joleeka leaned forward and looked earnest. "Is not religion a thing for a country and people, not a God? You live in England, worship their God. You live in Eastern India, worship your God. There is one God. The Christian priests say the same thing. Who is right?"

"I grew up under the care of mission teachers."

"Have you ever asked yourself why you did not grow up under the care of a Muslim? We're not the Christians the ones who practiced charity?"

"I grew up in colonial Bengal. The government controlled

everything."

"And did your Allah protect your people? Did he see to your care and well being?"

"And has your Jesus seen to yours?" Ayan did not like the questions the man asked. "Has he protected you? Is it a God's purpose to make our lives easy, or to prepare us for the hereafter?"

"You have some good arguments," Joleeka nodded. "I make baskets and the Christians buy them for charity sake. I receive alms from the church each day, and scraps from the kitchens. And, on Christmas, I receive a meal. I do not see your Allah taking care of you as well."

The blunt statement offended Ayan. This was not the time to get into an argument over religion. Thankfully, Joleeka stood and bade Ayan farewell, and left the building on his way to mass. Ayan watched the dark door where the man disappeared. Was this shell of a man who lived only to curry favour from the English an example of the Christian God's care? Darkness swirled around Ayan's head. He did not like the questions the stranger asked. They disturbed him. He rose and left the building.

The bitter wind cut through his clothes and burned his skin. Several hours later Ayan lay in another corner, sheltered from the wind. He dozed, comfortable in both body and stomach. He remembered that a Muslim fed both men tonight, not a Christian. He remembered being freed from The Bengal. He remembered finding love in Phoebe's arms. He flexed the strength in his arm and smiled. He would rather sleep comfortable, and remain a strong man following Allah, than to sleep in a warm bed, if it meant that he must return to the hollow existence of a man-servant, if it meant he must become a shell of a man, weaving baskets and living in the dark. Such a life may suit men like Joleeka, but Ayan knew he would never survive.

Ayan smiled and rolled over. He was now glad that Joleeka asked the questions, for now he had the answers.

CHAPTER 24

Ayan rose from his prayers. The salt air stung his nose. For a moment time stood still. The great steamers lay in the summer sun, like they had so many years ago when he and Kazi rummaged through broken crates and garbage for food. The acidic tang of smoke floated above the waves, signalling another ship heading east to the Americas. Another ship of Lascars bound for the slave markets.

Ayan turned before the unpleasant memory disrupted his moment's reverie. He wandered through the crates, unwilling to leave the familiarity. Countries may change and people may build great cities, but harbours around the world looked and smelled the same.

He stepped around a pile of rotting fruit, an experienced eye checking for an edible section.

Ayan smiled. He longed to return to the sea as a merchant marine and return home, but only white men were paid to work on ships that headed east to Eastern India. The only ships with berth for Ayan travelled west to the unknown and slavery.

Ayan watched the purple hue give way to a crimson strip. Every morning he tried to watch the exact moment that the morning dawned. He would watch with eyes wide, for minutes. But it always seemed like the sun breached the horizon at the exact moment Ayan blinked. Still, he returned to the docks each day. It was the only place he could truly find the east and pray with a heart full of peace.

The morning clamour of working men and horses invaded Ayan's thoughts. It was time to start the day. He moved quickly past The Constantine. She was a familiar sight and a comfort for Ayan. She carried spices from the Orient and Eastern India. She smelled of cinnamon and curry powder. Some days her load spilled and Ayan could scoop up a couple handfuls of fine curry powder to flavour his food.

"No. It is not fair," a man yelled.

"Fair? What does that matter to me?" the dock master replied.

"It is my cargo."

"What is on the docks is your cargo. The rest is mine."

"I paid for it all." A slight Bengali accent caught his attention.

"I work hard to earn the money to buy this curry powder."

"Course you work hard, darkie. That is all your kind are good for."

The dock master laughed and shoved the slightly built man hard enough to trip him over the pile of sacks in dispute.

Ayan moved to lift the man and brushed the curry dust from him. He turned to the dock master and stood full height, arms crossed. "The order is short."

The dock master's eyes narrowed.

"Please, do not . . ."

Ayan put a hand on the man's shoulder. "We do not leave until we have our master's full order."

The dock master's chin rose as if struck. He stuck a thumb at the small man. "I thought the order belonged to him. "

Ayan laughed. "This much curry powder belongs to a house servant? Would you like me to watch the order while this man fetches the master?"

The dock master turned without comment and called orders for another five bags to be added to the pile. Ayan bent down and helped the smaller man pick up his load, twelve bags in all. He prayed to Allah that he did not just help a thief make off with a man's weight in curry powder.

"Tell me we did not steal this curry powder." Ayan slowed his pace and set down the heavy bags.

"Peace and blessings upon you, my good friend." The small man turned and smiled warmly. "You are an answer to prayer. Would he, in all his wisdom, send you to aid a vile thief and wretch of a heretic?"

Ayan laughed heartily.

"This," the man waved his hands over the bags, "is the product of my labour. I paint ships and get paid. Then, I save my money and buy curry powder. The curry powder is sold and I make more money."

Ayan's brow shot up. "You are a merchant?"

"Most assuredly," the small man bowed.

"I was man servant to a merchant at one time."

"And yet, you did not learn enough to start your own business?"

"I did," Ayan suddenly felt like a child. "The man died but did not leave me a place in his business."

"And why should he." The little man stretched and started to pick up the bags. "Does not Allah teach men to work for their own gain? That righteousness is found in hard labour? You should start your own business."

The small man reached for the bags at Ayan's feet.

"Do not worry, I will carry these," said Ayan.

"Ah!" The small man looked up and grinned. "How am I to know that you are not a thief? You do not look like a merchant. You are too well fed to be a beggar."

Ayan wanted to say he was a street performer, or something that might impress the man. Instead, he looked at his feet and picked up the remaining bags of curry powder. "I...I work for men like you. Earning what I can by the strength of my arms."

"And a strong set of arms Allah granted you." He flexed his own arms. "Allah gives us gifts according to his wisdom."

The man scurried through the streets. Ayan knew the route well, as it led to Whitechurch.

"My name is Malik a humble purveyor of curry powder and a ship painter."

"I am Ayan Miah."

"Well, Ayan Miah. Do you have a roof to sleep under?"

"I sleep at the hostel."

"Then you must inspect my abode and see if it suits you."

Ayan looked down and frowned. "You would share your home with me?"

"Ah," Malik sighed. "A single man living in a small apartment is no home. An abode must be shared with friends and family before it becomes a home."

A wave of relief enveloped Ayan when Malik turned down a stairwell leading to a basement apartment. He had never been able to ascend to the upper level of any building without opening the wounds Phoebe's absence left on his soul.

"Welcome, friend." Malik opened the door with a flourish.

Ayan stopped dead in his tracks. His mind played tricks. Before him stood a Bengali tea room, rich spices assailed his nostrils while vivid coloured silks caught his eye, piled high to one side of the room. Malik chuckled and pushed Ayan through the door, closing it securely behind.

"I will own my own store soon." Malik boasted his eyes glowing with pride.

Ayan's hand reached for a silk before he could restrain himself. "You are indeed a wealthy man."

Malik waved away the comment. "We will have some tea, and then we will discuss our future."

"Our future?"

"Yes, friend," Malik poked the coals in the stove. "We will discuss how we will bring our ambitions to life."

Ayan sat down. The room mesmerised him. "I have no ambitions. I work hard."

Malik sat back on his heels and looked at Ayan seriously. "Friend. I have watched you pray to Allah every morning for months. I did not approach, for at first you shamed me, for I allowed my own devotion to waver. I do not believe that mere chance brought us together." Malik turned back to the glowing embers. "Allah brings me a man with the strength to build and the knowledge of a merchant. A man who can stand before a white man without fear, I wondered at first if you were not a vision sent by Allah to condemn my cowardly behaviour."

"I meant no offence." Ayan leaned forward, handing a pot to Malik.

The small man smiled, again. Ayan liked Malik. His smile twinkled deep in his eyes, as if he possessed a secret that protected him from the cruelty of life, and could not be snuffed by the cold or hunger. Malik nodded and accepted the pot.

"I did not take offence. I asked myself, Allah, is this your guiding hand? Have you sent me a friend and business partner who possesses strengths where I possess weakness?"

"My hands are my only strength." Ayan flexed his callused hands.

"And yet," Malik laughed heartily, "a humble man, do you think these eyes missed you checking the manifest? Do you think I did not see the way you understood the words there and knew the dock master robbed me, though I did not say by how much? Is not the ability to read words written on paper and in English, a strength that will be far more valuable to our endeavours than your courage or the bands of steel in your arms?"

Malik took a chair across to the small table and eyed Ayan seriously. "I thought to myself. If this man is a trial from Allah, then I will accept my fate. If he be a thief, then I will rebuild and restore what he stole. If he be a blessing, then I will see that we both prosper and fulfil Allah's destiny for our lives."

"How do I help?" Ayan looked around, unsure how he should answer the charge that Allah chose him to be a blessing. He only brought death to those he loved, and poverty to those he tried to protect.

"You are strong. I can find you work painting ships. Together we can save more money and buy more supplies. Then, when we have plenty, it will be time to open a shop and sell."

Malik grew animated as he described his plans. Ayan admired his new friend's vision. He remembered the large number of

Eastern Indian men and Jewish families moving into Whitechurch. To offer items for sale from home and make people's lives more pleasant seemed like a good plan. Ayan had to admit that he would go hungry to save ten pence and halal meat instead of settling for the blood pudding and pork cakes eaten by the other beggars.

Malik passed a bowl of warm stew across the table. Ayan eyed the white meat suspiciously. "It is halal." Malik responded to the unspoken question. "Does not Allah say, 'If any is forced by hunger, with no inclination of transgression, Allah is indeed Oft-Forgiving, Most Merciful?"

"Does he?" Ayan's head shot up. "Does he?"

"Yes." Malik frowned. "Yet, the meat is rabbit."

"I ate much forbidden meat while a Lascar and a beggar."

"A Lascar? That is an interesting story for another day. But, eat hearty. Allah did not wish you to starve. How is it that you grew in Allah's grace without understanding his teaching?"

Ayan savoured the stew for several moments before replying.

"My father died when I was young. My brother, Kazi and I lived in a Christian mission. Then we were forced to beg in the villages of Sylhet. After that, we moved to the mountains where necessity forced us to travel far to hear teaching. I signed on as a Lascar when a very young man. After that, I settled here."

Malik nodded with understanding. "Fear not. There are many here who are suffering such as you. Just understand that Allah only wants his best for the righteous. The hereafter will be a blessing to you, and Allah will ensure that you receive rest for the suffering you endured."

A tear edged Ayan's eye. Malik turned away, intent on some small speck in his bowl.

"A shop?" Ayan cleared his throat. "My brother and I dreamt of a shop."

"Your brother is here?"

Ayan shook his head. "I believe my brother is dead."

Malik's sad eyes mirror's Ayan's soul. "Then let me fill the void left by your loss. We will be brothers and will build the shop. You will see. Allah will use this shop to bless us in more ways than we can imagine".

* * *

Malik looked at Ayan with sympathetic eyes. "My friend, we have worked together for five years and only now you tell me about a wife? I do not know who I feel worse for: you or me."

Ayan and Malik smiled and touched palms. It had been a long time since Ayan met an equal in strength and honour. Malik arrived in England as a curator, employed by an archaeologist. His journey to England never took him into the bowels of a ship. He travelled in the stern of the ship, attending to the artefacts.

"What man does not tell his best friend and partner about a wife?" Malik grinned and looked Ayan in the eye.

"It is personal." Ayan met his friend's glance evenly, neither giving quarter or responding to the jest. After decades of protecting, it felt good to meet a man who matched him in strength and size.

"One does not tell a fellow Sylheti that he possesses a wife?"

"You tease me friend."

"Friend? And business partner and still I do not learn about this wife?"

"I don't know why, but she was in my head this morning," Ayan said. "The other day I was outside the shop and there were a group of boys hanging about. They weren't doing anything, just jostling like boys do. One of the boys had dark skin, and it made me think about my wife, and my child. Some days, do you ever wake up with ghosts in your mind?"

Malik pretended to shiver. "I can't say I have, but I feel I will tomorrow. First a wife, and now a child? Is it a son?"

"I do not know, Malik. I just found myself thinking about things that I shouldn't. Things that only cause me pain."

"You know you can talk to me about it, if you choose. It may help."

"And now you are sounding like the women in my village! Do not worry about me, my friend, I am not going to allow ghosts from the past to spoil the life we have here and now. Come now, Malik. We do not sell anything if we do not open the shop."

"True, my friend, true," said Malik, as he took one end of a table that Ayan reached for. They carried it to the front of the shop, revealing its piles of goods to all who passed.

The sun shone especially strong on this day. Ayan stood upright after setting down the table and basked in the glow, accepting the welcome ease in his back.

"Does your back trouble you?"

"More each year."

"I have heard many stories about the life of a Lascar. I do not believe I would have survived."

"Few did," Ayan said with a wry smile. "The sun makes me strong again."

"Your dreams must agree with you." Malik smiled. "You look years younger today."

Ayan stood up and flexed his muscles, revelling as his muscles rippled. The supple strength moved down his back, flowing like it had when he was young and hard muscle covered every inch of his body.

"Your wife…did prison separate you?"

"Yes," Ayan answered, not quite sure whether he told a lie, or not.

"Her father did not approve. He accused me of stealing from their home. I was imprisoned for five years."

"Debtor's prison?"

"No."

Malik frowned. "What type of man was her father?"

"Wealthy."

"Ah." Malik nodded, understanding all.

They worked in silence for several minutes.

“I wrote to her. She did not write back.”

“Did she visit?”

“No.” Ayan hesitated. “A woman arrived at the prison one day near the end of my term. I could not see well. A hard life weakened my eyes. I called to her but she did not reply.”

Moments later, Malik spoke again: “Do you think,” he said, “it was she by the prison gate?”

Again, Ayan shrugged. “The part of me that likes the sunshine believes, yes. But, as for the part of me that knows the rain…”

“Hmm.” Malik nodded with understanding. “I think it was her, Ayan.”

It fed Ayan’s emotions. The words touched his soul like a balm, but deep down Ayan knew Malik was simply being a good friend. Quietly, he said, “I’m glad to hear it.”

A noise alerted both men. They sprang in time to see three boys, none older than sixteen, exit the shop in a hurry.

Ayan grabbed for one boy, his fingers wrapping around anything he could, grasping at cloth, hair, skin, it did not matter. A scuffle ensued as the boys fought to escape, one boy catching Malik in the thigh with a hefty kick. The man roared with rage and pushed the boy to the ground, still maintaining a tight grip on a second boy.

Ayan tried to catch the remaining urchin. It so happened that it was the boy Ayan had told Malik about; the dark-skinned urchin that had brought old wounds to the surface. The child’s agility and fear made it impossible to find a secure grip. Ayan thought he had him twice, but each time he managed to wriggle free and make a fresh break for freedom.

By now, Malik had subdued the two other boys. Ayan had cornered the dark-skinned boy, who was now breathing hard from the exertion.

“Empty your pockets,” Ayan cried fiercely. “Empty them, now!”

Ayan towered over the boy’s, hoping to convince them he was

not a man to be fooled with. All three turned out their pockets. Three pairs of socks suddenly appeared.

"We do not keep them," one of them cried. "They are for Scour."

Ayan sighed. He knew of Scour, a worthless man if there ever was one. When not drinking, he beat the boys who stole for him. Even as the boys risked hard labour and the lash, Scour slept off his drunken stupor. It was no secret that he beat more than one boy to death. Others he starved. For the boys, prison was a relief from their horrible existence under Scour's care.

Ayan's mood lightened. He taunted the boys, "If I ever get robbed again, I hope it's by you three."

"You talk clever," muttered the boy to Ayan's left, the one who pocketed the socks, "but you left the back door open."

Ayan and Malik traded a silent glance, each blaming the other.

"Instead of looking for open doors, look for employers who are offering work. Then you can earn your socks rather than stealing them."

"You're lucky we don't fetch the police," Malik chimed in, matching Ayan's lenient stance.

"He's right," Ayan said. "Half our competitors would have had you arrested."

"We're sorry," wheezed the smallest boy Malik had caught. "But we must steal the socks."

"Why is this?"

"If we do not steal the socks, Scour will beat us."

"He will lock us in the basement," the older boy continued quietly, the thought of Scour's punishment sapping his bravado.

"He will forget that we are there."

Memories flooded Ayan's mind. He thought back to the Lascar days. The lost hope. The beatings. Then he thought of his times on the street, begging, because he did not realise there were opportunities. He looked into each boy's eyes and then realised the truth. "I broke free when I realised that I must be my own master. Not until I worked to make myself a true man, and learn all I could, did I set myself free."

"A man cannot set himself free."

"You can," Ayan nodded. "You can. You stand up one day and say, I am a man."

"I am a man," the smallest boy chirped happily.

The tension eased from Malik's shoulders. His compassion overrode his common sense. Ayan knew his friend could not bring himself to make the first move, to release the boys.

"Okay, think about what we have told you,"Ayan said with a laugh. He reached out to pat the dark-skinned boy to his left on the shoulder. The lad smiled up at him.

A flash of gold caught Ayan's eye. A locket from the shop's jewel case peeked out from under the boy's collar.

Ayan tore the locket from the boy's neck, breaking its chain. "Thief," he growled. "Malik, look at this." His anger made it almost impossible to speak. How easily this boy conned him, playing the innocent while planning to steal away with the locket.

"No," the boy panicked, "No!" He lunged for the locket. "Give that back! It is mine!"

Malik stepped to Ayan's side. Malik studied the locket and shook his head. He bit the locket. "Not one of ours, my friend. This is precious gold."

"Mine," the boy cried. "Mine. It is all I have."

"It is his," the oldest boy whispered.

"How?" Ayan looked at both boys. "You expect me to believe that you have hid this from Scour?"

The boys nodded. "For a long time," the oldest said boldly.

"A long time," the second chimed.

A hot wave of embarrassment swept Ayan's body. "No, look at it. I ordered these in the winter. They came with drawings of horses."

Ayan snapped open the locket, expecting to be met by an image of a horse.

Instead, he was surprised to see a pretty English woman on one side, and the strong dark features of an Indian man facing her. The woman wore a pretty summer dress. The man wore a tunic top like every Bengali man Ayan had ever met.

"Where did you get this locket, boy?"

"My mother gave it to me. Please, do not take it away. It is all I have left of my mother and father."

Ayan's fist closed over the locket. His eyes closed as he tried to regain control of his emotions. Here was a boy who could be his son. The similarities in circumstance were uncanny. When Ayan opened his eyes again, the other boys had left.

"So this is your mother?"

The boy shrugged. "She died couple of years ago. Been on my own since then."

"And your father?"

"I don't know much. Only what my mother told me. She said he was a tall man with large hands and kind eyes. He came from the other side of the world and travelled on a ship. He escaped when the ship caught fire, here in London. My mother said he gave her the locket after I was born. She knew I was his kid 'cause of my skin colour. She wanted them to be together, but he died."

"I am sorry to hear that. You know his name?"

"Amar." The boy said confidently.

Ayan couldn't recall an Amar from The Bengal, although that was not surprising. He smiled inside, happy that other Lascar's had benefitted from what he and Akbar had done that night.

Ayan pulled the boy closer. The boy resisted for a moment, then drew into Ayan's warmth.

"Your father was a brave man. And what is your name, boy?"

"Arthur. It's what most people called my father, too."

"Arthur. It is a good name. Well, Arthur; will you come inside for some tea? When did you last eat?"

"Not so long ago. I can look after myself."

"I am sure of that," said Ayan. "It is just that your father and I are very similar. If our situation was reversed, I would want him to look out for my son. I am sure he would want me to do the same."

"I guess so," said Arthur.

"I am Ayan, and my good friend is Malik. Come inside. Malik keeps special treats in a drawer."

"Do you have peppermint? My mother gave me peppermints when I was little."

"I do believe we have peppermint. Do you like stories? I can tell you stories of far off places where women wear beautiful silks that flow like water. There are elephants there and mountains that touch the sky."

"Ok then, for a short while. I am little hungry."

Ayan gestured to Arthur that he should follow him into the shop. He led the way through the rows of tables full of bright fabrics, and through the heavy cloth that divided the store from the living area. Ayan and Malik shared two rooms in the rear of the store. A door led out to the back alley. To the right, bunk beds lined one wall. Two trunks were slotted under the lower bed. A wood-slab table and two chairs fit on the opposite wall and a stove sat neatly in the corner.

Malik opened the door to let the morning air into the room. The aroma of a pungent tea filled the room, mixing delightfully with cornmeal and fruit mixed biscuits. Ayan signalled for Arthur to take the chair closest to the stove. He set out two china tea cups, complete with their saucers. A small pot of jam and a pat of butter finished the tea.

Ayan lay out the warmed biscuits while Malik poured thick milk into a mug. The boy stared hungrily at the frothy, warmed drink. Ayan sprinkled a light veil of cinnamon on top and set the drink on the table. Arthur stared at it for several moments while Ayan poured the tea. He took the opposite chair. Malik sat on the lower bed.

"Do you like milk?" Malik asked.

Little Arthur's eyes widened. "Mother gave me milk in the morning."

"Enjoy," Ayan smiled

Ayan watched Arthur as the milk slid down his throat, the gulps long and drawn out as the boy tried to make the good taste flow over his tongue as long as possible. Ayan poured some tea in his saucer and blew on it to cool it. Malik also used his saucer to drink his tea.

"Mother said drinking tea from a saucer is the old way," Arthur said when he stopped for a breath.

Both men smiled at the innocent rudeness. The boy's voice shook with uncontrolled emotion when he mentioned his mother.

Ayan put a big spoonful of fruit jelly on a biscuit and passed it to the boy. He wolfed the food down and licked his fingers. Malik pulled some cornmeal and couscous pudding from the pot, poured milk on it and set two bowls on the table.

"More?" Arthur's head tilted slightly, suddenly cautious.

"Eat." Malik pushed the bowl closer to the boy.

"I do not have money to pay for this." His hand touched the bowl to push it away.

"You do not need to fear anymore. I will take care of you."

"Why would you do that? Why should I believe you?"

"Because your father and I are the same," said Ayan. "My child was taken from me. Now Allah has blessed me with the chance to be a father once again. This I truly believe."

"Scour said he was my father." The boy said uncertainly.

"Scour is not your father. He is a bad man who does bad things. If you stay with me and Malik, he will not bother you again. I promise you."

Arthur said nothing. He pulled the pudding bowl closer and slowly starting eating.

"Just think about it Arthur. You can work with us here in the shop. We could do with a strong pair of hands, isn't that right,

Malik?"

Ayan realised he had been making promises that Malik might not agree with. He smiled at his friend, hoping that he felt the same way.

"Of course, my friend. We were only saying the other day how we were struggling with some of the heavy cloths. Ayan is so strong, but I have a weak back."

"You see, Arthur? You don't need to do those bad things for Scour. You can work with us, and I am sure we can fit another bed in here."

Ayan subtly nodded to Malik, pleased that his friend had not disagreed with his proposal.

"I...I could think about it. I don't know..."

"Don't pressure the boy, Ayan. We were just chatting nicely before you put all these thoughts in his young mind," said Malik.

"I am sorry, Arthur. I do not mean to pressure anyone. Please, tell us more about your mother."

Arthur seemed to relax.

"Mother sewed for fine ladies. They paid this much for a pair of lace gloves." Arthur drew coins on the table to represent the payment. "I grew older and she became sick. That is when she took me to my grandfather. They lived in a big house, bigger than anything I've ever seen. He started shouting at mother, something about her taking advantage of his generosity and that he should have kept her at the house, instead of letting her live in London. He wanted me to go to the kitchen and mother grew angry. She said she would never darken his door again. Grandmother said the church turned its back on me, but I don't know what that means. I never go to church now. They make me stand at the back. When I went with mother they gave us a bench near the front."

Ayan sighed silently to himself, thinking about Arthur, and also what his own child would have been exposed to.

"When mother died, I was sent to Grandpapa and

Grandmamma, but they didn't like me. I hated working in the kitchen."

"They really made you work in the kitchen?" Malik shook his head in disbelief.

"Grandpapa said I might become a house servant if I polished my manners. I liked the jolly boys in the stable better. They told jokes and were great fun. I stayed there until I got old enough to survive on my own. Then I left."

"Why?" Malik asked before another uncomfortable silence filled the room.

"A gentleman came into the kitchen one day. He laughed at me and said I didn't belong, called me a bastard, he did. I was takin' none of that so I popped him one. Right on the chin." Arthur smiled boldly. "Grandpapa told me I should be grateful for my cousins and that I needed to learn my place. He sent me out with the groundskeeper who cuffed me a good one. I spit on the ground and walked right out of there. T'is more than a man can take, having his own blood treating him as if he was nothing."

"I can imagine the trouble you caused." Malik chuckled as the boy told his story.

"I pulled some ripe capers. I stole an egg a day for Molly. She scrubbed the pots with steel wool every day. Cook hated her and made her work through meals often. I slipped her an egg when I brought wood in. Cook pinched my ear and hit me with a spoon but I didn't care. I didn't care about none of 'em. 'Cause the shade of my skin, they treated me as if I was nothing."

An old anger boiled deep in Ayan's soul. The grandparents treated Arthur with the same disdain that Phoebe's parents had treated him. And worse still, they probably treated his child in the same way. The feeling coated his mouth with a bitter taste, as the parallel stories reopened old wounds. Ayan bit his lip, and held the anger where it lay.

"And so how did you end up here?" asked Malik, clearly

intrigued by the boys precociousness.

"I headed for the docks when I got to London. Figured if my father worked the ships, then maybe it's in my blood. I was fine for a week or so, but then Scour found me and made me one of his gang. You don't get no choice if he says that's how it is. He beat me a few times at the start, said I was useless and I had better start paying my way, or he'll replace me. I saw him replace another boy, a little while after. Me and Henry had to get rid of the body."

Malik shook his head. "It should not surprise me that we treat people so badly. But still I can't believe a child is rejected by his family, or exploited by criminals. What a world we live in, Ayan."

"Well, from now on you will stay with me, Arthur. You will quickly learn that I do not treat people that way. For I am a man, a man of..."

As Ayan's eyes met those of Arthur, all he could see was his own son.

"Ok then, "said Arthur, "I'll give it a go. Gotta be better than sharing a room with all those other boys. And I ain't that good at stealing anyway."

A powerful force swamped Ayan. He felt aggrieved and grateful in equal measure. Aggrieved because of all he had lost, grateful because of all he gained. Tears flowed unabashed down his cheeks. The tears cooled the hot bitterness upon his tongue as they passed his smiling lips.

* * *

Lady Achala entered Ayan's thoughts. He saw her sitting upon her chair, that knowing look upon her face. Her smile mocked him. Eyes flashing, she took a bite of sweet fruit and nodded her approval. No doubt she had passed away, leaving countless people to live on, each one grappling with her predictions.

Ayan smiled. He no longer grappled with her words or her wisdom. Lady Achala told him the truth. His logic had not decided whether the woman was psychic or not. Akbar and his brother died before they became men. Mr Jennings ruled his house with a quiet but firm hand, but despite a solid head for business, he never learned how to stand tall like a man. Mr Jennings was nothing without his business. Mr Hillary was nothing without his title. The Cruel One, nothing without his whip. None of these men lived long enough to understand what it meant to be a man.

Ayan Miah was a modest man, but he was a man, indeed.

CHAPTER 25

The summer breeze promised a gentle season. Ayan longed for a warm period to ease his aching back. He worked hard, but slow. Arthur took the brunt of work, moving the tables and fetching crates from the docks.

Malik and Arthur made a perfect team. Together they defied the shippers to short them, add fees, or bilk a bit of their cargo. They arrived back from the docks chatting about their latest find.

"Pardon me, sir." A well-dressed footman stood at the door. "Lady Winthrop to fetch her silks."

Ayan did not expect to find Lady Winthrop outside in the carriage. He accompanied the footman to the Winthrop manor to show swatches to the Duchess. Ayan put the silks in a box and wrapped it with lace. The footman took the box without comment and left the shop. Ayan didn't have room in his heart for anger or bitterness. He smiled at the footman's petty arrogance. There were more important things to live for than pride. Ayan went back to work, certain that the Duchess would call upon him again. He would grace her private parlour, using the skills he honed in prison to work his way into her good graces and earn enough respect to win sales that in the past would have gone to a white merchant.

"Salams, brother," Malik cried as the back door swung open.

"Pops," Arthur cried out the colloquial term learned from the American soldiers. Ayan smiled to himself. He felt warmth inside whenever Arthur called him that.

"Pops, you should have seen the Portman's face when I compared the manifests and found an error. He was so shocked to learn that I could count."

Ayan moved toward the rear of the store. He bowed politely to the women milling about the fabrics as he passed.

"You look good." Malik smiled.

"I feel better," Ayan said, flexing his broad shoulders. Time had worn away the strength, but not the breadth of his shoulders. "The weather agrees with you, too."

"I do feel younger. Must be this pup."

"A pup no longer." Arthur laughed as he flexed a youth's tightly muscled arm. "I'm taller this summer. I'll match you soon."

Ayan laughed at the boast and went into the small kitchen and poured tea into three translucent china cups. He placed a silver holder on the table which held three small crystal holders that contained salt, pepper and a small mustard pot. The warmed-over fish looked good with a citrus glaze. The current buns were warming on the stove.

"You are pensive." Arthur remarked.

Ayan looked up and smiled. "There is too much to do, too many jokes to exchange -"

"Many drinks to share," Malik chimed in.

"Meals to be devoured," Arthur sang.

"Walks to be taken." Ayan played his part.

"And futures to be dreamed," they all chimed in together.

"Too true, but I know you, Pops. There is something disturbing you."

Ayan smiled. "I think of Kazi lately. I turn expecting to see him standing behind me. I explore every avenue and do not believe I am developing a weakness of the mind. I do not know any reason for my melancholy. It seems that Kazi's spirit moves among us. Signs and reminders spring up everywhere." Ayan patted Arthur nose. "I hear him when you snore."

He looked down at his rounding middle. "Kazi's middle hung in a particularly absurd lump as if someone tied a loose sack around his neck. The skin hung from his body as if a perverse joke placed a large man inside a boy's body."

"A little less sweet meats and tarts will cure your middle," Malik taunted.

"It is not I who visits the market," Ayan defended himself. Despite his reverie about Kazi's presence, the truth remained that he simply did not know if Kazi resided among the living or had joined their father and mother.

Ayan studied Arthur. The boy lay on the brink of manhood. A thin shadow suggested a beard. The eyes promised intelligence.

"You cannot protect the child forever. The boy needs to know about his homeland, and what life is like there." Malik sipped his tea.

"I must close the store." Ayan returned to the front of the store. He did not like Malik's ability to read his mind. He moved around the tables tidying the piles and refolding the articles the customers left in a heap. He lit a lamp before he finished tidying the store and locked the door. He did not want to recount his life, but felt it was his duty to do so at some stage. There would never be a right time, so maybe now was as good a time as ever.

Ayan followed Arthur and Malik into the backroom and took a seat.

"I was a Lascar as my father before me and like your father was, too." Ayan began. A silence settled over the room as he continued. "My father drowned when his ship sank in a storm. My mother died shortly after that. My brother Kazi and I were committed to an orphanage." Ayan told of the dream that signalled the first change in his life, of snake charmers and elephants, Rajahs and the docks. He talked of the "little mother" who tossed sweet breads when they danced beneath her window in the dead of night.

Ayan leaned back in the chair. The lamp flickered. His eyes closed. The dank scent of the rice patch filled his nose. He talked of snakes in the bush and the purple mountain tops that ringed the world he knew. Arthur listened intently as Ayan described defending the betel nut tree from thieves. Malik listened closely when Ayan spoke of his encounter with Lady Achala.

Late into the evening, the trio sat as Ayan recounted his story.

He described standing by the table at the docks, waiting for his name to be called. It amazed him how clearly he recalled life aboard The Bengal. Ayan held nothing back. Emran's achievements became noble. Akbar, a loving brother, revenged his death. He described The Cruel One. He retold the escape, waiting under the dock, the rifle shot and treading water that was tinged with the blood of his friend.

Farook became a catalyst which defined the difference between greed and friendship. He preserved Louisa's angelic voice and her insatiable lust for life. It took some time to tell about life with the Jennings'. He had become a different man. He chose his words carefully, making sure that Arthur understood that Christmas gifts, warm beds, good meals, and favour of another man is only the illusion of success and life. Ayan carefully expressed the difference between surviving and thriving.

His heart took over and gave tribute to Phoebe's life. Each precious moment, in delicate detail, celebrated her life. The words needed no narration or embellishment to express the divine nature that made his bride larger than life. Ayan spoke softly as he recalled finding the note from Mr Hillary, and the resulting court appearance.

Arthur sat mesmerised. The wonderful stories about Bengal could be about his own father, and Phoebe could easily be his mother. The sad ending to the tale mirrored his own story to some extent. How strange that fate had brought everyone together. Arthur knew very little about Amar's life before London. His mother always said that Amar told her that his life didn't begin until the day they met. The only detail he did know was that Amar, like Ayan, was originally from Sylhet.

"And when I returned here, after my spell in prison, I was fortunate enough to meet Malik. Allah smiled on me that day. And again when I met you, Arthur. I may not know about my child by blood, but you have been like a son to me. A son any man would be proud to speak of."

“Don’t be all soppy on me, Pops. You and Malik have been like family. You treat me like a son, and I respect you like a father. Malik, on the other hand; you are more like a jolly old uncle,” chuckled Arthur.

“I thought as much,” laughed Malik. “You always make fun of me. I dread to think what you two say about me when I am not here.”

The light-hearted ribbing eased the slightly tense situation. Ayan was glad that he had finally told Arthur how much he meant to him. Arthur’s response had reciprocated those feelings in his own special way.

“Are you to live all your life,” said Arthur, “without returning to your home and your family?”

Ayan and Malik traded sober glances. “You can count on Arthur to jump straight onto a different subject, eh Ayan,” said Malik.

The dawn’s sun had turned the room a pale grey. Without realising it, the men had talked the night away.

“Do you want to return home?”

“It is something we have discussed many times,” Malik ventured without looking at the boy. “It is an expensive journey. It will take at least two more years before we have the funds to embark on such a trip.”

“Why don’t you go put a sign out front?” said Ayan. He gave Arthur a pat on the knee.

Arthur rose to his feet and asked, “And what is the sign supposed to say?”

“A weekend sale,” said Ayan, scratching his chin as he thought it over. “Fifteen percent, off all items.”

“A sale? It is not a holiday? How do we earn the money to make an expensive journey if we offer our wares at a discount?” Arthur’s brow furrowed.

“Ah.” Ayan smiled. “I will teach you the ways of business. I did not waste those years looking over Mr Jennings’ shoulders. I know ways to encourage the whites to part with their coin."

"Twenty percent discount," said Malik, displaying his support.

"I do not understand." Arthur shook his head.

"Better a nimble pence than a slow crown." Ayan smiled at his son.

"Yes." Malik nodded, tapping his colleague on the elbow. "Twenty is good."

"Great journeys begin with one step," Ayan said. "Allah willing."

"A man might buy three tickets to travel comfortably if we sold the store."

"Sell the store?"

"We have no need of it if we return home." Ayan waited a moment for Malik to consider selling the store. "Enough for three tickets and enough to engage in a business enterprise when we return home."

"When you return home, do you have a plan?" Malik asked.

Ayan's eyes travelled around the room. Pale china cups with vivid roses lined a shelf on the wall. Rare silks and "up and coming" novelties waited in the store. Chinese lamps hung above the counters. "I made a plan many years ago. A rice store with exotic treasures from around the world. My brother and I talked about selling rare teas and fine rice to important merchants."

"There are many rare curiosities in our store," remarked Malik. "Not all needs to be sold. Some can travel home with us."

Ayan nodded. "There are plenty of wares to stock the store for a new owner, and to ship home, to build a new business."

"A tea store is a good investment."

"Yes and selling good rice. Women will walk a long distance to purchase good rice."

"A man may be considered wealthy if important men travel a great distance to drink tea in his shop."

"A man may be considered wealthy indeed." Ayan nodded.

"And your brother?" Malik's voice rang hollow.

"Kazi," Ayan whispered. "I will still hope that he waits on the front step, longing for my return."

"And if he is not?"

Ayan turned to Malik; sure the man's words hid his true meaning.

"What are you asking?"

"I wondered," Malik swallowed. "Can enough wealth be earned from a tea store that serves rich teas from china cups and sells fine rice amid rare silks? Can enough wealth be earned to share three ways."

Ayan stood. "Come, brother." He reached out his left hand.

The men clasped left hands, the universal signal for eternity.

"Do not fear." Ayan smiled. "I may have lost one brother. I will not risk losing another."

Malik stood and smiled. "Come, brother. It is time to go home."

CHAPTER 26

Ayan awoke early. Today was the day. He rose quickly and dressed. His days of shivering in the cold English mornings would soon be over. Within months, he would again bask beneath the sun and walk through the jungle's shadows.

"Albert." He turned to see why his son didn't answer. The young man's cot was already empty and rolled against the wall. "Arthur?" Ayan looked around.

Malik still slept. Ayan decided to let the old man rest a little longer. He had not been healthy lately. Arthur spared Malik the heavy work. Ayan did the cooking so Malik could rest after tending the shop.

The shop had grown way beyond their expectations. Not only did they sell it for a good price, they had learned enough about trade with Eastern India to ensure their future once they returned home.

Arthur opened the door. He wore the beggar's clothing he felt most comfortable in.

"You will not need to dress as a beggar to feel safe when we return to Eastern India."

"Maybe."

"You will be in your home." Ayan stopped wrapping their bedding and turned. "No. You will be among your own people."

Arthur shrugged. "There are rich and poor everywhere. A beggar can travel invisible."

Ayan dressed quickly. They worked together letting Malik sleep. They were almost ready before Ayan walked over to his friend. He shook his shoulder and lifted the blankets.

"Malik, come my friend. It is nearly time to leave."

Ayan stood completely still for several moments, until he turned to Albert with an empty gaze.

"What is wrong?"

"Malik is dead."

"No, this cannot be!" Arthur crossed the room. "Get up, Malik. It is time to go."

Arthur sat down with his head in his hands. They were supposed to ship out today. Their passage paid, their luggage loaded the night before.

"What do we do?"

Ayan shook his head.

"How much will a funeral cost?"

Ayan looked up, startled. "I do not know. I need a shroud."

"Shroud?" Arthur yelled. "Where are we going to buy a shroud at this time of the morning?"

"It is the way,"

"We are going to miss our ship." Arthur paced the room. He walked faster and faster. A few minutes later he stopped dead. "We will leave him here."

"It is not possible. We must help him."

"He is dead!"

"Only his physical body. He is in heaven now."

Arthur continued pacing as Ayan sat and looked at Malik.

"We do not leave our friend."

"We have no choice."

"He must be prepared."

"I thought he had to die in Makkah."

Ayan shook his head as he answered. "Only facing Makkah.

"Awe," Arthur threw up his hands. "No one can talk to you when you get all religious."

"Arthur!"

"I'm leaving."

"Where are you going?"

"It looks like I'm going nowhere," Arthur hissed.

"Son!"

Arthur stamped outside and slammed the door. Ayan sighed. He knew that their ship left in seven hours. He felt helpless.

There would be no hero-stone for his friend. He deserved one. He earned one. Malik's body lay lifeless and calm on the worn-out mattress. Ayan looked around the room. There was nothing left. They had sold everything.

He stood up and fetched a jug and poured some water. Malik's face was placed in the direction facing east, towards Makkah. It was time to purify his friend's body.

He would not sit at the banquet tomorrow. He would not walk to the grave. He would not toss dirt in the grave or say, "We created you from it, and return you into it, and from it we will raise you a second time."

Malik's other friends would walk that journey alone. He was not a relative. He jumped as the door opened.

Arthur walked into the bare room followed by several men. They walked in quietly and looked at the bed in the middle of the room. Ayan knew all of them from the temple. Each man nodded. The men carefully washed Malik's body and wrapped him in a white cloth. Each nodded in approval as they examined the dead man's glow on his face.

Ayan stood still, his mind racing as he struggled to come to terms with what he was thinking. A lump formed in his throat as he said the words without knowing if he meant what he was saying.

"Arthur, go without me." His mind screamed that if he remained then he would suffer the same fate as his friend. It was his duty to care for Malik. He looked up at Arthur.

"No," Arthur shouted. "You must come. We planned this for years."

"Your friend would not want you to stay," replied a long-time customer and friend.

"I should be here. I am all the family he has. It is my duty."

"That is not true," an elder contradicted.

"He has us," a small woman smiled. "We will take good care of him."

"Pops," Arthur begged.

"What is this?" A large voice boomed.

Everyone turned to face the landlord.

"I told you to be out by early morn."

"There has been a death in the family," Malik's only other friend replied.

"That isn't my affair," the grubby-looking English man snapped. He spat on the floor. "You'll be out in twenty-minutes or I'll have you thrown out."

"Patience –"

"I don't think you heard me." The burly man stood over the smaller Eastern Indian. "Twenty minutes. Or me and my mates will lend a hand."

A silence hung over the room for a moment.

"It appears that we need to move the body," the woman said quietly.

"We will take him to my house." Malik's friend smiled. "He was my friend. As close as two fingers on one's hand. He was a brother."

A few heads nodded in agreement.

Ayan turned to protest as two dark men walked into the room. Each was thin and hungry. They looked around unsure. "We were told that this room was empty."

The second man hesitated, "We already paid our money."

The elder held up his hands. "Rest assured, friend, you have not been robbed. We must take care of our old friend. Once that is done we will leave you to your home."

The men looked at each other.

"I see that you are from Eastern India," the elder continued, his voice friendly and his manner welcoming.

"We finished our three years." One of the new men said. His voice held the truth of the horrors he suffered.

"They did not take us home," the other replied.

"No." The elder shook his head. "Every year, more and more

Lascars are left in England. But, do not fear. You are among friends now." He turned to Ayan. "You see? Allah has made everything work out."

Ayan's head tilted. He looked at the elder, then back to the two men. The elder turned back to the new arrivals. "Will you allow us to prepare the body?" The man pulled two apples from his pocket.

The new men stared at them greedily and nodded. Ayan's stomach turned as they grabbed the fruit. Arthur stepped back. Ayan saw alarm in the boy's face. The boy grew up knowing the Lascar stories. This was the first time he had seen a Lascar straight off the boat.

"You are all Lascars?"

"No," the elder smiled. He pointed to Ayan. "This man is the only one who was a Lascar. Until recently, the only way to leave a British merchant ship was in death or to run."

The men looked up at Ayan and paused. Their eyes registered respect. "You are brave."

Ayan never thought of himself as brave. He did what he needed to survive.

"We must go." Arthur stepped over and nudged Ayan. "It's all right now."

"Ah," the elder smiled. "Is it good to abandon a journey you started? It is a question to be pondered in another lifetime." He took Ayan's elbow. "In this lifetime it is time to take the journey."

Ayan let Arthur lead him out of the house. A few feet away he exchanged goodbyes. His friends reassured him that they would follow the traditional ways.

Ayan walked blindly through the streets of London for the last time. He never felt a twinge of loss at the thought of leaving London forever. The only thing he wanted to take on his journey was the memories of love he had for Phoebe and the great friend that was Malik.

The docks were not as crowded as Ayan expected. They

climbed the gangplank and found their room. It was not a stateroom, but comfortable. Ayan let Arthur take the bottom bunk. He lay on the bed and wondered about death. Ayan thought of his brother and of his past as he stared at the ceiling.

"It will be all right," Arthur interrupted his thoughts.

"We have abandoned a friend to satisfy our own desire," Ayan replied sadly. Arthur smiled. "We did not abandon him. Everyone else is with him."

"It was my duty."

They looked out of the grimy porthole together. One last look at London. So many bad memories being left behind, yet Ayan had found true love here. Arthur by his side would always be a reminder of all that was good about his time in England.

"I tell you one thing. I will not mind leaving the English behind."

"We are in agreement on that."

"We will be home soon," Ayan promised.

"I will like living in a country where men do not need to work from sunrise to sunset for a few pence or where men do not judge you for the colour of your skin." Albert said with excitement.

"Men must work everywhere. A lazy man is soon ruined."

"You made life on your farm sound like easy work," Arthur said. Ayan smiled.

CHAPTER 27

Arthur savoured the salty taste. The sea air cleared his mind and England's harsh memories faded into the same, dark fog that swirled in the ship's wake. The red dawn capped the waves with a myriad of colours. Only the ship marred the morning's beauty.

Arthur smiled. It was too perfect a morning to ruin with words. He didn't want to ask questions, but one burned in his heart. "Will Eastern India be the same?"

Ayan looked at his son and frowned.

"What if things are different?" Arthur challenged.

"Eastern India will never change," Ayan said firmly.

"What if everything is changed?"

"Eastern India has not changed in thousands of years."

"All British colonies change," Arthur said matter-of-factly."The ways of England are the ways of the world."

Ayan turned. "It is strange hearing you quote English sayings."

"It is true." Arthur shrugged.

"And you know this to be a fact, how?"

"Everyone knows it. Isn't all of Eastern India an English colony?"

Ayan smiled. "Not if the English built their colony for five hundred years. Eastern India is a vast land of jungles and mountains. A man could travel a lifetime and never reach every corner."

Ayan spread his hands wide. "England is a very small country. There are cities in Eastern India that are bigger than England."

Arthur leaned over the railing and looked into the water.

"The world is a great place," he said lazily. "We do not even need to go to Eastern India. We have enough money to live comfortable anywhere in the world."

Ayan frowned but did not look at Arthur. He gave the boy time to finish his thoughts.They stood silent for several minutes.

"You have experience as a seaman."

"Of course, Arthur."

"You could help us get hired on a merchant ship."

"Why?"

"We have our whole lives to live. It would be a sad thing to be one of the few people in Eastern India who knew the opportunities available on every port, but never to be bold enough to grasp them."

"It is not good to abandon your faith to chase your desires." Ayan's lips pinched. He had the look of a man deep in conflict.

"A merchant seaman can explore the world while being paid."

"Lascars sign for pay but are never paid."

"I've seen that myself," Arthur smiled. "Merchant seamen are different."

"Merchant seamen are white."

Arthur shook his head and laughed. "Look around you. The men on this ship are all colours." He paused for effect, "And well fed."

Ayan turned slightly. The nearest sailor was a Nubian. He grinned at Ayan as he wound rope into a neat bundle. Ayan nodded politely. The Nubian grinned wider.

"Why is there a rush to return to Eastern India?"

"I am an old man," Ayan sighed. "I need to return home before I die."

Arthur started to laugh and then stopped. It was as if the words opened his eyes for the first time. Ayan was old. His weathered face looked over the sea. Scarred hands hung loosely over the rail. Only his muscles remained hard as steel – and the hard, determined look in his eye.

He wondered what it meant to be old. Ayan still did a full day's work. Malik did not appear to be older than Ayan, despite spending the last few years as a frail man. Arthur tried to compare Ayan and Malik. Ayan was cut from steel. Malik was the son of wealthy people and never bore the same constitution.

"I do not see an old man when I look at you," he said honestly. Ayan's grin betrayed his feelings on the subject.

"I feel old."

Arthur felt a pang of fear. "Are you well, Pops?"

Ayan put a hand on his Arthur's shoulder. "I am well. It is just that old bones hurt in the morning. Some days it takes a lot of effort to rise from my bed."

* * *

The crew fell into a slow rhythm that matched the waves the ship rolled over. Silence fell over the morning. A silence Ayan had long forgotten. Years ago, in his distant memories, he remembered the soothing effect as the deep green jungle fell silent when the night chased the sun over the mountains. The purple evening held an almost tangible stillness.

The ease that their steamship cut through the waves reminded him of that moment. The fifty-man crew seemed caught in the spell. Not even the gulls followed them into the blue horizon. Ayan studied the edge of the world, where the sky melded with the ocean in a glossed haze. He smiled. It would be easy to shout with joy and run, as he once done as a young man.

Time took its toll on Ayan. His muscles did not rejoice at the thought of racing through the jungle. He settled deeper into the coarse sacks and enjoyed the morning with an understanding and solidarity that evaded him when he was a younger man.

It seemed impossible that this ocean with its power and beauty gave birth to his old nightmare, the miasma of fear and horror where the water filled a sinking ship, taking Ayan's father away from him forever. Today, the sea held no horror.

The days settled into a steady rhythm. The waves marked time. Ayan felt more relaxed as each day passed. He did not realise how tight and worn life in England had made him. With each day a little of the stiffness seemed to leave his body, until after about a week he woke feeling refreshed and young. He lay in the coarse net bed as it rocked in the belly of the ship. The good sleep had enabled vivid dreams to manifest themselves in the night. Dreams about his previous life in the belly of the steamship. Voices from the past echoed in his mind, as vividly as if they were in some distant corner of the ship. Ayan rose to escape the unpleasant memories.

He strode easily up the wooden stairs toward the night sky. His legs had strengthened as the days passed, and he did not need to steady himself as he rose from the ship's dark belly. The stars covered the sky like a bride's lace veil. It had been a lifetime since Ayan saw more than a few glimpses of the sky between the thick trail of smoke which hung over London's lower side. He didn't notice the cold as he stared hard at the sky. He was almost afraid to blink, fearful that the stars would disappear and he would, once again, be in the slums of England, or the bowels of the Lascar ship.

He didn't block out the memories tonight. He let them slip through his fingers. It felt like the stars were pulling the dark tangles from his soul and casting them to the ocean.

He let the fear grow. It brought back the faces of his mother and father. It flowed through him like water, making him feel strong. He looked at his worn, wrinkled hands. They did not look stronger. This was a different strength; the same as the ocean possessed, invisible on the surface, but hiding in the depths was something that would never be harnessed. No white man, no whip, would ever possess the power to control this strength. His body shivered, though his heart warmed.

"Pops?"

Ayan turned. Arthur stood behind him, shivering. He looked around the deck, bewildered. Ayan smiled and touched the railing beside the spot where he leaned. Arthur stood close. Ayan leaned in close, protecting him from the breeze.

"Why are you on deck?"

"I remembered a day when I was a young man."

"In Eastern India?"

Ayan nodded. "Eastern India is a land of mystery. It is ancient. Not like England."

Arthur leaned forward. "I dream."

Something in the boy's voice caught Ayan's attention. He waited. Arthur bit his lip but did not continue. "It is better to speak of the things that trouble you. Pain turns to poison when hidden in your heart."

"I know, Pops."

"You have grown into a strong man. A son any man would be proud to call his own." Ayan took a deep breath. "In the last few days, you seemed like the lost boy who caused so much trouble in the few first months after we found you."

Ayan smiled at the embarrassed look that crossed the boy's face. He let the silence engulf them as they stood and watched the stars. The steamship cut effortlessly through the waves. Ayan wondered at the boy. His life held far more promise than his ever had.

Arthur leaned forward and looked at the water. "Do you have dreams?" He took a deep breath. "Dreams that are so real you feel they would drain your life away if you didn't wake up."

Ayan stood silent, watching his knuckles turn white. "I," his mind went blank. No words would come. He was the boy's father. He must talk honestly. "I dream. I have horrid dreams. Some there are nights when I believed I had died. Some nights, I wish, I had."

Arthur stared with wide eyes. He nodded slowly.

"When I was young, I dreamed that I was trapped below a ship. I could not escape the dark prison that was nothing more than just a long narrow space. Water flooded in." Ayan stopped. The breeze blew his damp hair into his face. He stood shivering. A seaman walked the deck behind, intent on his duties. Ayan's heart sank.

"I understand now, my son. You will not follow me to Eastern India."

Arthur looked up. A haunted look shadowed his eyes.

"This is your dream? This is the nightmare that haunts you?"

Arthur's mouth pinched. He nodded his head slightly.

"Then we must ensure that you escape your nightmare." Ayan wanted Arthur to know that he would help him avoid a life of suffering, no matter what the personal cost. He said the words slowly, a promise to himself that he would not condemn Arthur to several lifetimes at the bottom of society.

"I do not want to anger you, Pops."

"I do not want you to suffer because I am afraid of hearing. You are a man now. It is time for you to make your own decisions."

"Even if they pull us apart?"

"Even if they pull us apart," Ayan repeated.

* * *

Arthur sighed. "That is the problem. You've been so many places, and seen so many things, but you've never experienced them. You've never ... I do not know how to say it." He stared across the ocean.

Ayan saw a flash of passion that reminded him of Phoebe. He bit his lip to maintain his composure.

"You do not know how to live," Arthur said. "Really live. You are alive. It is not the same."

"You seek wealth?"

"No," Arthur shook his head. "It is not about wealth and pleasure. It is more. I do not know how to explain it."

"Phoebe tried to explain." Ayan watched the red sun snake over the black water. "She took me to see art and museums. She'd sit in the park and paint life. One day she painted a family. She said she captured life. I just saw a park."

Arthur put a hand on Ayan's shoulder. "Life has been hard for you. I do not expect you to understand. You've never wanted anything except to go home."

"Home is a good place," Ayan defended.

"I am sure it is. But, it is too ancient. And it is not my home." His hand spread across the waves. "There are new lands out there. The colonies. They say that it is a new world where any man can 'make do himself.' "

"Any white man," Ayan corrected.

"There are opportunities for us too. In the new world ... slavery is against the law. A white man must pay for the wages of a dark man." He turned. "An educated man who can write is respected. He can work and earn good money. He does not need to be an indentured servant working for a master."

Ayan shook his head at such nonsense.

"You could be your own man in the new country. Paid to teach the things you know. You could write a story and have it published in the newspaper."

Ayan laughed, "Arthur, you are dreaming. You have your mother's passion and her wish to chase the clouds. There is no happy life beyond the horizon. You will not find anything different in the colonies. You will be treated the same as you are here. As a servant. As a Lascar."

Arthur sighed. "Pops. It is the chasing that makes life worth living. It doesn't matter where you are. You made a good life for yourself in Eastern India, as a servant, in the slums. You made life good for everyone around you."

"I worked hard."

"No one denies that. I appreciate it. But you have another life. You can teach what you learned from your white family. You can teach people how to read."

"Who do I teach? No rich man will hire me to tutor his heir. No college will hire me." Ayan shook his head. "You do not think these things through."

"And you do not explore the world. You have a chance to be someone. In America anyone can set up a school for rich or common worker's children. You can find a place where Lascars live and start a school there."

Ayan's head snapped back. "No one would let me teach the poor how to read and write."

"Why not?" Arthur's exasperated sigh ended in a woeful gasp. He shook his head. "The new world does not run on the rules set by the old. All a man needs is the courage needed to take what he wants."

"Take it?"

"Fight for it." Arthur explained. "Nothing happens if a man doesn't make it happen. That is the only difference between a rich man and a poor man. A rich man does not accept the dictates of another. He makes his dreams come true."

"It is not always a good idea to make your dreams come true."

Arthur paused. "Do you know what happens if a man doesn't work to make a dream come true?"

Ayan's head shook slightly.

Arthur stepped away from the rail. "Nothing." He put a hand on his Ayan's shoulder. "That is what happens if a man does not use what he has to make something better - nothing."

"I would not say that." Ayan said softly.

Arthur shook his head. "So what are you going to do? Are you going to travel to Eastern India, build a hut and eat rice for the rest of your life?" Arthur looked hard at his father. "Your life hasn't changed at all. You are the same man who lived under the betel nut tree."

"What change should I have? What should I be chasing?"

"Everything. Anything. Phoebe showed you so much beauty and love. She opened a whole world to you. You should wish to be a better man just to honour her memory."

"I honour her every day in my prayers."

"The old way."

"Do not scoff. Have a care."

Arthur held out his hands. "My hands, I see. I believe my hands. My strength, I see. I believe in my strength. You've spent years in prison. Your most dearest died while you were in jail.

Did Allah free you from the steamship? Did prayers heal your brother?"

"NO!" Ayan yelled. His chest heaved. "You speak of things you do not understand. You speak as if I was not given strength, wisdom, and life. You speak as if life happened by mere chance."

"There is more than belief."

"There is more to the balance of life than a man's strength."

"You cannot have one without the other," Arthur recited blandly.

"I have taught you well."

Arthur's tension softened into a half-hearted smile.

"I gave you the strength." Ayan watched the sunrise. "Your strength comes from the things I taught you. The things I learned."

"I know."

"You were lost when you came to me. When we found you."

"I know."

"There is strength in the ancient world you despise. You've never seen it. You've never seen the mountains or stood still as the sunsets silenced the jungle."

"You've never stood and looked through jungle at a temple that is older than the trees. A place where people once worked and played. Where children were born. Where Rajah's ruled."

"You've never stood on an elephant walk as the mighty beasts went to the river for water. You've never looked into a giant's eyes and have it quietly usher a child off the path with the gentle touch of a mother. Arthur, you cannot say that you've lived and known the meaning of life until you build a house and are responsible for everyone in it."

"I am not doubting your wisdom, Pops."

"There is so much for you to learn."

"Be that as it may be. I do not want that life. I do not want to build a home and be trapped for the rest of my life, working hard from sunrise to sunset to feed those who live inside. I want to live life. I want to experience everything there is to experience."

"What could fill your heart more than a home and family?"

Arthur looked around. "Look at these men. They will see new places. Meet people. They can stay on this ship, or choose another one. They can choose to live anywhere they want."

"Can they?" Ayan asked. The hollow sound of his voice stopped Arthur. "Can they?" he asked, suddenly tired.

Ayan turned to the upper deck where several young boys were learning how to use sextants. "Look at those boys. The third and fourth sons of wealthy men." He pointed to one young boy, about seven years old. "That child is learning to be a naval officer because he did not have the luck to be the first boy born into his family. He will live on this ship. When he grows he will be put into the service of the British Crown."

Ayan turned back to Arthur. "He is white. His father is wealthy. This affords him a private place to sleep. An officer's education. Better food than we eat." He put his hand over Arthur's heart. "Have I not offered you more? You have something that boy will never have. I gave you freedom. You must never forget to respect what you have."

"Clear the deck!" A loud voice boomed behind them. Ayan turned.

The seaman's weathered face snarled, "Passengers belong on the aft deck."

"And why is that?" Ayan asked in a soft voice. "Is there a reason why it is important that we move to another part of the ship?"

The man opened his mouth then slammed it shut. He stuck his thumb in the air, indicating the direction he wanted them to go. Ayan and Arthur watched him move down the deck.

"That man is not free. He is a merchant seaman who you respect, but he is not free," Ayan whispered. "He barks orders like a jungle bird, with the same understanding." Ayan turned and leaned over the railing again.

“I figured.” Arthur crossed to the aft deck with the other passengers.

Ayan remained where he was, unmolested by the seamen. He did not understand why Arthur did not see the truth. In Eastern India Arthur would eat when he wanted. He would choose when and where he would sleep. If he wanted to be a wealthy man, with a beautiful young wife, he would only need to work harder than the men who were not wealthy. Arthur was educated. He could even become a town elder if he chose.

Ayan did not see anything on the steamship that he wanted. The men were paid. They worked on the deck. They were white. But, they were still Lascars.

CHAPTER 28

The Moorish port was unbridled chaos. Stacks of goods littered the docks, as men moved around everywhere like worker ants. Some piled crates two or three high, while a steady procession lined up and carted them off to who knows where.

Ayan had never seen men like these. They were dark, with black hair and piercing eyes. They wore long robes and moved with the grace of animals. They were civilised – but they were as fierce as the sun overhead and as dangerous as the cliffs that lined the coastline.

The passengers were herded off the ship with very little of the respect they had been given onboard. The captain had fulfilled his duty. He had delivered the passengers, and it was clear that he felt no more responsibility for them.

Ayan stood on the dock, patiently waiting for the local government to process their paperwork. He could taste the salt in the air and it tasted just as sour as it did in London. Arthur shuffled anxiously nearby, his eyes taking in everything.

Casablanca stood on the edge of the ocean, like a stain on a bride's dress. Ancient and dirty buildings marred the coastline as far as the eye could see. The heat hit Ayan like a wall, sucking the water from his body. His skin prickled with the heat instantly. The burning sensation became overwhelming.

"Papers."

Ayan pulled out three packets of papers then put one back in his pocket. The official barely looked at the papers for several minutes. Arthur paced impatiently.

"What are they waiting for?"

Ayan shushed him. "Patience."

"Incompetent-"

"Patience. It is how things are done."

"There is no need to make us wait."

"They believe there is."

"This one." The official flicked Ayan's papers across the desk. "You are not English. Why do you have English papers?"

"I spent many years in England. I obtained English papers to maintain my position."

The man sneered. "Your position?"

Ayan realised the truth would only cause more questions. He let his shoulders drop and took on the old manners of a lower servant. "My master needed me to handle papers and documents."

The official's eyes narrowed. He shrugged, stamped the papers and shoved them across the table.

Ayan picked up the papers and moved past the piles of sacks, cartons and groups of merchant seamen. They passed several Scottish and English sailors with red faces, fierce men with tattooed faces, short men in silks, with yellowish skin and narrow black eyes.

Ayan had never seen such dark-eyed people. Their skin was light. They dressed in long robes and wore turbans, albeit of a different style than Ayan's. The men carried curved swords.

The ancient city closed in. Ayan choked on the heat and the smell.

"How long do we stay here?" Arthur asked as he shouldered his bag, keeping it out of the dust.

"Until we can find a suitable ship to get us out of the port."

"I saw them." Arthur looked over his shoulder. "The Lascar ships."

Ayan nodded.

"They say that an English ship can only have twenty-five percent Lascar workers."

Ayan held his tongue.

"They say that a Lascar is paid well, and freed after three years."

Ayan fixed his eyes on a group of tables ahead. Tables and

food usually meant an inn of some sort.

"Father."

"Arthur." Ayan realised he had been ignoring Arthur.

"Why don't we travel on another steamship?"

"There are certain laws for travelling on different steamships. It was difficult for us to secure passage on the one we took to get here. We can't change to another ship easily. There are laws for white men and no law for us darkies. That's what we are in their eyes – slaves. We have to make our own sacrifices to obey their law." Ayan put his bundle down.

"What is written on a white man's piece of paper is for their law. I saw this many times working as a gentleman's servant. They write up long papers to protect their wealth from law. It does not reflect what happens."

"They have to obey the law."

"Why?" Ayan pointed back to the ships. "Why? Are you going to make them? Will you tell them to feed the Lascars? Will you tell them not to trade Lascar slaves in the Bahamas for black slaves to take to countries where it is still legal?"

"It is not right," Arthur said.

"Much of this life is not right." Ayan shook his head and looked down at the ground. "I am just saying that it is the wrong time of year to take a steamship around."

"Around where? The Cape of Good Hope?" Arthur said.

"The southern part of Africa. The storms sink many ships. And if you survive the passage, you pray that you make it past the pirates." Arthur picked up his father's bundle.

"We could travel to Cairo, on another steamship, across into the Gulf of Suez and then into the Red Sea. From there a ship can follow the coast to Eastern India," Ayan suggested.

"It sounds like a long journey," said Arthur.

"It will take months."

"We could wait here, Father." The passion left Arthur's voice. "We could, couldn't we? We could find work. In a port like this, there is always a need for merchants." Arthur turned down a street.

"Not that way." Ayan grabbed his arm. "Not that way."

Arthur looked down the narrow street. The buildings were the same reddish sandstone buildings. Arthur looked back at his father and shrugged.

"Slavers." Ayan nodded to a group of men cowering in the recess of a wall, where their street met the main one. These unfortunate souls were looking down at the ground waiting for orders. An Arab man, in a headdress, pushed and shoved two of them down the street.

"The slave markets are that way." He turned and led the other way, without another comment.

* * *

Arthur followed Ayan through the streets. He shoved back when the crowd pushed on him. He wished Ayan would let him take the lead. They would make better time. Ayan waited politely. Arthur never figured out whether Ayan's deep religious beliefs made him passive, or if his extreme politeness was the result of years as a servant.

The bold men with dark skin and fierce eyes suited Arthur better. Their quiet manner belied the fierceness that burned deep in their eyes.

They passed women dressed in flamboyant silks. Their doe eyes made promises that tempted the strongest men. Except, Arthur noticed, his father. Ayan walked past them without noticing.

"There," Ayan motioned to the left.

They walked into the dark inn, which looked exactly like one found in England. Dark wood tables filled the room. Meat roasted on a fire. An old man served ale from a jug. Ayan moved though the tables toward a counter at the back. He waited patiently for the Master of the House to address him.

"Juice," Arthur ordered.

The merchant looked up, but kept wiping glasses. "Don't serve your kind."

"Our kind?" Arthur put two coins on the table. "We just disembarked an English steamship."

"He don't look like no seaman."

"He's..." Arthur looked at his father. "He's a Holy Man."

"Arthur," his father scolded softly.

The innkeeper huffed and put the two glasses he had been cleaning on the counter. He filled them with a thin looking fruit juice. He put down a round loaf of hard-crusted bread and signalled the old man who brought over two thick slices of meat.

"Stay here," the innkeeper said with a nod. "They might not warm to your company. They're from Yemen. "

Arthur looked back at the room. There were seamen all squatting on the floor. The room was dark. A few men looked at Ayan, although he could only see their teeth, and the whites of their eyes. Some whispered murmurs hinted at hostility. Arthur smiled at the innkeeper. "I'll take that to heart."

Ayan ate quickly. Arthur was too excited to eat. He wanted to get into the city and see everything.

"We need a room," Arthur said.

"This is a good place to stay." Ayan replied as he wiped the last bits of meat dripping from his plate.

"We stand out here," Arthur objected. "There are many places where we would fit in. Why stay in an inn where we draw suspicious looks."

Ayan nodded. "Where would you stay?"

"Deeper into the city, until I can find a ship to take us to Cairo. We have nowhere else to go."

Ayan looked down. Arthur knew his father did not feel safe going deeper into this mysterious land. He wanted to take the trade route to Eastern India. A good plan, if they rode a steamship.

"You looking for a berth?"

“Passenger,” Arthur called back without looking over his shoulder.

“Darkies as passengers,” the seaman laughed. “What will they think of next?” Laughter rolled through the room.

Arthur did not rise to the bait. He ignored the insult, more interested in his meal, which he appeared to have finally noticed.

“They will get passage, in the galley of a Barbary pirate ship.” Another roll of laughter burst from the men. Ayan and Arthur smiled to each other. It was hardly the first time they had faced open hostility and this was pretty minor compared to some situations they had endured. They washed down the meat and bread with a second cup of fruit juice, and discussed their next move.

“We should move on. There will be many more places we can stay.”

“Ok, let’s go.” Arthur picked up both their bundles and walked out. He stopped in the street and turned to Ayan.

“It is a shame. It was a clean inn.”

“Why stay where we are not welcome. There are many inns that will welcome us.”

“We need new clothing.” Arthur moved off. “We can find a market deeper in the city.”

Arthur led the way through the streets until they found an area with goods for sale. It appeared that there were no shops in a Moroccan city. All the merchants hawked their wares from tables set against the wall, with a short canopy for shade. Food was sold in the middle. Arthur had never seen such rich foods.

“Arthur,” Ayan cried out excitedly. He had stopped at a cart full of a colourful array of fruit and vegetables. Ayan picked over the pieces, carefully selecting some of questionable quality. He looked up and smiled. “This,” he held up a yellow fruit, “is from Eastern India.”

Arthur watched as Ayan bartered for the food. Several gestures flew in rapid succession before the merchant agreed on a few pence.

Arthur saw the merchant he was looking for and shoved through the crowd. The man behind appeared more dark African Berber than the Arabs that filled the market.

"English?" Ayan asked.

The man stared blankly. This was not going to be easy. Arthur pointed to a couple of people who were dressed in the local custom. Then he pointed at a rail of similar clothes on the stall. The man nodded and moved his hands together in a universal signal for money. Arthur fell into a hand language conversation with the man.

"What are you doing?" Ayan asked.

"Grandpapa taught me," Arthur replied without missing a beat. After a moment the merchant held out two outfits. They were not as grand as the Arabs wore, but they were of better quality than the Berbers. Ayan nodded at Arthur, signally that the clothes were fine enough to gain suitable housing.

He counted out the coins and reached for the clothing. The merchant put his hand on the clothes and signalled for more. Arthur shook his head, no. The merchant shrugged and started to move the clothing back to the rail. Ayan countered by scooping the coins off the table, letting the coins jingle in his hand.

The merchant's eyes narrowed. He grunted a few times, but his eyes never left the money. Arthur added one more coin to the offer and then moved his hand forward. The merchant hesitated. Arthur picked up a very nice dark-blue silk scarf and put it on the pile. He then added one more coin. It was a ploy used by his grandfather many times.

The merchants wanted a certain amount of coin, the amount or type of product might not be as important. Sometimes they were willing to part with more goods in exchange for the extra coins. It worked with this merchant. He grunted and grabbed the money.

Ayan took the clothing and turned to leave. Arthur grabbed his shoulder. He gestured loudly and held up the clothing.

"Do the same. Appear to be happy that you bought these clothes."

"Beautiful," Ayan said in a loud voice.

Arthur praised the goods and held them up until he drew a few glances. He turned back to the merchant and smiled broadly, nodding ever so slightly. Then he bundled everything together and walked slowly away. They cleared the market before Ayan asked why they made a public spectacle.

"What was to stop the merchant from taking our coin and then calling us thieves?"

"That is dishonest," Ayan said.

"It is what it is," Arthur responded. He led them into an alley. "We can change here."

"I wish I could bathe," Ayan sighed. "It has been a long time since I was so filthy."

"We will bathe soon," Arthur promised. "We need suitable accommodation. It is late."

"I do not want to be outside when this city grows dark."

"That would not be wise."

Both men wore a white under tunic that hung to their feet with an overcoat. Over this was a black robe. It took several minutes to wrap the new style of turban around their head and let it hang over their shoulders.

"You look like a light skinned Moor," Ayan said.

"You look like - Ayan." Arthur smiled. "Your dress will never change how you look or who you are." His father did not look proud and fierce under his turban. Arthur thought the new clothing made him look nobler, more like a Holy Man.

The difference was immediately noticeable. Arthur and Ayan strode side by side. The crowd moved out of the way to let them pass. The narrow sandstone buildings gave way to wider streets with large stone walls. As they walked further from the harbour and market area, the city stench faded. The scent of roses and jasmine filled the street. The scent was strongest when a litter passed. Most carried wealthy women hidden behind silk screens, upon the strong shoulders of six large Moors or Berbers.

Even the slave women and men were well dressed. Fruit trees laden with succulent looking wares peeked over many of the walls. Arthur recognised date trees, though the others were foreign. He wanted to taste them all. They came to a smaller market, surrounded by several buildings.

"This is a good place." Ayan nodded. His mood lightened.

"I agree."

Ayan took the lead. He headed straight to a small inn. They moved through the small door into a dark room. It took a couple seconds for their eyes to adjust to the dim light.

The floor was covered with low tables and pillows. The bluish haze of cigar smoke hung over the room. Men lounged around the edge, watching as a girl danced in bored rhythm to some music. She wore a chain on her waist and bells at her feet and a fine sheer fabric wafted around her as she moved. Her eyes were hollow and haunted.

"I do not like this place," Ayan whispered.

"It is different," Arthur whispered. "That is all."

"It is not the type of place for respectable men."

Arthur turned. "It is the type of place where men mind their own business. It is a good place to stay until we find passage on a ship."

"It is better to stay away from this type of men."

Arthur stepped back, out of the doorway. He felt better in the shadows. He knew Ayan was right. He wanted to run and to walk forward at the same time. A small man approached. His hands wrung as walked towards them.

"A room?" the man said in broken French.

"Yes," Ayan replied in English.

"Ah, you are English gentlemen."

Arthur didn't like the gleam in the man's eyes.

"A room," Ayan stepped forward.

The man held out his hand.

Ayan put a coin in it. He turned to Arthur and nodded. Arthur picked up their packs and followed. The small man led through a curtain made from red and gold beads. The dark hall beyond turned twice to the right before the small man stopped and opened a door. The room beyond was hot as an oven and had not been cleaned in the recent past. A small window was high on the wall. Too high to climb out of, but big enough to let in fresh air.

Arthur immediately left the room. The small man look confused, then smiled. He pointed and jabbered. Arthur looked down the hall and then followed the direction of the man's hand. A wooden door opened into a small garden. It was as unkempt as the inn, but it was cool.

He returned to the room to tell his father about the garden.

"I've ordered a bath," Ayan greeted him. The baths are on the roof."

"We should both bathe," Arthur said. "I suspect that baths are costly, but with this heat, and the time since our last bath I think it will be worth the expense."

A few minutes later, there was a knock at the door, and they followed an old slave up to the roof. The air was noticeably cooler. A slave girl stood at the side of the bath but Ayan signalled to the old man to take her away. He returned a few minutes later with a boy. Arthur stopped him at the top of the stairs and sent him away too.

Arthur could see the disgust written across Ayan's face. He had never told Ayan that he had a slave nanny before his mother died.

They bathed slowly, enjoying the evening air. A small bundle of money inside a dirty leather wrap hung around his neck. Ayan made sure that this was not getting wet. They were just dressing when another man came to the roof and started taking off his clothing. Arthur looked at his father, who ignored the man.

"Turkish Corsairs," the man said as he unwound his tunic.

Arthur looked up.

"Corsairs?" the man said in a strong accent. "Turkish Corsairs." He paused, thinking. He tried again forming his words carefully, "Barbary pirates?"

Ayan shook his head. "English."

The man nodded, seemingly unconcerned.

"Merchant seamen."

The intruder's eyes narrowed slightly as he nodded. He spoke a stream of indecipherable words. He stopped and waved to the sunset. "Red Sea?" Then he swung his hand to the right.

"No, Eastern India," Arthur said confidently. He knew his father did not approve the moment the words escaped his lips.

"You signed on ship?"

"The steamship Berthard," Arthur said

The man nodded. Ayan nodded politely and walked away. Arthur followed his lead. He heard the man step into their dirty water. The naked slave girl passed them as they descended the stairs.

They entered their room before Ayan spoke. "Do not share our business. It is always best to avoid anyone who is concerned with our business."

Neither man reacted with surprise when they saw their bundles had been searched. The thief had not bothered to hide the fact, and so clothes lay strewn all around the room. Arthur picked up their filthy British clothing. "We should have destroyed them."

"We may need them."

"Yes, but they are traveller's clothing, not merchant seamen's clothing." Arthur stuffed the clothing back in the bag. "It would be better to be mistaken as a seaman."

"I think it is better to leave as soon as possible."

Arthur nodded in agreement. The city's allure had faded with the sunset.

CHAPTER 29

Ayan sat on the roof staring across the city. He leaned heavily on his knees. The strange clothing disturbed him. He felt unsettled. Nothing made sense. Arthur grew more and more restless. He stayed out later each night. He spent the day searching through the palm-lined streets and the tall white towers of the Moorish castles. It intrigued Arthur that the white city, which stretched beneath a flawless sky, was the most depraved city he had ever visited.

He spent hours exploring the lace-covered arches. The Moors built the most beautiful buildings in the world. But, there was a very different world to discover behind those white doors. Ayan only accompanied Arthur a couple of times. He begged him to stay away, but the boy's curiosity would not be sated.

Ayan did not like the way his son hungered to spend hours in the smoke filled dens, sampling fruits while dark-eyed women danced in the shadows. He watched the sun sink. Arthur would leave soon. Something in the boy's habits mirrored Kazi's. Ayan feared this. He struggled helplessly to prevent history from repeating itself.

Ayan turned to the building across the alley. It was an exact duplicate of the roof Ayan sat on. A white cat jumped on the wall and looked over the edge into the alley. It was white as snow with long soft fur. It turned and looked in his direction. Ayan stared into the clear green eyes for several moments before the Persian cat looked away.

The cat circled on the spot, seeking a comfortable position. Eventually it settled down, sat perfectly still and stared directly at Ayan. Its tail wrapped tight and twitched. They watched each other long after the city awoke. The cat looked over its shoulder then back at Ayan. It rose and walked to the edge of the roof, pausing a moment before jumping back into the street.

Ayan watched for several minutes before understanding the significance. He experienced a sudden clarity and understanding beyond anything he understood before.

The cat did what the cat was born to do. If Ayan set his son free then he would follow the path he was born to follow. Allah called him, but Ayan had been too focused on his own life and comforts to listen.

A surge of strength lifted his spirit. He rose as refreshed as if he'd slept all night. Ayan left the coolness of the roof and walked through the dark halls and into his room.

Arthur snored lightly in the grey light. Ayan left him to sleep peacefully while he went to fetch some fresh fruit, and when he returned, Arthur was sat on the edge of the bed with his head in hands.

Ayan sat down on a stool beside his son.

"Do not start, Pops."

Ayan sat in silence until Arthur's head lifted.

"Pops?"

"I have decided that we've stayed long enough in this city."

Arthur lifted his head and eyed Ayan suspiciously.

"We are not going to Eastern India."

"No?"

Ayan shook his head and leaned forward. "I have decided to return. You will sign on a ship as a merchant seaman."

"Pops!" Arthur rose to protest. "We've talked about this."

"And I did not understand. You have your own destiny. I cannot force you to walk mine."

"You are going to Eastern India?" Arthur's shoulders drooped. "You are leaving me?"

"No," Ayan smiled and put a hand on his son's knee. "You are a good man. You will follow the sea to Eastern India. It is in all men. You do not need to be in Eastern India or make pilgrimages."

"Then stay with me," Arthur begged.

"No son," Ayan smiled. "It is what I must do. Your path lies in another direction."

"I do not understand."

"That is part of life. It will be clear to you soon. You will one day understand."

"You are not making sense."

"One day it will." Ayan rose. "It is time to leave. We must escape this city. If we stay then we will destroy our faith." He started packing their bundles.

Arthur followed his lead. Ayan pulled a large citrus fruit from his pocket and handed it to Arthur.

"There is no saying that we can find berth on a ship today.

"We are not seeking a berth. You are. We will find a berth on an Italian or English ship."

"I will not leave you here."

"I will not remain. I will leave today."

"How?"

"I will be on a ship that will take me to Eastern India."

"You found one?" Arthur hefted the bundles onto his shoulder.

"Yes," Ayan lied.

"How?"

Ayan smiled. "A cat told me the way home."

Arthur's lips narrowed. "How are you getting home?"

"I have worked as a seaman, in some capacity. I will travel as a seaman again."

"Why don't we sign on the same ship?" Arthur cried.

"No," Ayan shook his head and led the way out of the inn. "You are heading to America. I am travelling to Eastern India." He pushed into the crowd before his son could question him further.

They travelled through the crowds silently, savouring their final moments together. Arthur's mood lightened as they broke free of the city stench and smothering heat. The cool ocean breeze brought a spring to his step.

"Pops!"

Ayan turned to the boy.

"The ships to America are over here. I have waited days for one."

Ayan looked at his son suspiciously. Could it be that his son did not spend all his nights in squalor? He felt a sense of joy as he realised Arthur knew the dock well. He did not spend his nights in the evil dens. He was here, among the ships.

Arthur led them through the piles of goods and crates, jumping from wharf to wharf as they navigated the maze of docks and warehouse buildings.

Ayan realised the boy knew the docks by heart and was heading toward a particular ship. Ayan felt a sense of pride as he followed his son. Ayan slowed his pace. He wanted to prolong the time spent with his son, to savour their time together.

CHAPTER 30

Arthur stood on the wharf as Ayan approached. The morning sun burned his skin. The salt air stung his nose. The years of dreaming seemed surreal. Today a dream would become reality. Sailing to America? Arthur wondered what would happen after arriving in America. He might travel across the continent. He might travel to China. Nothing would hold him back once he was a merchant seaman.

"Over here," he called. "The Pittsburgh is heading for America today." Arthur elbowed his way to make room for his father. "I talked to the shipmaster a couple times. He said he would take me on."

"You already made plans?" Ayan looked surprised.

"Yes, Pops," Arthur shrugged. "I spoke to the Shipmaster. I have to plan ahead, just like a man."

"When does she sail?"

"At the tide," Arthur replied.

"Is there time to share before you board?"

Arthur sighed. His head lowered. "No, I should be onboard soon."

Arthur looked at Ayan. Ayan's eyes had a hungry gaze Arthur had never seen. "What is wrong, Pop?"

Ayan shook his head. "I just want to remember the way you look today."

"I will not forget you."

"I will not forget my dear boy."

Arthur looked at the ship then back at him.

"You are the best thing that my life has yielded. I would have been lost without you."

Arthur's throat choked. His mouth opened but no words came out. Ayan stepped forward and hugged him. Arthur felt like a boy again. Ayan's strength always made him feel like the street urchin who stole socks and food. Emotion overwhelmed him until he finally found the strength to unfold himself from his Ayan's arms. He grabbed his bundle and tore across the dock toward the ship. He crossed the gangplank and stood on the deck before he turned.

Ayan stood in the same place. Arthur thought that his father looked lost for the first time.

"Name."

Arthur turned to the deep voice. He looked up at a tall black man.

"Name," he repeated. His low timber rumbled through his chest.

"Arthur –"

"Not on the list."

Arthur panicked. The man didn't even look at the list. "I talked to the cook..."

The man stood in his way and sneered. "We take no Lascars on this ship."

Arthur's muscles tightened. "I am no Lascar," he snarled.

"You look Lascar."

Arthur dropped his bag. A white grin lightened the man's face.

"What is this?" a smooth voice drawled.

They both turned to face a white man, who was obviously an Officer on the ship.

"He be a Lascar off one of them British steamers," the black man replied respectfully.

"Perhaps his father was too." The white man smiled. He was well-dressed but did not have the arrogant standing of a rich merchant or the stiff countenance of British nobility. Arthur stood stiffly, unsure how to address this newcomer.

"I am no Lascar," Arthur replied.

"Of course you're not." The man leaned lazily on a barrel. "You can tell by the gentleman's English that he is educated. I bet he has even been to school. Can you write?" Arthur nodded.

"There, you see Bo. This is not a Lascar."

"Martin, can you please tell me what the holdup is."

The man stood at attention. "Just a wannabe deckhand, sir."

Arthur quickly followed suit. This man needed no introduction. His very manner and the way everyone treated him betrayed him as the Captain of this ship.

"I need no deckhands," the man said politely then turned to leave.

"Sir," Arthur said politely.

The man turned surprised. "It is not my habit to be addressed by darkies."

Arthur stiffened. "Sir," he said again. He lost his courage under the captain's steady gaze. "I beg your pardon, sir. I talked to the cook. He lost his assistant to dysentery. He said he would recommend me for a position."

The captain looked him over carefully. "You ever been on a ship before?"

"Yes, sir," Arthur faltered. "Once, sir." He didn't mention that he had paid for passage.

"Indeed." The captain turned. "You need two things to work on this ship. You need to remember your place. And you need your name on Mr Bo's list."

The captain turned and walked away. Arthur didn't move until Bo stuck out a board with paper on it.

"Make your mark."

Arthur wrote his name and picked up his bag.

"Can you find the cook?" Bo chuckled deep and walked down the gangplank.

Arthur turned to watch him go. It took a minute to realise that Ayan was still standing on the dock, watching.

The thought of sailing had consumed him for weeks. Every night he had ventured down to the wharf and talked to the men. Every night he had listened to the waves lap on the ship's hulls.

Now that it was real, he realised that it was permanent. He

understood why his father stared at him so hard. Arthur would never wake up beside his father again. His heart sank. He had a bright future ahead of him but his prospects dimmed at the thought of the cost.

CHAPTER 31

Ayan stood on the dock until it was impossible to make out the waves from the ship that carried his son away. His heart turned to stone. What seemed so clear this morning now stole his strength. He walked slowly to the cargo holding area, and was lucky enough to find an official who spoke English. Ayan produced his chit that declared he was the owner of a crate that was being held in the port.

"I can't let you open the crate, Mr...Mr Miah? Is it?" The official was scruffily dressed, and Ayan could sense that he was quite low down on the scale of importance.

"I just need to check that my wares are ok after the voyage. And, also, I saw the way it was unloaded. The men were very rough with my goods," Ayan said in his most haughty voice. "I would just like to check my silks and my tea. If they rot while I am doing business in the city, my partner will be most upset."

"Partner?" said the official curiously.

"Yes, my English nobleman partner. He is in the government in England," Ayan lied. "I am to meet with possible new trade partners here, but there seems to be some hold up. Maybe I can spare some tea for your trouble. If you could be so kind as to show me to my crate?"

The man studied Ayan for a few seconds, as if trying to work out if it what he said was true.

"How do you come to be in partnership with an Englishman, Mr Miah?" He finally said.

"Look, my family have been merchants for generations. I helped set up a family import and export business in London. We did a lot of business with my partners' family business, so it seemed natural to do a joint venture. Money does not see colour, sir. If you can't help me, maybe I am talking to the wrong man...."

"I am sorry sir, I just…"

"Don't be fooled by my attire sir. I do not wish to stand out as wealthy. Now will you help me, or do I need to speak to a supervisor?"

"No need for that Mr Miah. Some tea, you say? My wife would be very grateful for some tea. And if you have some silk, maybe some samples? She would be very happy sir! Follow me."

The man led Ayan through a massive holding area. Crates and containers were stacked on top of each other on both sides, making a towering channel that hid both men from any outsiders view. Ayan tried to see a pattern to how the goods were laid out, but if there were a method, its key eluded him.

Eventually the port official turned down a short passage, and stopped to study a pile of crates.

"Should be around here somewhere….there we are!" he exclaimed happily. "That wasn't too hard to find sir. First time I've had to locate a single crate sir."

"Thank you….what is your name?"

"Ahmed, sir," the official said proudly.

"Thank you Ahmed, I will not forget this."

Ayan pulled the leather wallet out from around his neck, and took out a key. He placed it into the padlock, and made an almost audible sigh of relief when the key turned all the way in the lock and the padlock clicked open.

"One minute please, Ahmed," he said, insisting on some privacy. Ayan quickly checked that everything was fine. All the tea had been well packed in waterproof and airtight containers. The silks had been bundled tightly together, and were well covered and protected. Ayan chose several packets of the less expensive tea, and put them in his backpack. He opened a bundle of silk, and realised he had nothing to cut a length off.

"Here, Ahmed. Make your wife smile with this gift," Ayan said as he turned and handed over a twenty metre length of silk. Ahmed's eyes lit up as he realised the quality and quantity of the gift.

"Mr Miah, sir, this is most generous....I...I don't know how to thank you."

"I may need to come here again Ahmed. If these business meetings keep being put off, I may be here some time. My goods are safer here than in my lodgings. I know you will keep an eye out for any thieves."

"Of course sir. I will look after them for you. If you need me again sir, I am here all day, until ten at night."

"Thank you Ahmed. I hope your wife likes her gift."

Ahmed led Ayan back through the maze of goods, until they were back at the holding area entrance. Ayan bade the man farewell, feeling a little guilty that he had misled him with his fanciful story of a business partnership. 'Well,' Ayan thought to himself, 'it was the only way. And anyway, it is my tea!'

Ayan made his way back to the Inn, and paid the owner for another week. Hopefully he could find a passage back to Eastern India soon. The long day had tired Ayan. Saying goodbye to Arthur had drained him more than he realised. Before he could even take off his clothes, he flopped onto the bed and drifted off to sleep.

The next day, Ayan rose with the sun. Refreshed and purposeful, he decided today would be a day of action. First of all, he arranged with the Inn keeper for breakfast to be provided every day for the next week, in exchange for a container of the exotic tea in his backpack. After breakfast, Ayan headed towards the port area once again, to see some ticket agents about a berth back to Bengal. As luck would have it, The Eastern Star was due to leave in four weeks' time, with cabins available. The ticket price was high, and Ayan would have to pay for a whole cabin to himself, as no white passenger would share with him. Still, it was not an unobtainable price. Ayan would have to raise the money in three weeks. He handed over every last penny he had, as a deposit, and then headed off to find Ahmed.

Ayan realised that he had little time to waste. He bribed Ahmed once again, and loaded himself up with as much tea and silks as he could carry. He made his way to the market area, found a small space against a wall, and carefully arranged his goods around him. Ayan's experience as a merchant served him well, and by early afternoon he had sold all his tea, and several lengths of silk. He took the remaining silks back to the Inn, and persuaded the keeper to allow him to leave samples behind the bar.

The next two weeks were played out in much the same way. Each morning he would go to the ticket agent and pay off more of his cabin, and then he would find Ahmed and load himself up with more goods for the market. The days passed in a blur, as Ayan kept his routine going. He had sold three-quarters of the crate, and would need to sell most of what remained. Things had not turned out quite as he had expected, and he would be returning home with a lot less than anticipated. Still, it would be worth enough to pay for a doctor for Kazi. If Kazi is.... Ayan let the thought drift away. It was not something he wanted to dwell on.

Eventually the day arrived when Ayan could pay the last instalment of his ticket. The agent took the money and pulled a large stack of papers onto his desk, and thumbed through them until he found the one concerning Ayan. The man called over a young boy, and gave him an envelope with several pieces of paper stuffed inside.

"The boy will get your ticket, sir," said the agent. "You want to collect it here? Or you want the boy to bring to your lodgings?"

"I will collect it here, thank you. You have a receipt for my final payment?"

"Of course, Mr Miah."

The agent handed Ayan his receipt, and shooed the boy away. Ayan thought about following the boy, to make sure he was doing as he was supposed to, but shook off the paranoia, and opted to treat himself to a fine lunch. Today he would sit at the best restaurant and eat the finest food they had to offer. There was no need to save his money any more. He walked to a place just up the road from the agent's office. Ayan had passed the restaurant almost every day for the last three weeks. The aromas had enticed him every time, but he had fought against the seduction. Today he would submit to temptation.

He sat at a table out front, surrounded by jasmine and roses. An Arab looking man walked over to take his order. Ayan laid down enough money to feed three men. The man's eyes widened in appreciation and he rushed away.

The first course included iced fruit and a refreshing drink. Ayan still enjoyed the fruit when the man brought three types of cheese with several types of sweet bread. This was followed by dates and cream.

Ayan finished with a savoury meat meal.

The meal ended with an assortment of sweets and creamed cakes served with a sour drink Ayan had never tasted before.

Finally, when Ayan felt like he could eat no more, he left the café and headed back to the Inn. He informed the owner of his departure, and paid for his room up to that day. He ordered a bath, and went to his room until it was ready. Ayan felt a great sense of achievement. It had been a mighty task to raise the sum needed for his return to Eastern India, and he had passed the test with time to spare. There was a knock at the door, and Ayan went up to the roof to soak in his well-earned hot bath. There would be time in the next week to tie up any loose ends. He could not afford to pay for any cargo in the hold, so he would take what he could carry, and dispose of the rest in a way that he saw fit. Ahmed had not been a greedy man. He was obviously badly paid, and had been grateful for the small gifts Ayan had given him. He had never tried to get any more out of Ayan, than Ayan had freely offered. He would be rewarded for his good nature. Some of Ayan's more expensive tea and a whole length of silk would bring a huge smile to Ahmed's face and that of his wife. The off-cuts of silk that had been left at the Inn would be shared out among the girls who danced there. Their job may not have been pleasing to Ayan, but the girls were sweet and friendly, and did the job out of necessity rather than for pleasure.

Ayan filled his bag with the most exotic and expensive tea that he had left, and bundled up as much silk as he could carry. He put aside enough of the remaining tea to sell over the last few days to raise some funds for his last week onshore, and the time he would spend on The Eastern Star. Everything that was left, Ayan bundled up in several small bundles. Each night Ayan took one of the bundles and headed towards the market area, where he gave it to one of the beggars.

The day finally arrived. The day Ayan would return to Eastern India. It had taken a lifetime to get to this point. Or so it seemed. There were so many questions that would soon be answered, but Ayan tried to put them all to the back of his mind. He had dreamed of this moment for years, walking up to the house, with Kazi running to greet him, Faiza and Mirvat waiting excitedly by the door. He could picture his return no other way.

Ayan said his goodbyes at the Inn. The owner was sorry to see him go. A mutual respect had grown between the men in the weeks Ayan had stayed there. The owner, Hasan, has seen how Ayan quietly and respectfully went about his business. Ayan had been impressed by how Hasan ran his Inn. There may have been a slight unsavoury air at times, but it was the nature of the business. Any Inn in a port area would have a similar vibe, but Hasan kept a clean and well-run Inn, and treated his staff fairly. Ayan had stayed a lot longer than most men and had always paid in advance. He had been friendly and courteous at all times. Hasan called one of his sons and told him to help Ayan carry his luggage to the docks.

Once again, Ayan found his papers were scrutinised more carefully than the other passengers. Eventually, with a huff, the required stamp was given, and Ayan walked up the gangplank, on to the deck of The Eastern Star.

"Tickets. Tickets," shouted a deck-hand.

"Excuse me, where do I find my cabin, please," asked Ayan.

The boy glanced at the ticket, then up at Ayan. "Far side stairwell, two flights down, turn left, sir," replied the boy, without hesitating.

Ayan crossed the deck. Any moment he expected to be challenged. But, the stairs came into view, he descended two flights as he'd been told and found his cabin. After several hours, the ship finally pulled out of port, and began the long journey back to Ayan's home. Ayan spent the first couple of days in his cabin, just looking out to sea. There was no need to leave for food, as he had filled his pockets with dried fruits and snacks at the Inn. The longer he could delay mingling with other passengers, the safer he would feel.

The weeks passed, and Ayan had a routine in place. He still spent most of his time in his cabin, leaving only to eat and to watch the sun go down. He would lean on the rail and wonder how Arthur was faring on his own. The boy had a fire and determination that matched his own. He really could be Ayan's son. As the journey's conclusion drew nearer, it was hard not to think about Kazi and whether he would be at the house when Ayan walked past the betel tree and up the path. The sun disappeared finally; Ayan buried his thoughts for the night and returned to his cabin to pray. Shouting from outside the cabin disturbed his thoughts. Ayan stuck his head out the door as a couple of young deck-hands passed.

"What is the disturbance, young man?" Ayan asked with a respectful nod.

"We've just entered the Hooghly, sir," the boy replied. "We 'ave to be on deck all night, to make sure we don't hit anything"

"Really?" said Ayan.

"Aye sir. There's lots of islands and stuff we 'ave to navigate through."

"Well good luck. It would be a shame to ruin a lovely journey at this late stage."

"Sure would, sir."

The boy's hurried off to their duties, and Ayan closed his cabin door to the world and let the conversation sink in.

The Hooghly River. He was almost home. It was too dark to see much from the deck and anyway; Ayan had no references from when he made this journey in the opposite direction. There had been no portholes or windows in the bowels of The Bengal.

It would be a restless night. As Ayan dressed the next morning, the ship's siren sounded with several sharp blasts. Ayan could hear people hurrying down the corridor outside his room. As he opened the cabin door, he could just make out cheering and shouting from the decks above. He slowly walked up the two flights to the upper deck, still wary of being among the other passengers. Everyone seemed to be congregating at the front of the ship. The ladies appeared to be wearing their finest dresses, the men wore their best suits and hats and even the servant boys had been scrubbed and put into fine clothing. Ayan gently slithered his way through the throng of people until he found a space at the rail. He put his hand up to shield the morning sun. There in the distance, on the right-hand bank of the river, was the unmistakable sight of the spectacular High Court of Calcutta. Ayan stood open-mouthed and oblivious to the noise around him. People jostled him, trying to share the view, but Ayan gripped the railing tightly with white knuckles. This was a place Ayan knew. The Eastern Star would berth within the hour. Tears welled in his eyes as the realisation dawned that his journey was over, and he was finally home.